T0115015

My Brothers' Footsteps

Historical Fiction of Six Brothers in World War 1

A story inspired by true events.

GLORIA MARSHALL

BALBOA.
PRESS
A DIVISION OF HAY HOUSE

Photo provided by, Joyce Jackson
Map produced courtesy of www.greatwar.co.uk

Author Credits:
Winner of International Poetry Contest 2007. Poem published in Forever Spoken published by The International Library of Poetry, Ownings Mills, MD 21117

Balboa Press books may be ordered through booksellers or by contacting:

Balboa Press
A Division of Hay House
1663 Liberty Drive
Bloomington, IN 47403
www.balboapress.com
1 (877) 407-4847

Printed in the United States of America.

ISBN: 978-1-4525-1796-4 (sc)
ISBN: 978-1-4525-1797-1 (hc)
ISBN: 978-1-4525-1798-8 (e)

Library of Congress Control Number: 2014912184

Balboa Press rev. date: 8/26/2014

DEDICATION

In loving memory of my father
Percy Harold Swinimer
Proud veteran of WW1 and WW11

MAP OF WESTERN FRONT AND BATTLEFIELDS 1914-1918

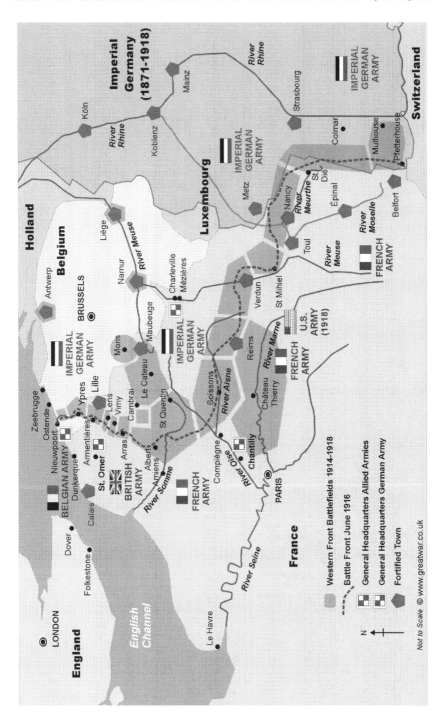

Epigraph

Notes taken from Professor J. A. Cramb's series of lectures on relationships between England and Germany in 1913, which were published in a book, <u>Germany and England</u>, reveal an astounding revelation.

"And if the dire event of a war with Germany – if it is a dire event – should occur, there will be seen upon this earth of ours a conflict which, beyond all others, will recall that description of the great Greek wars:

> **"Heroes in battle with heroes**
> **And above them the wrathful gods"**

And one can imagine the ancient, mighty deity of all Teutonic Kindred, throne above the clouds, looking serenely down upon that conflict, upon his favorite children, the English and the Germans, locked in a death-struggle, smiling upon the heroism of the children of Odin, the War-god!"

Excerpt from <u>Germany and England</u> by J.A. Cramb
Professor of modern History, Queen's College, London
Published: John Murray, Albermarie Street, W. London

Contents

Acknowlegment

First, and foremost, my heartfelt thanks to the daughter of the late Sergeant Harold Lantz. Through her, I was privileged to learn about the Lantz family and their chosen paths after the war. She also gave me permission to use her father's diary, which I had previously found in a box of old books belonging to him. This diary is the building stone of an amazing journey. It has now been returned to his daughter who saw it for the first time, one hundred years after it was written. Looking through the Lantz family photographs with her, I discovered that we were long, lost cousins. I am an avid genealogist and was surprised to find my paternal great-grandmother and her paternal great-grandfather are first cousins.

Second, a big thank you to a dear friend and my late daughter's childhood best friend, Sandra Barry, for her much needed advice and her help with writing this novel. Although very busy with her own endeavors in the literary world, she always had time to edit my first attempt at writing and offer valuable advice.

Third, my family who waited patiently for me to finish (which I am sure they thought would never come) my first novel. For all the dinner invitations and family gatherings I missed as I was so engrossed in my research and writing, thank you for your support and understanding.

Last and certainly not least, to my support team at Balboa Publishing, who guided me patiently as I struggled through the complexities of writing a novel worthy of the subject matter and bringing to print a compelling true tale in one of Canada's greatest historical endeavors.

Introduction

When England declared war on Germany in August 1914, it called on all its colonies for recruits. This touched the lives of every Canadian and they responded from every corner of Canada. This story follows the Lantz family in Nova Scotia and is typical of the households whose sons and daughters answered the call to serve King and country. Descendants of German Protestant settlers who came to Nova Scotia in 1753, the father, a strict Baptist, watches in despair as six of his ten sons go to war. Three sons volunteer in 1914 when the first call for recruits ring out around the country. Harry, a sensitive, caring man, is assigned an orderly in the 1st Canadian Field Hospital unit as he refused to kill the enemy. Harry witnesses the brutality of the war through the wounded soldiers he treats. He develops a fear of the battlefield as he listens to their stories. Burdened by his father to protect his two younger brothers, Harry finally succumbs to shell-shock after two years on the Western Front. Returning home before the end of the war, he is filled with guilt and a deep sense of failure. His brother, Orrin, earns the respect of his commanding officers with his natural ability on the battlefield. An officer in the famous 85th battalion, made up of Nova Scotia soldiers, he is thrown into the thick of fighting. As he becomes battle hardened, Orrin is consumed with a hatred of the Germans. Watching his childhood friends killed in battle changes Orrin from a kind, self-confident man to one driven by passion. He seeks satisfaction and revenge on the battlefield. A decorated hero, he clings to the edge of sanity as he becomes more aggressive to defeat the enemy. The youngest brother, Gordon, is assigned as batman to the chaplain of the ill-fated Nova Scotia Highlanders. While he is disappointed that he will not be in the trenches, he cheerfully carries out his duties. His desire for his *baptism of fire* is known to the chaplain who deliberately keeps him away from the killing fields. Gordon's youthful innocence and antics are the delight of senior officers but a worry for his brothers and his father. Canada's controversial Conscription Law in 1917 brings the three older brothers into the war. One brother, Havelock, refuses to go overseas and is posted to the garrisons in Halifax. He witnesses the Halifax Explosion in December 1917 which destroys half of the city. The two older brothers, Lenley and Everett, serve in non-combative duties until the end of the war.

Overcoming the British skeptics, the Canadian soldiers, who were tagged by the British generals as "barbarians" and "drunken Canadians", prove their worth on the battlefield. They never lose a battle and before the end of the war, Canadian soldiers earn the respect they deserve.

Prologue

Reverend George Lantz sits at his desk and ponders the news that Britain has declared war on Germany. He is greatly disturbed that Canada has been requested to send troops to support the war effort. The year is 1914. The father of ten sons and one daughter fears this war will have an impact on his family. The late afternoon sun heats up the small room which contains books and papers necessary for him to conduct his sermons. Reverend Lantz always feels a certain peace in this room and his mind drifts back over the past years. When his beloved wife passed away seven years ago, he was left with eleven children to care for. It is a burden he accepts without rancor. But the years have been difficult for him; the youngest child being only three years old when he lost his mother. While his daughter was young, she stepped in to fill her mother's shoes. Reverend Lantz knew he placed too much responsibility on her but he resisted the pressure on him to remarry. His love for his departed wife still burns deep in his heart.

A noise outside the window breaks his reminiscence. Reverend Lantz slowly gets up from his chair and goes to the window. He watches the boys return from a swim in the brook that runs by his mill. He smiles as his youngest son, Beecher, tries to outrun his two brothers. These boys are the youngest in his large family and still attend the local school. They are enjoying the last weeks of their summer vacation. The hot August sun offers many relaxing days by the cool waters of the fast flowing brook. Two of his sons, Harry and Orrin, have already left for college where they are studying theology. Reverend Lantz returns to his chair as he worries how the war will affect these two sons. His four oldest sons are over twenty-five years of age but only one is married. They help him with the work at his mill. He is relieved that the government is recruiting only one son from each household.

The kitchen door bangs shut when the boys race excitedly into the house. Hearing his daughter threatening her brothers, who are dripping water over the newly scrubbed kitchen floor, brings a smile to Reverend

Lantz's worried face. "Ah, yes", he says to himself, "a war cannot touch this family. One of my sons may have to do his patriotic duty but I expect the others to stay home with me."

He moves toward the door as the noise in the kitchen erupts into loud taunts. Three brothers against one sister always end in tears. All thoughts of war are brushed aside as Reverend Lantz seeks to restore peace in his beloved home.

PART ONE

The Great War: 1914-1915

FOOTSTEPS OF SERGEANT HAROLD LANTZ:

T he student lounge at Acadia College, a Baptist school established in 1838 in Wolfville, Nova Scotia, is packed as I push open the door. Everyone is excited to hear Prime Minister Herbert Asquith speak on the latest war news. War fever is sweeping the campus. I glance around to see if my brother, Orrin, is in the room but with so many heads bobbing this way and that way, I give up and push my way through to the center. I notice all the chairs are pushed back against the wall and everyone is standing. In the center is a table with bowls of apples and pears from local orchards. But my focus is on the Marconi radio turned up to full volume so that you must shout to be heard.

I squeeze as close as I can but elbows and shoulders are pushing against me, forcing me to stand and search the room with my eyes. I can hear well enough and I look around the room again for Orrin. This time I notice him over by the south window in deep conversation with several of his friends. It is futile to get his attention so I focus on the student trying to make his voice heard over the noise.

"They say in the papers that the Germans are sacking all the towns they take, killing women and children," he shouts. I do not know him as he is younger and not in my classes but I remember seeing him in the cafeteria numerous times. I look for a familiar face closer to me and spot a fellow classmate, Ted Moir. Catching his eye, I push my way over which brings me closer to the table. Just then the radio crackles and snaps, and a British voice announces Prime Minister Asquith. We had heard him speak many times in the past few weeks. The room became quiet as all ears poise to hear the latest war news of the British Expeditionary Forces. The deep, British accented voice of the Prime Minister came on the air filling the room. "Good evening to all; my news tonight is very bad," he paused. "Austria-Hungary has declared war on Belgium. Japan has declared war on Germany so we have a new player in the field. Germany has a big army, as you are aware, and it is deployed in several areas. Our British Expeditionary Forces which arrived in France 16ᵗʰ of August, are engaged at the Battle of Mons but it is a big battle with Germans outnumbering our Forces. Commander-in-Chief Field Marshall Sir John French reports high casualties. Our Navy has sunk the first German submarine 'U-15' in the North Sea. One of our fleet, HMS Amphion, was sunk by a mine off Yarmouth. It was a heavy loss. We have concluded a Naval Convention between France and Great Britain and the French Admiral is to command the Allied Naval Forces in the Mediterrean." Again he gave a long pause. "We are expecting our troops from the Colonies to arrive in England in early October. I am more than pleased with the promises of troops from Australia, New Zealand, Canada and India. We must stop this madness by the Kaiser before it reaches our soil. God will prevail! Now I must say goodnight." There was a spurt of static and the announcer came on again advising us that the Prime Minister had finished his message. A tall, dark haired student near the table reaches over and turns off the radio. The room immediately erupts into loud voices with everyone excitedly talking at the same time.

While Ted Moir and I review the war news, Orrin spots me and pushes his way towards us. Ted asks me if I have seen the recruiting poster on the bulletin board yet. Since I had just arrived at the Academy a week ago and was busy with my courses for the term, I had not seen the poster.

"There will be a recruiting station on campus tomorrow," he says. Orin hears the last part of the conversation and after saying hello, asks Ted if he is going to join the army.

"Hell, yes! Just about everyone here plans to sign up. What about you two…will you go the aid of your King?" Ted looks at us expectantly. We both look at each other before I answer.

"We will have to discuss it, Ted. This is my last year at college. Orrin, let's go to my room and talk about it," I finish. We both say goodbye to my friend and push our way out of the crowded student lounge.

The next morning is busy as the students gather in the cafeteria prior to the opening of the recruiting station. All classes have been suspended to allow everyone a chance to sign up for the Army. Orrin and I discussed the pros and cons until after midnight and finally decided we had to help protect King and country. Since we were both studying theology, we agreed that our role in the army would be non-combative, if possible. The thought of killing another person even if they are the enemy is offensive to me.

The recruiting officer glares at me. It is late in the morning and he had started very early to review the hopeful candidates in line. Orrin had gone before me and was quickly passed through. "Haar...umph." The officer cleared his throat. "What brings you here, young man?"

"I wish to join the Cause, sir. To serve my King and country, sir." I hope I sound brave as I am unsure of myself. But I stare back as the officer's eyes look straight through me. I can see he is sizing me up as a worthy candidate.

"Well now, lad, you and hundreds more like you. How old are you? Does your mother know you are here?" His voice lost a bit of its bite but his eyes are staring into mine.

"I am 24 years old, sir, and in my third year of study." I did not respond to his comment about my mother. She had passed away in 1907. The doctor claimed she was worn out having babies; she had mothered twelve children by the time she was 42 years old. At 43 years old, she closed her eyes forever one night; the cancerous tumor in her stomach claiming her life. My father was left with eleven children to care for after burying my mother in the community cemetery beside my three year old brother, Irwin. He had died two years previous from an unfortunate accident in the mill.

I jump when the officer's voice brings me back to reality. "Well, young man, go over to the registration desk. There will be more questions to answer but you look healthy enough to be a soldier. God be with you." He gave me one last glance and then waves the next candidate forward.

Two weeks later, I am sitting on the Intercolonial train on my way to Valcartier Training Camp in Quebec. As the train chugs through rural Nova Scotia, I think back over the past two weeks. The hardest challenge was telling father what I had done. I stare out the window as the fields and woodlands pass by and think of that eventful night. We were sitting at the kitchen table when my brother and I broke the news to the family. We had just finished dinner which my sister Hazel had prepared with such care. I now wish we had waited for a better time but Orrin blurted it out before I could warn him. Our father sits at the head of the table stunned while our younger brothers clapped for joy. I watched his face carefully for any clue of his reaction. Gordon immediately decided he was going with us and suddenly all the attention was turned to him. It was mayhem; my father's face grew more severe by the minute. Orrin looked down quickly when I glared at him. Our father was a strict Baptist minister who initiated all the decisions regarding the family. Both my brother and I were studying theology as he wanted his sons to follow in his footsteps. It wasn't a life I would have chosen for myself as I liked working the land. I knew that our younger brother Gordon was expected to follow the same career path as well. Orrin was already arguing with his younger brother when our father finally spoke.

"You are too young for this great burden, Gordon. What would your mother in heaven think of me letting you go to war? You are starting college this year, son. Give the war a year or two and if they are still recruiting, then do your patriotic duty." He looked around the dining table at us. I noticed the hurt and disappointment in his eyes. Our father's eyes fell on our only sister Hazel who looked so much like our mother. She immediately excused herself and, taking the two youngest boys, she went into the living room. We were all against Gordon enlisting; he had just celebrated his eighteenth birthday. But he would not change his mind; Gordon could be very stubborn if he didn't get his way. Our mother could always bring out the best in Gordon. Her sweet nature is greatly missed by our father in handling the children. Father looks at the three of us and, in great despair, he retires to his room. We were left sitting at the table looking at each other. We all knew that our father would kneel on the bare wood floor throughout the night praying for our misguided souls. Any joy we may have felt was soon replaced with guilt.

I watch my younger brother Gordon as he makes the rounds with the other recruits on the train. This is an exciting time for him as he has never been anywhere except school and church and now he is on his way to Valcartier Camp in Quebec. As I watch his excitement, a feeling of dread sweeps over me. I promised my father I would watch over him; it is a promise I know will be hard to keep. The look of despair on Father's face is still fresh in my mind. I am surprised that he came to the train station this morning to see us off. Father is good at hiding his emotions but his blue-grey eyes misted slightly as he embraced us and wished us "Godspeed".

Our sister cried openly especially when she said goodbye to Gordon. She and Gordon were always close, not only in age but also in sibling love. I gave her an extra strong hug to let her know I will miss her too. I promised to write her every week.

The Intercolonial steam train wound its way through the villages and towns picking up recruits at every stop. Fresh faced and eager for excitement, the recruits fill our car before we get to Windsor. I knew this government owned railway was making a special trip from Yarmouth, travelling through the Annapolis Valley and will reach Halifax. I had not been to Halifax so I was anxious to see this city. At the main station in Halifax, more cars are added to complete the journey to Quebec. I soon become bored with the slow progress so I make my way to the dining car which is crowded and hot.

"Harry..Harry..over here!" A voice calls to me from the crowd.

Pushing my way through, I see my friend Ted Moir waving at me. He has an empty chair beside him at a table next to the window. This is my first trip to the dining car and I expected it to be half-empty or, at least, quieter. As I push my way over to Ted's table, I wonder how anyone will be served meals in this crowd.

"Harry my boy. God, it is good to see you!" Ted exclaims as he slaps me on the back. "You are the first familiar face I have seen since I boarded in Kentville. Where is Orrin? Did he change his mind?"

I breathe a sigh of relief as I sit down on the red velvet cushioned chair. "This is insane!" I shout over the din. "I thought it would be quieter in here. What car are you in? I left Orrin back in the car with our bother Gordon. They haven't stopped talking since we boarded hours ago." I look around the dining car to familiarize myself; I notice that most of the recruits are drinking ale or pop but there is no food in sight. I turn my attention back to my colleague. "So what is the latest news on the war, Ted?" I ask.

We had to put our heads close together to hear each other. "Someone told me the British Forces had to retreat from Mons. German Forces were just too strong. The British Navy has been more successful. It sunk three German cruisers that were off the coast of Heligoland. The German Army is pushing back the Allied troops at every point." Ted gives me a concerned look and shakes his head.

"What do you expect at Valcartier? How will the brass hats ever organize this crowd?" The latest war news worries me. The war had seemed so distant and unreal but I know once we reach the training camp, it will become very real. I am still a little undecided about going to war. I do not share the same enthusiasm as my colleague. Leaving our father without our help with his mill disturbs me. "Were you expecting this many recruits?" I ask him.

"Harry, this is a small sampling. When this train gets to Quebec, there will be thousands on board. I heard they were adding extra cars in Truro for all the recruits from northern Nova Scotia. Just about every Scottish lad in Cape Breton signed up. And we still have to go through New Brunswick. I read that Colonel Hon. Sam Hughes is in charge of the training camp at Valcartier. He is our Minister of Militia and is highly regarded by our Prime Minister. I have an idea what to expect but we will soon know in a few days. Ahh..finally..some food!" Ted's gaze is diverted to the back of the dining car where a wide door above a counter has just been opened.

As we get in line to receive our dinner, Orrin and Gordon enter the dining car. I wave to them so they can find me later; we had not eaten since early in the day as had most of the recruits on the train. The smell of a chicken dinner is drifting through the crowd and all thoughts of war vanish.

When the Intercolonial Railway train pulls into the Truro station, a great excitement stirs. I am lucky to be sitting next to the window facing the platform but those on the other side of the train are getting out of their seats to cross over. We all know that hundreds of recruits from northern Nova Scotia are boarding here but nothing prepares us for the spectacle that awaits our anticipation. The platform is overflowing with recruits and spread out along the railway lines. As the train hisses to a stop, the recruits are shrouded in a cloud of steam. Then we hear the sound of bagpipes and out of the mist, stand the Scottish lads from Cape Breton dressed in their ancient tartans. The plaids of every clan stand beside each other: MacDonald, MacDougall, MacPherson, MacLean, MacLeod and their colors of blues, reds, greens and yellow make a spectacular scene. Each clan has its own piper and the mournful squeal of the pipes adds to the eerie sight. There is a magnificent white goat with superb curved horns standing beside one of the pipers. It also wears a plaid blanket. I stare in amazement. Every voice is hushed as a hundred faces stare out of the train window. We are all transfixed by this incredible sight.

"Mother of God, Harry, they are going to war dressed in skirts!" exclaim Gordon, breaking the stunned silence. He is leaning over me looking out the window but everyone hears him and laughter erupts.

"Gordon, they are Scottish kilts. That is their traditional dress for fighting," I explain gently because my brother's embarrassment is evident. "If you are ever talking to one of them, please don't call their uniforms "skirts" or you will get a broken nose or worse."

"They are going to fight dressed like that!" It is all too much for him to take in. "But Harry what will the Huns think?" he questions, still dubious about tradition.

I smile at his use of the slang term for Germans which he must have heard from one of the recruits but my response is cut short by an older recruit standing behind us. "They will put their tails between their legs and run like hell. The Scots are known fierce fighters and the Germans have met them before on the battlefield. These lads will take no quarter, I bet. They learn how to fight while still in their nappies."

With the excitement dying down, everyone returns to their seat but I still watch the scene on the platform. By now the Highland recruits are boarding the train and each clan is piped on. They fill two cars, such is their number. As the cloud of mist dissolves, I study their faces. They are young and healthy looking with wide shoulders and big chests. I feel they will become as fearsome fighters as their ancestors. There is no doubt in my mind that the Germans will not want to face them in hand combat.

"I wonder what Colonel Hughes will think of this bunch, Orrin. It will be interesting to see his reaction to the kilts." I turn to look at Orrin but he just nods; he is in deep conversation with the fellow in front of him. I settle back in my seat. It is still a long trip to Quebec and the excitement has drained the last remnants of energy from my body. I close my eyes and think about the events I have witnessed this day. The nagging thought of war stays me.

Two days later we arrive at Valcartier Camp at mid-afternoon. Although we were well fed and rested on the train, everyone appears apprehensive. Three officers meet us at the railway station and divide us into groups that reflect our province. Making our way on foot from the train station, I am surprised to see that the Camp is newly made. Thousands of tents are uniformly lined up in a big field as far as the eye can see. I study the scene before me with trepidation; my future is now sealed. I am going to war.

****

As we make our way on foot from the train station, Orrin, Gordon and I walk together. While the camp is close to the Port of Quebec City, we cannot see the port which I had expected. Instead a beautiful valley lies before us and when I first see it, it looks like a mirage. Thousands of canvas tents are set up in formation on many acres of grassland. I knew that Colonel Hon. Sam Hughes, Minister of Militia and Defense, had been give the almost impossible task to have the promised 22,000 soldiers ready to leave for England by the end of October. As I look at the scene unfolding in front of me, I wonder how he could have accomplished this incredible achievement in four weeks.

"What happens now, Harry?" Gordon asks me.

I get a strong sense that Gordon seems too young to be here although there are thousands here about his age. "We begin our training, I suppose, Gordon." I look at him. "I want you to stay with me if possible. I am not sure what lies ahead but we should stick together for a while. Agreed, Gordon?" My promise to my father is a heavy weight on my shoulders. Gordon nods in agreement.

I turn my attention back to the vista before me. I see a large parade square, a huge rifle range, buildings, and lots of newly made dirt roads. But it is the tents that capture my attention. There are thousands and thousands of them all lined up neatly.

"What an impressive sight," says Orrin as he stands beside me.

The officer in charge of the recruits from Nova Scotia motions us toward the parade square. Colonel Hon. Hughes is waiting for us to gather closer. He is sitting atop a beautiful white stallion and is handsomely attired in his uniform. I notice his medals from the Boer War proudly displayed on his chest. After the Highland recruits are ceremoniously piped onto the parade square, the Colonel addresses us.

"You are here today freely, you have volunteered willingly. This is a great moment in Canada's history." His voice carries an authoritative tone which sends a chill over me. I glance over the parade square where recruits fill every inch. I am overwhelmed with the reality of war. It has been a long day and I long for the comfort of my bed. Now our divisional officer is addressing us so I concentrate on his words.

"Proceed to the Administration Office to receive your uniforms. Your kits will be found on your bunks in your assigned tents. Familiarize yourself with the items. Six soldiers to each tent. Mess is served at 6pm sharp; don't be late. The evening is free but you will present yourself here, on the Parade Square, at 6am in full uniform tomorrow morning. I suggest an early turn in because tomorrow is a busy day." Sergeant William Sparks looks around before concluding.

"From this point on, you are soldiers! You will act like soldiers, think like soldiers, live like soldiers. Get to know your comrades because your life will depend on them. Dismissed!"

Later that evening after a wonderful supper, we find our assigned tent. Gordon, Orrin and I study each other with amusement. We are smartly attired in our dress uniform.

"You look like a general, Orrin!" exclaims Gordon. "You just need a mustache!"

Both Orrin and I laugh but our demeanor is more serious. Just then three more recruits arrive in the tent. Ted Moir slaps me on the back as he comes in. Laughter and conversation fill the tent as we familiarize ourselves with the contents of our kits. We are issued two changes of utility uniforms, and one set of dress uniform and a wool overcoat. Also in our kit are service caps and a helmet, web belt, ammo cases on a belt and a bayonet. The low-cut brown combat boots bring lots of comments but the putties that we wrap around the tops of our boots to our knees are a source of merriment. Trying to demonstrate, Gordon gets the putties all tangled up and finally calls on me to help him. Everyone reads the sheet of instructions twice to make sure we have wrapped the putties right. For parade, drill, rifle and bayonet practice, we are instructed to wear our dress uniform. All other duties, called "details", we are required to wear our work uniforms which are plain khaki pants and shirt. Most of the details include laundry, doing KP, raking gravel roads, constructing buildings and tents as needed. At the foot of our cots is a green wooden foot locker to keep our civilian and extra military clothes.

Having exhausted ourselves, we turn in. I quietly say a quick prayer and try to calm my anxious mind. Tomorrow a new life awaits us. *I am a soldier now*, I think, and finally fall into a deep sleep.

The next four weeks are filled with drill, rifle practice, bayonet practice, and lectures. I find it extremely exhausting work and when I am detailed to KP or construction work, I feel a little miffed. Every minute of the day is filled and no time to relax. Lectures prove to be popular at first. They are least demanding but soon there are tests that are more stressful than drill. I like the lectures best as it reminds me of college. The topics cover everything from personal hygiene to combat tactics. The rifle range is my least favorite although it is most popular with the other soldiers. Orrin excels at the rifle range much to his delight. At the end of three weeks, divisions are formed based on the assessments of the British training officers. As I had hoped, I am assigned to the Medical Corps, Orrin is assigned to the Infantry and Gordon is assigned as a Batman to the Chaplain of the Nova Scotia Highlanders. This came as a surprise to us all and even though Gordon complained bitterly, nothing could be done to change the assignment.

"What did I do wrong?" he asks me as he flings his haversack on the cot. "I can fight as good as the next fellow. I know I am not very strong but I am a pretty good shot. Harry, can you do something? I want to fight in the trenches with Orrin."

"Gordon, it is a surprise to me too. Did you say you wanted to be a minister in your interviews? Frankly, Gordon, trench fighting is a lot harder than you think. And part of your job is to be a bodyguard to the chaplain. He will be in the front line dressing stations and in the trenches with the troops so you will see lots of action." I watch my brother carefully, hoping I can settle him down before going to dinner. "Besides, Gordon, you will be with the best fighters in the war. Lots of excitement, I think, to keep you happy." I glance over to Orrin who keeps silent.

"But I am not even going with the first load of troops. Why did Colonel Hughes keep the Highlanders back if they are such good fighters?" Frustrated and tired, Gordon throws himself on the cot pushing his haversack to the floor. That look of stubbornness is on his face and Orrin and I exchange looks.

"He's keeping other battalions back as well including mine." Orrin finally joins the conversation. "There are only thirty ships and that is not enough for the thirty-two thousand troops here. The government did not expect such a large number of recruits. You will be on the shipment next month, Gordon. Besides we have to spend time in England to finish our training. You won't miss any action, I bet! We will all go over to France together. Now pull yourself together and act like a soldier. What was the lecture today? Obey and Don't Ask Why. Our officers call the shots, Gordon. Remember that and you might survive this war."

The fall rains that came a week before the scheduled departure created a muddy mess for everyone. The new roads are impassable for marching so we board trains to get to the ships lying in harbor at Quebec City eight miles away. It takes three days to get everyone on board including horses and equipment. By the time it is finished, any excitement that we felt is replaced by short tempers and frustration. It seems to me that the embarkation of us is badly muddled. I watch as ships are overloaded and unwary troops get on wrong ships.

A long gruelling eighteen hours in pouring rain takes its toll on my unit which is the last to board. What awaits us soggy and tired soldiers is not the warm welcome we expected. We are surprised to find the Princess Patricia Regiment on board and it is clear that they consider the SS Megantic their private ship. As most of their Regiment is experienced soldiers, they did not associate with the volunteers at Valcartier Training Camp. In fact, they had little to do with Colonel Hon. Hughes. This Regiment had been given an impressive send-off ceremony by the Princess herself about a week ago. Her father, the Duke of Connaught and the King's representative in Canada, was on stage and gave a rousing speech. All the recruits were assembled on the Parade Square and watched a magnificent parade of handsomely attired uniformed mounted soldiers with their previous war medals pinned to their chests take the salute from the dignitaries on a hastily made platform. This group included the Prime Minister himself and I was very impressed with his speech. Now I discover they had been living on this ship for the past week and not too happy to have their space invaded by us. When we sat down for dinner that night, they were boasting of their importance to the war effort. Since I had been made Sergeant in my unit, I sit with the lesser officers of their Regiment and listen to their boasts of ousting the Germans before the end of the year. I wonder to myself if this is possible. When I learn that many officers are bringing their wives and families to England where they will rent homes or apartments and hold social events in London, I am amazed. This news is quite startling and I begin to wonder if the Germans might be defeated so easily.

Exhaustion overtakes me by the time I reach my cabin and I happily lay down my heavy kit before falling on the bed. As yet, I am unaware who my cabin mate will be. There is no sign that he has been here ahead of me.

I make my first entry in my war diary which I found in my kit, and I suppose every soldier is supplied one, before falling into an exhausted sleep.

Quebec. Sept. 26.14: Arrived here from Valcartier camp at 6pm. Embarked on RMS Megantic enroute to England as I suppose. Had a good supper and later turned in between white sheets.

The next day Colonel Hughes makes a surprise visit to our ship. As it is Sunday, we are resting from the exertions of getting onboard and are caught in an unfit state of affairs. Most of us are lounging in our cabins when the order from our commanding officer to appear on deck is passed on. I scramble up the ladder with the rest of my unit; I only had time to put on my jacket but couldn't find my cap in the mad scramble.

If the Colonel is shocked by our unprofessional appearance, he makes no mention of the fact. But I notice our commanding officer is quite disturbed as we try to make a formation in the tight quarters on the deck. The Colonel's address to us is brief but passionate.

"This is the beginning of a great adventure, soldiers." His blue eyes sparkle in the fall sunlight as he continues in his strong authoritative voice, "The soldier going down in the cause of freedom never dies. Immortality is his. What matters whether his resting place may be bedecked with the golden lilies of France or amid the vine clad hills of the Rhine? The principles for which you strive are eternal." I watch as Colonel Hon. Hughes surveys the deck of the ship where we stand in our ill-fitting uniforms and poorly made boots. Then he shakes his head as if to clear his thoughts and continues. "Today you are as fine a body of officers and men as ever faced a foe."

After the Colonel left the ship, I notice groups of men that are clearly upset with his address. Ted and I retire to our stateroom so we can discuss this unusual speech in private. "What is he telling us, Harry? Are we all going to die for King and country? God, he knows how to bring us to our knees." Ted is furious.

I have a different view as I speak quietly, "I think he genuinely cares about us. Look at it this way Ted, we were farmers, students, fishermen, lumbermen, lawyers six weeks ago. We knew nothing about being a soldier. He is right, Ted! Today we are fine soldiers even if we are half-trained but here we are, all thanks to this man. Many of us will not return. After all, this is hand to hand combat. Never lose sight of that!"

Later that night, I make my second entry in my war diary:

Sept. 27th. Sunday. Passed quietly. Anchored in mid-stream. In the afternoon had a visit from Col. Hon. Sam Hughes. Evening had a sing and at ten retired.

Several incidents happened after the visit that I assumed were direct orders from the Colonel. The Princess Patricia Regiment moved off the ship the next day and boarded the HMS Royal George which immediately set sail up the St. Lawrence River. And training continued; everyone is assembled on deck for drill practice. After drill, we proceed to the dining room for a lecture. We are in dress uniform every day as there are no "details" to perform. We are told this will be our regular routine until the ships reach England.

Sept. 29th. Tuesday. Dawned bright and warm. After dinner saw a hydroplane sail over the river and then drop to the river and sail ashore. A concert was held in the evening but did not attend.

Sept. 30th. Wednesday. Fine and warm. Usual routine carried out. Pulled in to dock at noon. Started to paint. Saw six or seven ships sail out and some empty ones come in. Another concert is in progress but got into discussions and did not attend. 10:30pm. SS Megantic leaving Quebec.

Oct.1st. 8:1 5am. Dropped pilot at Rimouski and continued our voyage. 9:00 am. Went on drill with life belts. 10:00 am. Lined up for vaccinations then were dismissed until 2:00 pm. 11:00 am. Washed underwear, towels, etc. and hung to dry in stateroom. 2:00 pm. Drill; some infantry drill followed by a lecture on discipline by our most unpopular officer. His remarks caused hard feelings in the ranks between city and country boys! Time passes very rapidly. Evening all lights are blanketed.

Oct. 2nd. 6:00 pm. We are in the Gaspe Bay and there are about 25 other ships, cruisers, etc. around us. Night…some more ships have arrived. There is quite a fleet here now. Expect to leave in the morning.

Ted and I shouldered a spot on deck to gaze out at the assembled fleet in the early dawn. All the troops are on deck to take in this spectacular sight. Fog hangs over the St. Lawrence River making the ships look like giant ghosts. I count thirty ships that are carrying over thirty thousand officers and men, about six thousand horses as well as guns, motor and horse drawn vehicles, and even bicycles. Last night, the SS Florizel joined the fleet carrying over five hundred officers and men from Newfoundland. As the ships start to set sail, we watch Colonel Hon. Hughes appear in a tugboat at the side of each ship sending up his good wishes. I am moved by this last act of the Colonel taking his final look at the 1st Canadian Expeditionary Corps that he created. For a man reputed to have little compassion in his military career, I think this is a wonderful gesture. Many of the men wave and thank him including myself.

I learn later that one ship, SS Manhattan, has been left behind in Quebec City, still being loaded. One of the officers said it is overloaded with horses, motor vehicles, and scores of equipment. When I ask him if it will wait for the next shipment to cross the Atlantic, he assures me it is planning to follow our Armada without an escort. The officers dub the unfortunate ship "Noah's Ark" because of it assorted cargo. They make bets on it reaching the shores of England.

Ted and I get a good look at the British four funnel warship that will escort us across the Atlantic Ocean. It is our first glimpse of a warship and I am so amazed by its size. The twenty-four 12 inch guns are clearly visible to us as it passes our ship.

"I heard it can reach speeds of 30 knots," I tell Ted who is just as impressed with the warship. Finally the ships start to pick up speed and we move out of the St. Lawrence River. We decide to go below deck. This has been an exciting day and I want to record everything in my war diary.

Oct. 5. Monday. Our fleet was joined this morning by a four funnel warship having a speed of 30 knots and carrying twenty-four 12 inch guns. A man was lost overboard from the Royal Edward-don't know whether he was saved or not. 11 am. Sighted an incoming liner on the North. The man just mentioned was saved. 2 pm. A vessel was sighted on the North and one cruiser sailed out to intercept. The craft proved to be a British merchantman and thinking our fleet German turned and fled.

Oct. 6. Tuesday. Quite a choppy sea but very few sick and usual drill is carried out. There was a man died on one of the other ships and he was buried at sea.

Oct. 7. Wednesday. Nothing of particular interest. Having some rather heavy seas but bright weather. Are making 210 miles per day. Read <u>The Golden Key.</u>

Oct. 8. Thursday. Day fine and bright. Usual drill. Ranks thinned by indisposition among the boys. Read <u>The Religion of Evelyn Hastings</u>. Very good indeed. Ranks joined by another ship. Had a turkey lunch at 10 pm in our staterooms on the side among six boys.

Oct. 9. Friday. Fair and mild. Usual routine. Today made a record run of 250 miles.

Oct.10. Saturday. On hospital duties today. Not much work-only two patients. Met a big oil barge. Joined by HMS Princess Royal – a super dreadnaught.

Oct. 11. Sunday. Third Sunday on board SS Megantic. Beginning to feel at home. We had church service this morning in dining room. Weather unusually fine and warm. Destination as yet not known.

Monday, Oct. 12. 1914. Fine and warm-making good progress. I had a try at instructing today and did very well. I had a close view of the Princess Royal tonight. She is escorting us now along with several more.

Tuesday, Oct. 13. 1914. Usual routine-drill and written exam in the afternoon. Sea slightly rough.

Wednesday, Oct. 14. 1914. Plymouth near at hand. Sighted land about 10 am – our eleventh day on the voyage. About 1 pm, we began to speed up. Passed Eddystone Light at noon. The sea is now alive with British Scouts and torpedo boats and all kinds of war craft. About 2:30 pm, we stopped at Plymouth Harbor to take on a pilot. Words fail to describe the scenery. The whole country looked like a large garden with its green grass and hedges, etc. Took several pictures but day was dull and overcast everywhere. Up the Harbor, cheers from thousands of throats greeted our ears welcoming us and showing the spirit that prevails whenever "Rule Britannica" is sung. We anchored at the Harbor and our sister ship SS Laurentia pulled up alongside so that passengers can shake hands on different ships. The chatter of acquaintances at the rails after supper was deafening. Then we had a sing in Second Class Saloon headed by Y.M.C.A. and retired.

****

FOOTSTEPS OF SERGEANT HAROLD LANTZ:

T he first of the fleet arrive in Plymouth on October 14th; the harbormaster is completely taken by surprise. All day I watch the biggest English-Canadian liners steam into Plymouth Sound and anchor in the inner waters. We are told that our arrival is totally unexpected as the fleet had been scheduled to disembark at Southampton but rumors of German U-boats forced the sudden change of plans. As the long line of big ships carrying the troops make for port, they are stretched away from the entrance of the Sound as far as Eddystone. It is a magnificent sight. I follow my comrades around the deck and stand by the rail. My eyes have never seen such a sight; the grey ships completely fill the sea. As each ship approach the harbor, it is taken in charge by a Government tug which tows it through the narrow waters of the entrance to the harbor and conducts it to the anchorage of the dockyard. Crowds of people line the public space adjacent to the sea front and piers; their cheers are met with great appreciation from our troops who line the decks of the ships. Each time the citizens of England cheer, our boys respond with "Hail Britannica". I am overcome with emotion. This is beyond anything I could have dreamed. The ships continue to arrive all day and each one is greeted formally by the Commander-in Chief, Admiral Sir Egerton. The SS Megantic is anchored at the head of the harbor and its sister ship, SS Laurentia, is anchored alongside. Both these ships carry the Canadian Corps Field Hospitals. We are glad to see our fellow comrades after the long voyage and the noise is deafening as we stand at the rail and chat loudly.

Bands on board the vessels play lively tunes as Canadians swarm everywhere taking in the sights on shore. Finally when evening falls and all the ships have been formally greeted and anchored at the dockyard, I make my way to the Sergeants' Mess for dinner. It has been an exciting day and I am exhausted and hungry. All we can talk about at the dinner table is the tremendous reception by the English people. As soon as we eat, we go back up on deck to chat and watch the scenes on shore. All the ships are aglow with lights and I am sure it must be quite a sight from shore. The piers are still lined with people cheering and throwing flowers in the water to show their appreciation of the arrival of the Canadian troops. Finally, I grow tired of the noise and confusion on deck and go below to the Second Class Saloon where the Y.M.C.A. is holding a sing. I think this is a perfect way to end one of the most exciting days in my life.

Two days later, it is time to disembark. My unit, 1st Canadian Field Ambulance, is headed for South West Down Training Camp. The unloading of troops and kits prove to be just as confusing and chaotic as the loading was in Quebec. About half-way through the day's activities, several men report to the Medical Officer with food poisoning symptoms. When the numbers reach around thirty, he declares a crisis and keeps half the regiment on board to administer to the sick troops. I am among the medical staff left on board much to my dismay. I am kept busy with the patients as some are in serious condition. The Medical Officer decides it is ptomaine poisoning and orders all leftover food to be destroyed.

When the order came to disembark at seven pm on October 16th, I can hardly contain my excitement. Even though it is evening, the streets are still lined with cheering people of all ages. They throw flowers and candy as we pass by on our way to the train station. Several young girls break the lines of restraint and run over to me, grabbing at my buttons for souvenirs. I push them away and keep on marching; to stop in this chaotic scene would be disastrous. The streets are lined with cheering onlookers all the way to the train station. They hand out cigarettes and matches as we pass through.

We keep up a smart pace singing every step of the way. When our troops sing "It's a long way to Tipperary", the crowd goes wild with cheers and whistles. After we reach Amesbury Station, the battalion is detained for about an hour before boarding. There is more chaos here than I thought possible. Thousands of citizens crowd around the station trying to touch us. It is hard for me to grasp how the English must feel when they see thousands of Canadian troops marching in their streets for the first time in English history. As each train departs, cheers ring out and our troops respond with our own cheers while hanging out of the train windows waving wildly.

Several of the horses, tired and frightened by the noise of the crowd, refuse to go up the ramp into the train. After standing in the dark hold of a ship for three weeks, the sudden brightness of lights cause them to panic. The handlers are getting frustrated as all efforts seem futile. I watch as finally one of the horses, head hanging low from exhaustion, makes the perilous steps up the gangplank. The other three quickly follow; herd instinct overriding their fear of the sound of shod hoofs on the steel ramp. A great sigh of relief is heard among the hundreds of troops waiting to board; we are just as tired and exhausted as the horses. At last we are on our way to Salisbury Plains training camp.

On our train are the three thousand nursing sisters and headquarters staff. We were the last to disembark. The nursing sisters look very smart in their navy blue greatcoats and hats and attract a lot of attention. Lady Waldorf Astor, wife of the elected Member of Parliament from Plymouth, met them at the train station and presents them with pans of Devonshire cream. On the covers of the metal pan is an inscription, "To the Canadian nurses from Plymouth" and a picture of the Union Jack. The Canadian nurses are so delighted and each one thanks Lady Astor for her kindness. The crowd goes wild. I learn that the nurses will be sent on to London to staff the Canadian Hospitals being set up for the wounded.

My train reaches the ancient town of Salisbury at four in the morning. Hoisting our heavy kits, we begin an eight mile march to the training camp. We are trained for night marches so our eyes quickly adjust to the grey light of the night sky. Even in this subdued light, I can make out the beauty of the countryside. *Finally I am walking on English soil,* I tell myself. What a letter I will write to my sister about this day. I regret my brothers are not here with me to experience the excitement of arriving in England but I know they will be on the 2nd Canadian Contingent. Just as dawn is breaking at seven, we arrive at our site.

This is Saturday, 17 October. Got breakfast at 9 am. Did very little except rest today.

Sunday, October 18. Wandered around today. No drill so read most of the day.

After a day's rest, our routine begins. At six-fifteen every morning, each platoon falls in and takes a little run. When we return, we fold our blankets, clean up our tent and perform other duties before breakfast which is usually over by eight o'clock. Then our troops fall in and go on a route march in full pack or drill until dinner time. The afternoons are spent in more drills until tea at five o'clock. By this time, as the days are short and candlelight being our only source of light, the men usually gather at the Y.M.C.A. until "lights out" is sounded. I quickly adjust to camp life although I feel the meals are lacking. Breakfast consists of tea and porridge, dinner is usually beef stew and a pudding, and supper is merely tea and bread with jam or cheese. After the wonderful meals on the ship, the adjustment to this light fare is resented by many of our men. By the end of the first week, it is apparent that training is brutal with route marches and drill all day long. My first letter home begs for a care package I can stow away to offset the hunger pains. The village is within a half hour's walk but is off limits to us.

I admire the rolling plains of Wiltshire downs and flat fields of Salisbury Plains. Some of the boys from Alberta tell me the landscape reminds them of the prairies and they feel quite at home in England. After a week of sunny weather, the winter rains come to Salisbury Plains. Tents leak and fields turn to ankle-deep mud. While we Canadians are used to severe weather, the cold, damp conditions of our current existence starts to show on our good nature. I shiver through the cold nights under a thin blanket and finally sleep in my greatcoat which gives me a small measure of warmth. Our route marches through mud and rain are almost unbearable. After several weeks of this weather, our boots start to fall apart and wet feet gives way to sores and frostbite. The British replace the inferior Canadian made boots with their own British issue. When the winds come, our flimsy tents blow over and we get a good soaking before we eventually get them erected again. Everything is wet inside the tent including our blankets. With the wet weather, came sickness and I am kept busy at the Field Hospital which spares me the agony of drill practice in the rain and mud. Finally, each tent is issued a kerosene stove to drive away the dampness. By the end of our first month in Salisbury, we are hoping for better accommodations.

The camp is abuzz with the news of a visit from the King and Queen. I started cleaning the Field Hospital as soon as I finished breakfast. All routine drill and marches are cancelled so the troops can be ready for inspection. There are several dozen patients with chest infections and foot infections who are being groomed carefully. His Majesty will be visiting the hospital as well as other points of interest at the camps. We are told that Field Marshalls, Lords Roberts and Kitchener, along with Sir George Perley, Canada's High Commissioner in London, and Sir Richard McBride, Prime Minister of British Columbia will be with the Royal visitors.

I nervously stand with the Medical Officer when the Royal entourage arrives at the Field Hospital. While I am being introduced to Their Majesties, my heart is doing flip-flops. This is beyond my wildest dreams. The King's brilliant blue eyes are like magnets; they seem to pierce my soul. The Queen Mary, a German princess, is incredibly beautiful. She keeps her eyes downcast and never once meets my gaze. Holding my breath, I bow low from the waist and I am amazed to see my reflection in the shine on the King's boots. I am held captive by the feeling of power that the Royal couple imparts. Only when the Royals move to the bedside of the patients do I find the strength to breathe normally. I glance over to the Medical Officer who is in deep conversation with Field Marshall Lord Roberts. They are out of earshot of the entourage; I surmise they wished privacy. It is a quick exchange as I catch the doctor discreetly hand a small brown bottle of codeine to Lord Roberts who just as quickly puts it in his breast pocket. I divert my attention to the patients enjoying their conversations with the Royal party. My thoughts are still on the scene I had witnessed with Lord Roberts as the Royal Party leave the Hospital and proceed to the Parade Square. I want to question the Medical Officer but I am unsure if that is wise. I decide to remain silent and follow the Royal Party outside.

The Parade Square is a sea of greenish khaki with splashes of color from the bright plaid kilts of the one thousand Toronto Highlanders, and the bright red jackets of the Winnipeg Grenadiers. I watch the King survey the fresh, excited, young faces of the Canadians with interest. His late grandmother, Queen Victoria, often told him as heir to the throne that England's strength lay with her colonies. King George V was made a monarch through unexpected circumstances. He was twenty seven years old when his older brother and heir to the throne died unexpectedly in 1892. Through his deep sense of duty, he married his late brother's intended, a German princess, as requested by his grandmother, the Queen. King George V was crowned in 1910 after the premature death of his father, King Edward VII, from typhoid. Now he is King of a giant Empire and thrown into a war that pits him against his own first cousins and his wife's family. Whatever he is thinking as he looks out at the thousands of troops from Canada, I am sure he must have felt hope that England will conquer its enemies in this war. He stood there in uniform, proud and straight, on a rare sunny day as we cheer loudly.

After a long inspection of the troops, the Royal entourage left amid the lusty cheers of the Canadian troops. I am sure that the boys who had a chance to speak with the King will be busy tonight writing letters home to their families. It is quite exciting for all of us and we chat excitedly at supper about the day's events. I sit with several comrades and discuss the role of the King in a war that puts him in direct conflict with his Royal cousins in Germany and Austria. We conclude it is a terrible situation to be thrust into and retire to the Y.M.C.A. for a game of cards to end our day. Card playing was not permitted by my father so I never learned how to play. Instead I sit with a group of friends in a corner discussing the prospects of creating a band. I hope we will be successful in convincing the commanding officer that band practice and concerts can help relieve the monotony of camp life. I volunteer to shop for band equipment on my upcoming three day pass to London. This suggestion is met with excited agreement by my friends.

Before I blow out the candle for the night, I record the day's events in my diary. It is a day I want to remember forever.

November 4ᵗʰ, 1914. Still in camp. Have endured the rain and now we have a fine day. His Majesty and the Queen inspected the Canadian Troops today at three different camps where they are encamped. They returned via

Amesbury amid the cheers of the lusty Canadian boys. Tonight about twelve of the boys met to organize a band. Prospects are very good and the officers promise their support.

I am sent to Pond Farm Camp to check out the 3rd Canadian Field Hospital. The three mile walk is quickly covered and I am delighted to be reunited with several of my colleagues again. The 3rd Field Hospital that had sailed on the SS Laurentia is set up in a hut and operating smoothly. They have quite a few patients with "Pond Farm Particular", a slang term used by the soldiers for the cough and chest infections from the raw, cold wet weather. After comparing notes on various ailments with the Orderly NCO, I make my way to the Y.M.C.A. hut to meet with some of my friends and catch up on the latest war news. Ted Moir is one of the first to grab my arm and lead me to a group of soldiers standing to one side of the room. The Nova Scotia Rifles Regiment is training here so I know many of them. My brother Orrin would have been here if he had come over with the 1st Contingent. I am introduced to several soldiers from the Falmouth area whom I had not met before. They have become great buddies with my friend, Ted.

"Great news about our Navy, Harry!" exclaims Ted. "The British have the best naval ships but we have lost a few though. And to hear the German Navy actually attacked the British coast at Yarmouth and Gorleston. The war is ramping up, boys. We'll be in the thick of it soon, I hope. I'm getting tired of drills and trench-digging practice." Several of the boys agree with him. I know Ted is anxious to get over to France and I wonder why he thinks killing the enemy is exciting.

I ask the group what they thought of the King's visit yesterday. Everyone agrees that the King had made quite an impression. When I relate to Ted that I saw my reflection in the King's shiny boots, they all laughed.

"Not a spot of Salisbury mud on them," joked one of the soldiers and we all looked down at our own muddy boots. No amount of polishing can keep them clean.

The room is slowly filling up with troops coming off drill practice and I scan the crowd for familiar faces. "Harry, do you get a copy of the "London Times"? There is a reporter here at our camp and he writes fantastic articles about us Canadians." When I respond that I had not seen a copy, Ted sent one of his friends to his tent to get a copy. "I was saving it to send home but you take it back with you so your friends at camp can read it."

"We have little news at our camp now that the Princess Pats have moved out. I hear they are going to France in a couple of weeks. Did you hear that, Ted?" I ask. "They are going to fight with the British Army. I always wondered why they never wanted to be part of the Canadian Corps. You knew that most of the officers' wives are set up in London and part of the social circles it seems." I check my watch and know I have to leave in a few minutes. "Oh, by the way, the officers are putting together a band at our camp. I have a three day pass in a few days and I am going to London. One of the other officers is coming with me and we are going to pick up some band equipment." This news brings a warm response from the soldiers and they wish me well on my trip to London.

"Do you have a Wet Canteen at West Down South?" asks one of Ted's comrades. "We have had nothing but trouble here since they opened ours. Fights and wrecking things. God, I don't know why men can't be civil when they drink. They have had to ship a few guys back to Canada. Kicked them out of the Army!" Some of the men shake their heads in disbelief.

I reply that we do have a Wet Canteen but so far the men have behaved themselves. "I think Major/General Alderson made a mistake with this one. I have strong feelings about drinking, being a Baptist and all. But our camp is going to get a cinema later this month. The boys are excited about that! Camp life is pretty dull in the evenings." I conclude.

After I say my goodbyes, I start the short walk back to my camp. It has started to rain again and I don't have my rain sheet with me. *I will be properly soaked by the time I back,* I mutter to myself. Stuffing the copy of the "London Times" inside my jacket, I pick up my pace. My mind is filled with all the news from Pond Farm Camp and if I hurry, I can share it with my friends at supper.

November 12, 1914. Today I am 25 years old. Got a pass to London with Corporal Hunt to purchase band instruments.

I am so excited I can hardly wait to finish my breakfast of porridge and tea. It is my birthday and I am going to London on a three day pass. Three days without mud and hospital duties. I meet with Corporal Hunt who is going with me to help pick out instruments for the band. Together we walk to Lavington Station in the nearby village to catch a train to London. Lavington is an ancient village; first known as Bishop's Lavington when St. Osmund was bishop in 1220. Besides the quaint railway station, it has an interesting pub called *Bridge Inn*, a village store and a doctor's office. There is an old stone church which catches my attention as well as old stone houses with thatched roofs. I feel I am stepping back in history as some of these buildings must be almost seven hundred years old.

The railway trip to Paddington Station in London is pleasant and I have my first look at the landscape outside of the camp. I find the countryside beautiful with its rolling hills and green fields. Lots of sheep dot the fields which are ringed with stone walls. I can see the occasional old stone farm hut which makes it a pleasant scene. I will have to write home to my sister and describe everything; she will enjoy hearing about my day.

Reaching London, we set out for the Union Jack Club on Waterloo Street and register for the night. After a late supper, Corporal Hunt and I walk around the streets for an hour before retiring. This is my first visit to a large city and I am fascinated with all the sights. At breakfast the next morning, we discuss our plans. Since we have a map of the streets where the music stores are located, we decide to go watch the changing of the guard at Buckingham Palace before shopping. Having met the King, I am anxious to see the palace and surrounding royal buildings. The Westminister Abbey, where the Royal Family holds all royal functions including funerals, is of particular interest. Corporal Hunt insists that all sightseeing had to be finished by noon so that we have the whole afternoon to select band instruments.

The changing of the King's Guards is so colorful and impressive that I am overcome with emotion. Learning that these soldiers are actually working soldiers who have the honor to be assigned to the King's Guard is even more impressive. It is the first time I witness the *slow march* which had once been the famous battle march of the British. Their band instruments are of particular interest as well; I feel they add to the excitement of the event.

Absorbed in the changing of the guard, I suddenly catch a movement in a window and my attention is drawn to the magnificence of Buckingham Palace. As I view the countless windows, my mind goes back to the day the King visited our camp a couple of weeks ago. I feel very small and insignificant as I stare at the exquisite stone building. The flag is flying along with the King's colors so I know the Royal family is in residence. As I gaze at the windows on the second floor, a shadow passes behind the sheer curtains. I catch my breath and wonder if the Royals are watching us. I am reluctant to leave the splendor of the red coated guards in their tall black beaver hats. After a quick view of St. James Palace, the official residence of the Prince of Wales, we proceed to Westminster Abbey. We can only view it from the outside as it is not open but the size and grandeur overwhelms us both. According to the plaque on the gate, Westminister Abbey dates back to Henry III in 1245. The Gothic style is most pleasing to the eye and I wonder why the British Kings need such large and extravagant churches to worship in. My thoughts drift to a small, plain, white clapboard church where my father gives a weekly sermon. I knew he would not approve of such a display of wealth to worship God. "It is not the way of our Savior, son," my father would have commented but I am swept away with the beauty of the white stone towers and its beautiful stain glass windows. Corporal Hunt's voice breaks into my thoughts.

"Only fit for a King," he said. "I doubt if the common people ever step foot in it. I've seen enough, Sergeant. Let's go grab something to eat and then find H. Potters Music store. I think band instruments will be much more interesting."

The afternoon is spent in selecting band instruments and then getting them to Paddington Station by five o'clock. I am glad to get back to the Union Jack Club and register for the night as the afternoon was more exhausting than I thought possible. After supper, we go to the London Coliseum to listen to a musical performance which is a charity event in aid of the war effort. The Coliseum, built in the style of Italian renaissance, is one of London's largest and most luxurious theatres that had opened in 1904. We took the underground to Martin's Lane in the center of London where the streets are banked by beautiful buildings. It seems a shame to leave this incredible sight to go into the theatre but once we are seated, I stare in amazement at the extravagance displayed everywhere. The walls and ceilings are painted cream with gold etchings. Painted angels hung over the stage; gold statues of Roman warriors in chariots are beautifully carved. The Royal Box which is situated close to the stage is extremely opulent with gold statues and red velvet curtains. I glance over at Corporal Hunt who is as amazed as I am and when our eyes meet, he shrugs his shoulders in agreement. The crowd is mostly soldiers in drab uniforms which juxtapose the Roman inspired surroundings of marble columns and ornate boxes. My uncomfortable feelings dissipate once the musical play begins and the lights are dimmed. I am thrilled with the performance, especially as it is my first live play. *What a way to end my birthday,* I think as I watch the spectacular performance on stage.

November 14. Sat. Got up at 8am. Had breakfast. Took the underground to Paddington. Caught the 10:30 train for home. The day is fine and the scenery beautiful – flowers and vines all bright and green. Arrived at Lavington about 1:20 pm where we found our band instruments. Hired a taxicab.

On our return to our camp late the next day, I learn that Field Marshall Lord Roberts died in France while visiting the Indian Regiment that is fighting at St. Omar. The report said he died of pneumonia and that he was 82 years old. This is quite a shock. My thoughts drift to the incident I had seen in the Field Hospital during the Royal visit and wonder if this had anything to do with the untimely death of a great soldier. I am curious why a sick man would go to France. I ask the Medical Officer if he knew that Lord Roberts was sick when he visited our troops ten days ago. I didn't feel right about mentioning the medicine bottle so I put it out as a general question. While the answer is a bit evasive, I feel the doctor had been consulted by the Field Marshall.

"He was born in India, you know, and commanded the troops there for years. I guess visiting the Indian regiment was like seeing India again and he died a happy man," replied the doctor.

Sunday 15. 1914. Today is my first service since leaving the ship. Really enjoyed the service. Captain Frost, a chaplain who lately joined us, was the speaker. He is a Methodist from Toronto. In the afternoon, had a blow on our instruments.

Monday 16. 1914. Fine day. Usual route marches. Had a band practice in the evening.

Tuesday 17. 1914. Orderly NCO today. In the afternoon went on a route march. In evening had an appreciation of Lord Roberts where Chaplain Frost presided. Got a letter from home, the second letter in the last two months.

The Y.M.C.A. hut is filled with troops. Although we had only met Lord Roberts briefly when the King visited, we liked what he said about the efforts of Canadians in the war. Few knew that the man that had stood so proudly in uniform was 82 years old. He seemed in excellent health so it is hard to grasp that he is dead ten days later. When Captain Frost begins the appreciation service, a silence descends on the hut. The Chaplain cites the history of Lord Roberts pointing out that he was born in India but educated in the finest schools in England. His father, Sir Abraham, commanded the 1st Bengal European regiment so when Lord Roberts finished his education, he joined the Regiment. From that point on, his military career was remarkable," comments Chaplain Frost: "He has been decorated with so many medals and achievements, he hardly had room on his chest to display them. The one most dear to him was the *Knight Grand Commander of the Star of India* in 1893. India always held a special place in his heart and to die while visiting the Indian Regiment fighting in France would have been his dearest wish. The King has bestowed a great honor on this wonderful soldier and man; the first non-royal to lie in state at Westminster Hall. He will be buried at St. Paul's Cathedral in London. Both his sons continued the family tradition of military service but they were killed in previous battles, unfortunately. He leaves a daughter to mourn his passing. This is a great moment in history that you have been privileged to witness."

Captain Frost concludes his eulogy and looks around the crowded Y.M.C.A. hut. It is so quiet that I am amazed considering that half of the troops are battling chest infections.

After the service, tea and biscuits are served. I make my way over to the members of the band in an effort to shake off a feeling of empathy that engulfs me. My mind is filled with the picture of this gallant soldier fighting a chest infection to get to his beloved Indian Regiment.

That night I dream of bloody battles and soldiers dying in agony. I wake in a cold sweat many times but the dreams persist. Not wanting to disturb the other troops in the tent, I lie awake in the cold pre-dawn shivering under my greatcoat. I think of the rumors about the war I have yet to confront. I try hard to suppress the fear that invades my doubts of being a soldier in a war that is becoming more real to me.

****

Friday Nov. 20. Weather squally and cold. No appreciable change in war events. Usual route marches, scrubbing our tents, etc. Yesterday was issued an oil stove to warm tent. This evening we had a short impromptu concert which was very good.

Friday again. Nov. 27. Nearing the end of the month and still raining. Have been quite busy lately. Was on duty yesterday. Had a close arrest prisoner to guard. Got a good book to read Seats of the Mighty by G. Parker. Just finished Life in a German Crack Regiment – very good. War reports favorable. Great Russian victories. Bulwark HMS lost by an internal explosion. About 800 lost.

Sunday, Nov. 29. We had service in the morning addressed by our recently acquired Chaplain Captain Frost. Topic: the place of vision in our lives with a reproach on the conduct of some of our ranks. A very timely admonition. Afternoon went to Y.M.C.A. to another service, largely song. Then hunted up Ernest Chappel, an old roommate, had a short chat. Returned to our quarters.

Monday, Nov. 30. Today has been one of the stormiest since we arrived. High wind with driving rain. A few tents blown down and no one moving. Mud here is simply awful. Rain falls every twenty-four hours.

The last day of November brought a furious wind and rain storm that wreaks havoc on our camps on Salisbury Plains. Most of us stay in our tents physically holding them down so the wind cannot blow them away. But the rains fall in torrents and soon parts of the West Down South is flooded. The Toronto Highland Regiment, who is camped in the lowest part of the field, are flooded out. They stand in knee-high water; blankets and tents completely ruined. It is an effort to save anything including the kits and rifles. Finally, in desperation, they are marched to nearby villages and housed in barns and houses.

I am at the Field Hospital when a sound like a freight train is heard. Some of the patients scream in terror; they have never heard such a howling noise. I run to the door of the hut but the force of the wind against it is tremendous. I can't budge it. Medicine bottles start falling off the shelves crashing to the floor as the wind shakes the fragile hut.

"It's a hurricane!" I yell over the noise. My hometown in the Annapolis Valley gets an occasional hurricane that would tear huge trees up by their roots and blow the roofs off the wooden barns. My father would try to calm us children by saying that God was just playing with bowling balls. Of course, we didn't believe him and continued our wailing. He would herd us all to the basement and start a singsong.

"Everyone under your beds!" yells the doctor. He is worried the roof of the hut might blow off as it is creaking and groaning under the force of the wind. "Sergeant, let's get some of the medicine in a safe place. I think we might get very busy soon."

The paymaster, situated in a large domed tent which serves as the Orderly Room, is busy with the month's payroll. Hundreds of soldiers stand in the rain and wind to get their month's pay. Most of them will go on a one day pass to Salisbury later so they are anxious to get paid. One last gust of wind, so strong that several of the soldiers are blown off their feet, rips the domed tent from its rigging and blows it across the water-logged field. The soldiers stand transfixed as thousands of English banknotes blow around them and across the fields. Realizing it is their money that is blowing away, they chase after it. The paymaster is desperately trying to hold down as much of the money he can but most of it is lost as the gusts of wind circle the exposed table. It is a disaster; hundreds of troops are now chasing the money, slipping and falling in the slick mud. Finally the wind blows itself out but the rain comes down in torrents. Drenched soldiers come back to the ruined tent holding sodden, crumpled and muddy paper money.

"Everyone go to the Y.M.C.A. so we can sort this out. Try to find as much money as you can or it will be a dry December!" yells the paymaster as he gathers up everything he had desperately saved from the wind.

It is days before most of the money is found. Some soldiers justify putting muddied money in their pockets saying that it is worthless. Later, when the muds dries and they try to wash it clean, the paper money crumbles much to their dismay. The camp is in such a state of despair that the commanding officer decides that huts need to be built to protect the troops from the winter weather. Lieutenant/General Alderson makes a rare visit to assess the situation and voices his concern that there will not be any troops healthy enough to take to the Western Front in the spring. The flimsy tents offer no protection and more than half the troops are sick with colds. Several cases of spinal meningitis are reported in two camps. We are issued oil stoves to heat and dry out the rain soaked tents and occupants but the mud is so bad that all drill and route marches cease. We are handed hammer and saws.

Soon poorly made huts which will sleep sixty men appear on the flat, flooded landscape. But even the huts prove disappointing. While they offer shelter from the rain, the wind blows up through the floor boards causing damaging drafts to the lungs of the sleeping soldiers. A fuel shortage causes many huts to go unheated and the field hospitals are swamped with sick soldiers. I have to do double shifts several times as our staff gets sick as well. A rotation of *one day leave* is issued so groups of soldiers can get a respite from the conditions. This helps the morale of the disheartened soldiers and eases tensions at command headquarters. While the soldiers are on leave, other accommodations are desperately sought. Salisbury Plains is totally flooded; not fit for human or beast.

As December progresses, farms and villages are scouted out and soon many of the regiments are billeted out. The Canadian horses are farmed out much to the delight of the local farmers who are used to cobs or mules. The beautiful, big Canadian work horses are welcomed and almost revered. But the rains persist and soon snow is added to the woes of us still left in camp. The Field Hospital is the last to leave I am told. I am not happy about this news but I know we have to stay until the last of the sick soldiers are moved elsewhere. Most of the huts are empty now and I wonder if the next contingent of Canadian recruits will have a better time of it here than we did. At least they will not have to contend with winter weather.

****

FOOTSTEPS OF SERGEANT HAROLD LANTZ:

D *ec. 2. Wed. Fine in the morn and then usual squalls. Decided to accompany Sergt. Teuridel to Salisbury on a day's pass. We had been paid last eve. We walked to Bustard then got a ride to Larkhill. From there we walked across a Lord's estate toward Amesbury. We were warned off by the gamekeeper. Arrived in Amesbury 12pm. Looked thru the old church. Then hurried to station, got ticket and rode to Salisbury. 8 miles by rail. Arrived about 1:20pm. Had dinner and then engaged rooms at 3 Swan Hotel. We then visited the St. Thomas of Canterbury Church built in the 16ᵗʰ century. From there we went to the Salisbury Cathedral. The oldest and highest one in England. Here we saw tombs of a great number of old lords, knights and bishops. The Priest of the Theological School showed us around. In our party was a Belgian and his wife. Refugees so called. They have lost one son and had another taken prisoner. We then strolled around awhile and then went to supper. In the evening, we attended a theatre where we saw a rather dull sort of comic play.*

The streets of Salisbury are busy with soldiers on leave. I notice that the pubs are crowded with khaki uniforms; some are very noisy. I am fascinated with the old cathedrals which are such a contrast to the churches in Nova Scotia. Sergeant Teuridel is interested in England's stone buildings; his father is a mason with big plans for his son after the war. The ancient town of Salisbury is located in the Valley of the River Avon, about 90 miles from London. After wandering through streets lined with ancient brick buildings, some dating back to the 13ᵗʰ century, we walk through the gates on High Street and enter the Cathedral Close.

Church of St. Thomas Becket, which is a 13ᵗʰ century Gothic church, is located in St. Thomas Square. It is the first medieval church we will explore. I find it hard to believe that this was built as a place of worship for the masons working on the 13ᵗʰ century Salisbury Cathedral which is close by. I realize that in medieval times, religion and worship controlled the lives of these people. *Times have certainly changed since then,* I think. As we walk into the foyer, a faded painting filled the walls above the chancel arch. We both stop and stare; the paint has faded but one can still see the figures and landscape. A plaque on the wall catches my attention and I read it out loud. *"The Last Judgment or Doom mural pictures Christ in judgment."* We both look closely, and even though it is high over our heads, we can clearly pick out the figure of Jesus. I wanted to linger longer but our group is asked to move on through the main door. The carved timber roof is also spectacular; it is made of crested and painted beams with more than one hundred angels in various locations. The south chapel displays a primitive mural of nativity scenes on its north wall and a fine classical redo and wrought iron screen. There were fragments of medieval stained glass in the windows, including the Virgin tending a garden of lilies. This scene really captures my attention. I always pictured the Virgin with the baby Jesus. The fact that she was painted without Him disturbs me.

"What an interesting scene for a stained-glass window," I say to my friend. I would have liked to stay longer but I know the Salisbury Cathedral will take the rest of the afternoon to see.

We approach Salisbury Cathedral situated in a low meadow on the banks of the River Avon. The famous spire, claimed to be the highest in England, overpowers the magnificent early English Gothic stone building.

"How could they build something like this in those days, Harry? My father would love to see all this stonework!" Sergeant John Teuridel exclaims. "It must be over three hundred feet high. We are talking 13th century!" He could not take his eyes off the beautiful spire.

There is a small crowd waiting for the next guided tour so we stand in the lineup. I see a few soldiers at the front of the line and I am pleased that we are not the only ones taking in the sights of the ancient town. A couple ahead of us turns around and asks me if we are going to France. I think this is an odd question but I nod my head. The man puts out his hand in friendship and I step forward to shake it. "We wish you well. Our son was killed when the Germans invaded Belgium and our other son was taken prisoner. My wife and I fled to England. Living conditions are very bad in our country."

I offer my condolences and tell the couple that my friend and I are Canadian soldiers and waiting to get called up to fight the war in France. We chat until the tour starts; some of their comments bother me. It is one thing to read about the Germans' unethical war tactics but hearing about it from an eyewitness unsettles me. I am glad when the tour begins. John gives me an anxious look as we proceed into the Cathedral.

Our group gathers in the Nave facing east as the young priest outlines the history of the Cathedral. "This wonderful work of stone masonry was completed in thirty-eight years; to be exact, from AD1220 to 1258. These beautiful slender dark columns are made from crystalline limestone, known as Purbeck marble. You will notice it is used in the column shafts of the nave and aisles, and in the vault ribs." Everyone looks up at the vault admiring the breathtaking arches of dark marble. "The other stone used in building of the cathedral is Chilmark stone," continued the guide. "Masonry was a craft in medieval times. As you can see, very little restoration has been done in seven hundred years. Known as St. Osmund, the bishop's tomb is here in the trinity Chapel as well as a wonderful statue of this remarkable religious man. There are statues of other saints as you will see in your tour. This nave is eighty-three feet long and eighty-four feet high. There are other tombs of important figures of the 13th and 14th centuries. The spire which was added in AD1310 to AD1333 is four hundred and four feet high and is the highest in England. There are 332 steps to view the inside and anyone brave enough is welcome to explore the tower. The beautifully carved oak used in the choir stalls was provided by King Henry 111. Please enjoy your tour and spend as much time as you wish. One other point of interest for you; there are 365 windows as in the same number of days in a year and 8,760 marble pillars which are the same number of hours in a year. When you finish inside, the Cloisters are of great interest as well as the library above them."

John and I step away from the group. We are anxious to start our tour. A glassed-in working model of the Cathedral catches our eye and we move through the arched columns to the south wall. We both view it in wonder. The various stages of completion were displayed plus the working scene of the masons as it would have been in the 13th century. John is especially interested in the making of stone bricks; nothing could have described the building of the cathedral better than the working model the master builder used. I leave him there so I can view the medieval murals painted on the walls. These are better preserved than in St. Thomas of Beckett church and I thoroughly enjoy the various scenes. From there, I view the statues of the saints and read the plaques beneath them. The marble statues are incredibly life-like. My friend catches up with me and stares in amazement.

"Harry, I am going to climb the steps inside the tower. I need to see how they did it so I can write my father. He will be so interested. Probably take a while but I will find you." I smile as John hurries off to the tower. I am more than happy to stroll through the cathedral at my own pace.

I come to the first of the older tombs that are lined up between the marble pillars dividing the nave from the aisles. I am struck by the wonderfully carved stone effigy of a knight. It is elegant yet humble and I have a strong desire to touch it. However, a wire rope encircles the tomb. I read the plaque and learn that the tomb belongs to Sir William Longspee, 3rd Earl of Salisbury and illegitimate son of King Henry 11. This is the first tomb to be buried in the Cathedral in AD1226; it is fascinating to me that this tomb is over seven hundred years old yet it looks new. The carved shield with the royal lions intricately gracing it is so well done that it fills me with wonder. As I read the life history of the Earl, I am amazed at his skill as a knight protecting his half-brother kings. Perhaps it is the fact that the effigy is carved with its stone eyes open that haunts me but I can only move away when several other people come to view the tomb.

Working my way down the south aisle where other wonderfully carved effigies grace the old tombs, I come to the most grand and opulent tomb of marble and gilt. It stands at the very east end of the south aisle. This tomb stretches to a great height. Above the effigies of Sir Edward Seymour, Earl of Hereford, and his wife, Katherine who was sister to one of King Henry VIII's wives, is a fantastically carved canopy. So absorbed in this regal display of wealth, I did not hear my friend when he first spoke.

"This must be a king, Harry," repeated John. I turn as I advise him it is only a sister to a king's wife. "What must a king's tomb look like, I wonder?" He questions.

"The kings are buried at Westminster Abbey and I cannot even imagine what their tombs must be like. Next time I am in London, I will certainly go see, though." I reply, quite intrigued by such splendor.

As I speak, I move to the next one which is very plain with no effigy and it contains the remains of Bishop Poore who was Bishop of Salisbury when the Cathedral had been built. Beyond that tomb is the Trinity Chapel that holds the very old and extremely plain tomb of St. Osmund, Bishop of Salisbury who died in AD1099. Now I felt anger stir inside me as I glance back at the opulent tomb of a rich Earl and compare it with the austere tomb of one of the greatest religious leaders in history. Then I remember the wonderfully carved stone statues of the saints on the further end of the south wall and feel a measure of gratitude that they had been properly immortalized.

I turn to my friend and enquire about the stairs in the tower.

"I found it extremely interesting, Harry. I think I figured out how they did it. It took the masons twenty-three years to build the spire so it must have collapsed many times before it was finished. What is interesting is that it has not moved an inch since it was built. Isn't that remarkable? One architect in the 1600's claimed it was starting to lean and supported it with steel rods but I couldn't find any cracks in the bricks to indicate any movement." John shook his head in wonderment as he finished talking. "My father will be getting a long letter soon about this amazing cathedral."

By now we are standing in front of a stained-glass window depicting a young girl holding a crown but also wearing one. The window is in a small chapel of white stone and a small stone tomb was placed in the alcove. I read the plaque out loud as there is no one beside us. "Margaret, Queen of Scotland and daughter of Norway." I look at the girl in the stain glass window again before I continue. "It says here her father was King of Norway and her mother was the daughter of the King of Scotland. Margaret was born in 1283 and her mother died in childbirth. When the King of Scotland died without heirs as his sons had predeceased him, his granddaughter inherited the throne at three years of age. While on her way to Scotland to claim the throne and to be officially betrothed to the Prince of Wales, she died on voyage at seven years of age. The Treaty of Salisbury declared her Queen of Scotland and that is why we have this stained-glass window in the Cathedral. Well, that is quite the story," I say as I turn to Sergeant Teuridel. "I have discovered that being royal is a hazardous life. Not only were they killed in battle, but they were poisoned or murdered while they slept. I think I have had enough of this. I would like to see the library above the Cloisters and I want to do some shopping if we have time. My sister would like a nice scarf for Christmas, she tells me."

By the time we finish our tour, it is too late for shopping. Leaving High Street, we walk down a narrow side street where the old brick houses are joined together. We are in the oldest section of Salisbury as we search for a pub or tavern. A sign hangs over the weathered door on a 12th century red brick building which read *The New Inn.* Happy to have found a quiet tavern in a very old part of the town, we enter the dark interior. We both notice the low ceilings and old oak beams and framing. As our eyes adjust to the change of light, we spot an empty table by one of the three huge stone open fireplaces. A wonderful log fire is burning, giving the room a cozy glow. A serving girl arrives at our table dressed in period costume and advises us of the day's menu. We both decline the offered pitcher of ale which surprised the serving girl.

"Home brewed," she says. "The ale is authentic here." In medieval times, taverns were drinking establishments where friends gathered for home brewed ale. Women were not allowed, only prostitutes which was a common trade in those days. We both choose a 12th century English dinner. We are served a steaming meat pie filled with savory pieces of wild duck and rabbit blended with chunks of potatoes and carrots. Flour had been added to the sauce to thicken it as well as delightful spices.

"This is so good, John. Our food at camp is going to be difficult to eat after this wonderful meal," I comment. For dessert, we both choose mince pies filled with raisins, candied apricots and cherries, apples spiced with cinnamon and nutmeg.

Sergeant Teuridel rubs his stomach and smiles. "You know, Harry, I find the English food extremely filling. If this is what the people ate in medieval times, I think they were well fed."

I did not respond but, so far, all we had seen in the churches and cathedrals were royalty, wealthy knights and lords, and bishops. I am beginning to wonder where the common people lived and worked. I ask the serving girl when she returns to gather our empty plates and am surprised to learn that we are now in the section where the tradespeople had lived. She tells us that anyone living outside the gates of the Cathedral was considered peasants or trades. John snorts at this news but I hush him before he makes an unsuitable comment. When we get outside, he lets out an expletive comment about English class system. I look around anxiously to see if anyone is nearby that could be offended but we are alone.

Later that evening, we attend a comedy play at a popular theatre which I find very boring. I find English comedy very difficult to understand; preferring musical plays. But we retire to the 3 Swan Hotel quite satisfied with our day in Salisbury. I want to find a beautiful wool scarf for my sister before we return to camp the next day.

Dec. 3rd. Thursday. Bright and fine. Had a needed bath. Breakfasted. Went shopping. Posted our mail and then boarded a motorcar for home. A 17 mile ride. Arrived at Amesbury. Here we stopped for supper. Finally arrived home about 7pm.

Dec. 15th. Sunday. Cold and wet. Had some snow in the afternoon. Court-martial was held today. Judgment reserved.

Dec. 6th. Sunday. Allies progress reported today. Cold and ground frozen today. I am on duty today so did not go to church. 8pm. Received orders to proceed to Aldershot in the morning.

The camp is in an uproar with rumors that the remaining soldiers are going to be moved. At the Y.M.C.A. every evening, speculation runs high on the pending move to the front. So when I get my orders to be ready to move out, I am not surprised. What did surprise me though was the destination. Aldershot Garrison in Hampshire is the training grounds of the British Military. I thought we would be going to France. I help pack up the field hospital; most of the patients had minor chest infections and were cleared for normal duties.

Dec. 8th. Monday. Set out for Bustard camp enroute for Aldershot. Left there at 11am via motor lorry. Arrived at Salisbury at 12:30pm. Took train for Aldershot arriving about 3:25pm. Marched to barracks, two of our party had become drunk and had to be put under armed escort. We felt proud of our party and the impression they made. It is said that in the firing line they or we are laughed about as drunken Canadians. To our shame it is well applied. Finally we are registered and shown to barracks and issued beds. Luckily I got a room for two.

It is a short three hour march to Bustard camp where the motor lorries are waiting to take us to Salisbury. There is a lot of excitement as we board a train for Aldershot. This will be our first exposure to the great British Military and I am anxious to meet the medical corps. I hope the British commanders will be impressed with us. However, when two of our party drank too much on the train and is put under escort guard, my hopes sank. I had heard the rumors that the British commanders considered the Canadians "uncivilized and undisciplined". Now we would arrive in disgrace because of the two drunken soldiers instead of the proud young men I knew them to be. The slang term "drunken Canadians" by the British soldiers is an insult to our hard working young men. So it is with great humiliation that we detrain in the town of Aldershot and march to the garrison. No one felt it more than me; my strict religious background is sorely affronted by the two drunken soldiers as we march through the gates of the Garrison in full view of the commanding officer, Field-Marshall Sir Evelyn Wood, and the Duke of Connaught, Governor-General of Canada.

Aldershot Garrison was established in 1854 by the War Department as a permanent training base for the army. Permanent wooden huts were constructed to house the soldiers. With a keen interest by Queen Victoria, a wooden Royal pavilion was built in which she would often stay to review the troops. In 1898, the Duke of Connaught, the Queen's son, was General Officer Commander. The Royal family took a keen interest in the training of the British military; quite often Royal members would be trained here themselves. The wooden huts were replaced with brick barracks, along with many other improvements to make military life comfortable. The Garrison has an excellent parade square, a Royal Garrison church, an Observatory, a library, an impressive Wellington statue, a military cemetery, and thousands of acres of open military training area.

After I found my barracks, and pleased that I share it with only one other person, I sit on the bed in total amazement. My emotions are in conflict; delighted to be with the British Army finally but hurt by the treatment we had been subjected to since we arrived in England. The comparison between the Salisbury Plains camps for the Canadians and this incredible training camp for the British is hard to put into perspective. I could not help but think General Sir Hughes was wrong to insist that the Canadian Corps stay together instead of being integrated into the British Army. I wonder if he knew the hardships he had placed on us by this decision. I decide to take a walk around the grounds before turning in; I cannot let negative thoughts ruin my first night in the new Camp.

Dec. 8th. Tuesday. On duty today. Went to Hipplodome in the evening. Really good show.

Dec. 9th. Wednesday. Change of hat at field kitchens.

Dec. 10th. Thursday. Read of capture of 3 German Cruisers in S. Atlantic. With a feeling of satisfaction. This evening made a few purchases for Xmas presents and mailed them. Got a taste of English FOG. People straying right past their own doors. We got coal today and are fairly comfortable now.

Dec. 14th. Monday. Last evening was to Baptist Church here. Today dawned bright.

Dec. 15th. Tuesday. Last day in field kitchen. Went to Royal Theatre in the evening. Saw a play Message from Mars. Very good indeed. Good morals and interesting.

****

FOOTSTEPS OF SERGEANT HAROLD LANTZ:

I sit in the expansive library at Aldershot Garrison and intently read the "London Times". *"At about 08:00 hours on December 17th, 1914, two German battle cruisers began shelling the town. Scarborough Castle, the Grand Hotel, three churches and various other properties were hit. People crowded to the railway station in an attempt to get out of harm. At 09:30 hours the bombardment stopped and the two battle cruisers moved on to nearby Whitby, where a coastguard station was shelled, incidentally hitting Whitby Abbey and other buildings in the town. Hartlepoole which was better defended was also shelled. Because of poor weather by then, only four British destroyers were on patrol. Shelling began at 08:10 hours and received return fire from the defending shore guns. A great gun battle pursued and the British destroyers, that had been patrolling the coastline, chased the German destroyers back to sea. Unfortunately, the attack killed 86 civilians and injured 424. The shelling by the Germans damaged steelworks, gasworks, railways, seven churches and 300 homes in Hartlepool. Poor weather and visibility hampered the British High Seas Fleet from catching the German destroyers that scampered back to safe waters. The entire attack resulted in 187 fatalities and 592 casualties, many of them were civilians. Britain is outraged by this senseless attack on its soil."*

I had heard the boys talking in the kitchens about the German attack but I am shocked at the damage they inflicted on innocent civilians. As we are leaving the library, I comment to my friend, John Teuridel, "Well, that brings the war closer to home. The Germans are really pushing hard to win this war and I think the odds are with them. They have pushed their army into France and now the front line extends to Italy. Did you hear, John, the Newfoundland Regiment is going to Italy?"

"Yes, I was talking to some of the boys from Newfoundland yesterday. They are quite hyped up about it. I think they are leaving the first of the year. I wish the British commander would make a decision about us," he complained. 'I am getting bored sitting around here not knowing what we are doing. What about you, Harry? Have you heard anything definite yet?"

"I think we are going to the Canadian hospital in Taplow in the next week or so. I heard the medical doctor talking to the commanding officer yesterday. Keep that to yourself, John. I am in the kitchens now so I pick up bits of conversation from the officers now and then." I patted my friend on the shoulder before we depart and go to our separate quarters.

Dec. 17th. Friday. Usual routine today. Raining again. Allies active but no decisive reports. This evening, the instructor received news of the death of his eighteen year old son who was a drummer and had just been awarded a D.C.M. the father's feelings can be easily imagined.

Dec. 19th. Saturday. Am detailed for dining hall duties today. Quite a number have gone on pass. Met some Australia boys this evening. There seems to be a mutual feeling between us.

Dec. 20th. Sunday. Real fine and clear. Had a frost last night. Went to Methodist Church in the evening. More heavy German losses reported tonight.

Dec. 21st. Monday. Orrin's birthday. Fine and bright.

Dec. 23rd. Wednesday. Wrote my examinations and left Aldershot for Taplow. Arrived about 4pm. And immediately took charge of the kitchen and served dinner at 6:30pm. Next few days passed quickly. Plenty of work and little spare time. Xmas and New Year passed unnoticed by ego.

Our orders came in and the Canadian Medical Corps is transferred from Aldershot to the Canadian Red Cross Hospital in Taplow prior to our move to France. I am anxious to see the home of Lord and Lady Astor who built a hospital over the grounds of their tennis courts for the Canadian soldiers. I have learned that the Duke of Connaught has been involved with this hospital and it will be named for his daughter. As we approach the north entrance to the Victorian three-story mansion, I only pause long enough to view the spectacular exterior of Roman cement and terra cotta balusters, capital, keystones and finials. The house sat high on the banks of the Thames River with incredible gardens and landscaping. It is beyond anything I could have imagined. I move on with the Corps toward the wooded area where we will be located for the duration of our stay. Lord Waldorf Astor has provided the use of some of the grounds to the Canadian Red Cross for the building of the hospital and the Lodge which had been used by servants at one time. The Lodge will be used to house the medical staff and officers. The ranks will set up tents in the nearby field. About twenty Canadian Nursing sisters who will work in the hospital are already housed there. All this I have learned is funded by the Duke of Connaught, Governor-General of Canada. I get a little satisfaction that we are finally being treated with better accommodations.

The Lodge is an impressive sight and almost hidden from view by the woodlands that had been planted in the eighteenth century on a barren cliff-top. A white, stately mansion stands before us, a scene of grandeur and tranquility. I wish I could linger and explore this incredible place but I have to rush to the kitchens as it is already four o'clock and I am expected to prepare dinner for the officers. So with mixed feeling, I leave with a guide to help me find the kitchens.

As I enter the front entrance of the Lodge, a huge foyer opens into a great room. The grand staircase dominates the high ceilinged, extravagant room. The staircase with a handsome carved newel post of dark oak, winds its way up two flights. The walls are covered in burgundy damask silk and a huge crystal chandelier hangs from the high ceiling. I am so caught up in the beauty of Taplow Lodge I have to be prompted by the guide to go through to the kitchens. There are two kitchens and I am told that originally they were for the upper and lower servants of the grand mansion who lived separately from each other. He tells me they used a tunnel to access the mansion. I am quite intrigued. The nursing sisters will be using one kitchen while I have the use of the other. Much to my surprise, the pantries are well stocked. With only two hours before dinner, I am hard pressed to decide what to cook and finally settle on a beef stew. My memories of the delicious meat pie I had enjoyed in Salisbury are still fresh in my mind. If I thicken the sauce and add dumplings and lots of spices, I feel the officers will enjoy it. Since I didn't have time to make fresh bread, I will make fluffy tea biscuits to dip in the thick sauce. With my plan in place, I quickly organize my work place and by six-thirty, I serve a very tasty supper to the hungry officers.

The next few days keep me busy. With no patients in the hospital, my time is spent organizing the kitchen and going on route marches. Christmas Day is close so many of the British officers are on pass. I organize a singsong in the great room on Christmas Eve; it is the first time the Canadian nursing sisters mingle with us. While the nursing sisters do not have rank, it is obvious to me that a senior nursing sister from Alberta, Elizabeth Pierce, is in charge of the younger nurses. She herds them like a mother hen, much to our amusement. But one young nurse is a bit bolder and approaches me with a cheery smile. I find Penelope Mullan charming and we engage in a lively conversation. She tells me she had been born in Scotland but her parents now live in Ontario. Her brown eyes sparkle with delight as I describe my travels since I arrived in England. We are so engrossed in our conversation that when the order to retire is given, it catches us both by surprise. Wishing her a Merry Christmas, I leave to check the kitchen before retiring. Later, as I wait for sleep to overtake me, my mind drifts to a modest house in a small village in Nova Scotia. I think of the happy times I spent there and I visualize my father and his beloved church. I wonder what my two brothers who arrived in England a month ago are doing tonight. I wish I could have spent time with them; this is the first time the family is not together at Christmas. I know Gordon is working in a hospital in London with the chaplain and that Orrin is training at Bramshott Training Camp. They had both written me to let me know of their arrival in England. *Everything is so uncertain*, I think, and the big question of when are the Canadians going to the Western Front weighs heavy on my mind. A wave of loneliness washes over me. I offer up a prayer for my family and finally slip into a troubled sleep.

Jan. 4th. 1915. Usual routine today. Some officers sick and some visitors. Quite floods along Thames towns and using boats in Maidenhead. An attempt to start a band being made.

I was in the Duchess of Connaught's Red Cross Hospital visiting several officers who had returned from their Christmas leave with severe chest infections. The unexpected arrival of Lady Nancy Astor with her personal physician threw the patients and nursing staff into chaos. Nursing Sister Elizabeth Pierce who is in charge of the nursing staff is exceptionally adept at keeping the hospital clean and tidy. She makes sure beds are changed daily. She is a kind and caring administrator and patients and staff love her. As she leads the unexpected visitors around the beds of the patients, I watch Lady Astor with intense interest. I had been told that she was an American aristocrat who married an English viscount, now a Lord with a seat in the House of Lords. I also know they are incredibly wealthy and that many of these wonderfully wealthy ladies are opening their mansions to injured soldiers as convalescent hospitals. It is their way to help the war effort. All this is done at their expense but Lady Astor stood out for the Canadians as her interest is strictly a healing place for wounded soldiers to convalescence before going home to Canada. It is rumored that she became interested in holistic healing after a series of surgeries and illnesses she herself experienced. While her beliefs do not sit well with many of the common practices of medicine, she holds steadfast to the belief that clean linen, fresh air, proper nutrition and loving care can heal almost anything including broken bones.

We are surprised to see her as we were told the Astors spend the Christmas holidays at Hever Castle located in Kent, near Edenbridge which is thirty miles south-east of London. Her father-in-law, Sir William Astor, a wealthy American, had purchased the run-down castle in 1903 and lavishly restored it to its former glory when King Henry VIII owned it in 1539. Its many gardens and mazes were a wonderful place for the children of Lord and Lady Astor to play so it became a family tradition to spend Christmas there. Now, as she graced the bedside of each patient, I am struck by her sincere and compassionate interest in each one. I am also amazed at her incredible beauty; she is like a vision in her tastefully designed ruffled white dress fitted over a trim figure.

As she approaches me, I find her more radiant up close and I make an effort to smile nervously. While we discuss nutrition for the soldiers and she offers advice on the healing properties of specific foods, it becomes obvious that we are both of the same thought. So our conversation becomes quite animated as we compare our own experiences. When Lady Astor concludes her visit and leaves the hospital, I notice how quiet it has become. She had so energized the room that her leaving left a void which we all felt. *What a lucky man this Lord Astor is,* I think. So deep in thought I was not aware of another presence close by until I glance up and find Nursing Sister Penelope Mullan smiling at me.

"She is a lovely person, Harry. We are so lucky to have her as our benefactress. If ever you need nursing care, I hope you can come here." Penelope's voice is hushed and her brown eyes shine with admiration.

I feel an uneasy stirring in the pit of my stomach and while my thoughts betray me, my voice remains steady. "I would think any of our soldiers would be very fortunate to convalescence here. How could one not get better in this fantastic environment?" I ask, trying to hide my feelings that threaten to embarrass me. Many a night I have thought of this charming young woman since the Christmas Eve party but this is the first time I have seen her again. As she is called away to attend to her duties, I quietly slip off to the security of my kitchens.

Jan. 14th. 1915. Have been under the weather 2 days but am better again. Nothing out of the ordinary happening but expect to move soon.

Jan. 18th. 1915. Went on route march to Windsor Castle – a fifteen mile march. We had a snare drum, cornet, flute and mouth organ and with these we furnished music. Did not get to see castle as we had not time. Saw some Eaton boys at Windsor. Very interesting and a pleasant trip. Day unusually fine for here.

A letter from home brought my world crashing down. My brother, Everett, wrote that things were not going well for our father. With three sons away in war, Rev. Lantz was having financial difficulties; his only source of income was the collection plate on Sundays. Many of the faithful parishioners were finding it hard to meet the cost of daily living and the church collections were dwindling. On reading his news, I immediately wrote a check for a full month's pay and sent a cheerful letter to my father. The other disturbing news was the health of our grandmother living in United States. Everett was thinking of leaving home to visit her and see if he could be of help. This would leave our father without any help in the saw mill mill as our younger brothers could do very little. He went on to explain that activity at the mill had slowed considerably since the war started and now would be a good time to leave. I was saddened by this news but glad that Everett had written me. I decided to write Orrin and Gordon so I could pass on the news and also encourage them to send money home to help our father. It was all we could do to ease the situation. The news of my grandmother's failing health prompted me to send her a cheerful letter with a little money enclosed.

Rumor around camp had us leaving for France in a few weeks. I had learned from one of the officers that the order had come down from the War Office. The 1st Canadian Corps was expected to leave for France but it would take a few weeks to make all the preparations. Everyone is excited including the nursing sisters who are going to work in the two Canadian base hospitals in Rouen and Boulogne. I had become good friends with Sister Elizabeth Pierce and learned that she was going overseas with ten other nursing sisters. Penelope Mullan was one of the ten. At first I was unsure of my feelings about Miss Mullan going to the Western Front. I had hoped she would remain safe in England but then I realized she would be closer to me and I might get to see her on weekend passes. The hospitals were far behind the frontlines so they should be safe from any enemy attacks. My deepening affection for the young nursing sister had grown since the visit of Lady Astor. We would sneak a few minutes together to walk through the wonderful gardens at Clividen; our conversations growing more intimate each time. I was delighted that Miss Mullan enjoyed literature and fine arts. We shared many happy moments discussing various authors and plays.

Feb. 1st. 1915. Are on our way to Southampton. Had anticipated spending a pleasant evening at Lord Astor's but the order came too soon and we had to move. However, Mrs. Astor came down and presented each man with scarf and socks and gave us a little counsel and extended good wishes, biding us Godspeed. We left Taplow at noon. Arrived at Southampton and are quartered in a school building for the night.

The ship, SS Hanchaco, was waiting for the Canadian troops when we arrived. I was surprised to find the harbor so active. Dozens of transports and a fair number of small vessels were guarding the route right across to France I learned from one of the officers. It seems that England has increased her naval activities after the surprise bombing of the coastal towns. Loading the ship was long and hard even with the use of electric cranes on the docks. Motor and horse-driven ambulances took a lot of time to load. I think we got out of shape while enjoying our relaxing time at Taplow. I was so exhausted by the time we went aboard at two o'clock I wondered how I would be able to prepare dinner for the officers. It was with great delight when I found out the ship's crew were doing the cooking. It took a while for the confusion of boarding to settle before we set sail for France at eight-forty that night. Standing on the rail with several comrades, I watch the coastline of England disappear. I think back to our arrival from Canada which seems much longer than four months ago. *We are finally on our way to war,* I think and a sudden chill spreads through me. I decide to do an early turn in as tomorrow will be just as hectic unloading the ship.

****

FOOTSTEPS OF SERGEANT HAROLD LANTZ:

I t is around noon when we reached the docks at La Harve, France and a number of longshoremen stand in groups watching the ship dock. I was expecting them to come forward and help with the unloading after we disembarked. But they make no effort to help and are very vocal. While I couldn't understand their French, I strongly felt our arrival was less than welcome. We cheerfully unload the ship, singing to drown out the angry shouts from the longshoremen. I later learn that the British Army had refused them the job of unloading the ship and they were very unhappy about it. When it is time to leave the docks, we are happy to begin our march to a camp set up six miles away. It is a moonless night and pitch-black by the time we reach an open field near a small village. I finally crawl into my tent at two in the morning and collapse from exhaustion.

Feb. 19ᵗʰ, 1915. Looking for orders to move any day. Meet lots of fellows from front – all say do not be impatient. Still cooking for officers on a simple style. Weather fair. Country better than England in regard to climate. More like home.

Feb. 20th, 1915. Still waiting and wondering when our turn will come. Saw a regiment set out this morning. Ash Wednesday.

Feb. 24ᵗʰ, 1915. La Harve, France. Quite a little fall of snow but fast going. Not much winter weather. Farmers plowing every day. Yesterday No. 1 Station Hospital left for front. Tomorrow we move. Night sleeping in sheds at pier.

Feb. 25ᵗʰ, 1915. This morning had breakfast of field rations. Our kits left in a boxcar by mistake so we had to go for them and returned to find train gone. Marched to another station and boarded an express for Rouen – arriving after a 3 hour ride at 3:30pm. The country seen was all clean and prosperous looking. Marched across Rouen which is a beautiful city to another station where we got something to eat and at 7pm set out again in boxcars for Boulogne. We were packed almost as well as sardines but got some sleep and arrived next day at about 10. We stopped at Boulogne where we soon joined our officers and outfits which we unloaded and at evening marched out to Convalescent Camp No. 1 where we were quartered in two large marquees.

Feb. 27th, 1915. Marched down to town and packed our outfit – a big job. Returned late.

Feb. 28th, 1915. Can see white caps in the channel from camp and at the back stands the monument of Napoleon. At 10:45, we fall in for service at Y.M.C.A. I think but owing to lack of accommodations only part would go so I fell out and went in the evening when we had a second service. Talked to some Canadians who had been up country. They tell some gruesome tales. Got a book The Scapegoat *by Hall Cain. Am also reading* Old Curiosity Shop. *Had mail from home tonight.*

Mar.1st. Monday. Fell in at 7am, again at 8:30 when we were dismissed for day so all I have to do is read and eat. Rained in afternoon but have good quarters.

Mar. 2nd. Tuesday. Calm today – no duties so read more of Scapegoat. *In afternoon, got a pass and with Sergt. McGill and S/Sergt. Burnett went to see the Napoleonic monument just across the way. It's a large circular monument with large bronze figure of Napoleon. At summit it is 176 ft. high. We went up inside to the platform. 265 steps – rather dizzy, tiring climb but the scene which stretches before one amply repays for the exertion. Then visited an old windmill which was grinding flour. A real old type mill but was successful withal. Truly this is a beautiful country – one hard to describe. Back at camp at 4:15pm. Expect to be moving soon again nearer line of battle.*

Mar. 4th. Thursday. Day very foggy. No duties for me today so read some and played checkers. 8pm. Got orders to pack and be ready to move in the morning.

Mar. 5th. Friday. Boulogne base. Rose a little early. Ready to start for town enroute for who knows where. 7:30am breakfast and immediately leave for station, arriving here we started loading, had dinner at 12:20pm and then finished loading at 3:00pm. We were joined by our five nursing sisters and then were shunted about on different tracks until about 3:45am *when we slowly drew out on our trip. We were riding in 2nd class cars – five to a compartment – did not get much sleep.*

Mar. 6th. Saturday. 7:30am. Stopped at Arques – quite a town – rather quaint looking. There is a canal runs thru the town and on one side there is a series of lifts. Shifted to another track and run to Aire. On the way, passed thru beautiful country. Saw some Indian troops killing sheep. Their manner was rather unceremonious and very casual. Arrived at Aire at 9pm. Waited here at station until 11pm then went by motor lorrie to a prison about 1 mile from station. We had the usual wet and mud to cheer us. Found lots of ambulances here. Started a mess in small kitchen in officers' quarters. Have now seventeen officers to cook for. Very busy time unloading and sorting stock and arranging for patients.

We arrive at the British First Army Headquarters in the town of Aire-Sur-L-Lays. When I step off the train, I am amazed by the sight of this pretty French town. To my dismay, our unit is loaded onto motor lorries and driven to an abandoned building which served as a French prison before the war. Fort Gassion is now occupied by the British troops as a rest camp. A British Motor Ambulance Convoy is also billeted here.

The Canadian Hospital Corps is to take over the old prison and make it ready for patients by Monday. As I walk around the old, filthy, dilapidated buildings, my heart sank. It will take a tremendous amount of work to make this into an efficient field hospital in two days. But we set to work and, while we are tired from our train ride from Boulogne, the work went fairly quickly. Once the equipment was unpacked and placed, it bore some resemblance to a working field hospital. The five nursing sisters with the unit put the finishing touches on the beds.

In forty-eight hours, fifty patients are admitted. This is my first look at wounds made by shells and shrapnel; I am horrified at the extent of damage done to the young British soldiers. The fighting at Neuve Chapelle is in progress and the Allied Forces are taking a beating from the Germans. When the wounded arrive, we care for them in a professional and cheerful manner but their wounds are appalling to me. The five nursing sisters attached to our unit are from Nova Scotia. I met them while we were at Taplow setting up the Canadian Hospital.

As I watch them carefully for signs of stress while they work diligently throughout the night, I am glad that Penny is working at the Canadian hospital in Boulogne. Sights here are not very pretty. I am so proud of these young women who are just as scared as I am to be finally within sight of the frontline. We can hear the guns while we work which add to our stress.

Mar. 9th. Tuesday. Everything well straightened out and the work going well. Colonel is sick in bed.

Mar. 10th. Wednesday. Colonel out today. Fine and clear. Heard the big guns very clearly last night. Big doings up country. Lots of cavalry going up by here. Today the British gained two miles and made up for yesterday's loss of territory. Can't hear the guns tonight.

Mar. 11th. Thursday. Much shooting today. There was some excitement last night when orders came to send men, NCOs and officers to aid the hospital at Merville which was overrun with wounded. We received some 128 wounded and tonight 90 men have been sent to Boulogne by motor ambulance. The horror of war is being opened up to the eyes of some our fellows who have been helping to carry and bury the heroes who are upholding their country's honor.

Mar. 14th. Sunday. Very little like a Sabbath today. Am very busy. Have lots of patients and expect to have a hundred more tonight making 395. Some pretty nasty cases among them. Mostly arm and head wounds. Heavy bombarding all day and evening. Can see the flashes of the guns and hear the awful roar. Had RC and CE services here today but could not attend because of duty. Our boys are working so hard and cheerfully. 9:55pm. Colonel just in for a bit of supper.

Mar. 16th. 1915. Very fine. Very busy. Hospital about empty. Talk of moving. Had a narrow escape today from been startled by hand grenade found in tunic about to be burned in incinerator. No heavy firing audible today, got a new tunic, also some badges.

Mar. 17th. 1915. Fine today. Busy as usual. Very few patients. Our boys played a game of football this afternoon. Alongside us here is a small loche in the canal which runs a hundred or more miles thru France. Would enjoy a trip in a barge along this. This is the 17th of Ireland and was remembered by the boys who wore green of different descriptions. Saw a farmer sowing grain today. Had new potatoes yesterday.

Mar. 20ᵗʰ. Saturday. Was out for an auto ride in the country about five miles buying eggs. Very lovely country, rather primitive in some respects. Our boys played a game of football with Eng. A.S.C. and were beaten.

Mar. 21ˢᵗ. Sunday. First day of spring. Very fine. Buds are opening fast. Farmers planting. Services were held today but was not able to attend. Afternoon, another football game again. Had chicken tonight for dinner. Expect to move in a day or two. Decided not to move as they had the option. Men are very sore about it and do not complement the officers.

Mar. 27ᵗʰ. Saturday. Have broken bounds and written a letter to Hazel. Only hope the spell with continue. Yesterday came the climax in the shape of a live turkey. I resented its arrival but became reconciled finally and got two fellows to kill and dress him and now expect I will have to try and make it OK for tomorrow. Today S.M. Roberts goes on duty and S.S. Morris is tried by court-martial for abusing S.S. Burnett. Have gotten a number of Canadians in hospital now – nearly all cases are rheumatism, etc. and not wounds. The enemy is not making any dashes just now but expect one soon. Tried stuffed Spanish onions last night – they went very well. I am handicapped by stove room but get along by maneuvering pots.

****

Sergt. Harold Lantz #3381
1ˢᵗ Canadian Expeditionary Force
France

Dear Hazel:

I do not often make the mistake of writing two letters in answer to one. I suppose you would have no objection providing they were interesting. Now I know that I owe you one this time and so am dispatching this so as to reach a few days after Beecher gets his of a few days ago. Beecher wanted to know if I had a snap of myself as he has forgotten just what I look like. He would hardly have known me with the heavy mustache, which I had been cultivating a couple of months but erased the other morning as it was getting cumbersome. May get him one soon.

Sunday evening: I started this letter Friday but was interrupted and at 10pm, am resuming my 'postal conversation'. It is not that I have been rushed so but just interruptions which prevented me from concentrating my thoughts.

The time of late has been very interesting for us and we have watched with interest every official item of news either from dispatch rider or "Daily Mail". We get all the English papers a day late.

Our Corps has branched again and part is running another station under canvas about twelve miles south from us. But we are only busy at intervals, however as warm weather approaches, we are sure to have more medical cases. We have a number of convalescent fellows on our staff now as we would be short otherwise.

Last night at 11pm. Practically our first Canadians came when our own ambulances brought us seven medical cases, four of which were measles cases and one of the four – a fellow from Paradise, N.S. so I am told by the name of A. Joudrie. I went to see him but he was sleeping at the time but will see him in the morning no doubt. I suppose or rather feel certain, he is Dave Joudrey's son. This may not interest you but you can hardly imagine what it feels like to meet a fellow 'from your own home town', even though you don't know him, after being in a foreign country among strangers for months.

The Canadians have been re-enforced but are not up to normal yet. The R.C.D. i.e. Royal Can. Dragoons; E. L. Caldwell's division, just came over as infantry about two weeks ago but find trench work hard after training for saddle work. We had a couple of said RCD's here now but could learn nothing of Lloyd from them. They have not been in action yet maybe soon. One fellow told me tonight that he was fourteen days in trenches without tasting hot food or drink, just field rations, i.e., canned corn beef, hard biscuits but mind you, they do not complain. You have all read, no doubt, about the 48th Highlander who was crucified on the door by the Germans. The Regiment will avenge that deed at first opportunity.

Fighting has been heavy lately and even now is going on but it is quiet where we are as we are not near enough to hear more than the heavy artillery.

Now I shall switch off the war news which are soon read and tell you that I have learned the rudiments of chess so that time permitting I can play a game. It is very interesting and good exercise for the grey matter. My Latin does not get much attention now but will still keep polishing up a little. I am, at present, sleeping in a tent with two other Sergts., and like it fairly well. Do you know that I think I will introduce sleeping on the floor as one really sleeps well there as I never slept better than when I had one blanket between me and the stone floor and am looking well too, at least, I think so.

I miss my glasses for reading but hope to be able to get another pair sometime soon from a specialist who serves in the force about a dozen miles from here.

Was glad to hear that you got that dental work started and suppose you will soon have it completed now and then you will be ale to get out. Say you must look a sight without them! Let's see, you would not be able to sing for a while, would you? Ha! Ha! Now don't get cross!

Now I am wondering what I will write on this sheet with the proverbial scarcity of news you complain of about then I have not told you about the weather which has been, and is, almost ideal if not quite. We have lettuce with mayonnaise dressing and cauliflower, spring onions, etc. of course in the Officers Mess. Now I have not told you that a Taube dropped a bomb in a town perhaps a half mile from us but it did absolutely no damage. Several have seen areoplanes being fired at by artillery up near the lines. From here on this evening, the boys could see the shells burst in the air.

Next: I received the papers O.K. which I now have perused with care. Do you know the 'Monitor' looks different after reading the 'Mail' and 'Times' every day but still they savor of home which is enough. There is a fellow by the name of Neilly with us from near Middleton, who managed the evaporator in Bridgetown for a year, who keeps talking about the farms and the farm life in the 'Valley' and is anxious to see peace so as to allow him to return to the furrow once more. He has the call of the land sure enough.

So you find brother Havelock quite adaptable too. Am glad he was able to help you. Your present work is like mine somewhat, only mine starts about seven and ends ten or eleven.

You would be surprised what we get in tins out here; roast fowl for patients, of course, mutton broth, beef as soup in powder, good stew dinners and other things too numerous to mention. And then I bake some beans every week. We have plenty of eggs and butter, and milk in tins. The men's breakfast is bacon, and stew or steak for dinner, and bread, cheese, jam and tea for supper. It sounds pretty good, does it not? But it gets monotonous after some months without variation.

Now I think I had better close and I will write again in few days when I may have accumulated some news. I have learned nothing of any of our 69th boys but they no doubt are in France now and may meet them any day.

Remember me to all inquiring friends, and boost Centrelea. Get something for the old foggies to take an interest in outside of hay crop and the weather. Easier said than done?

And now until next time,

Au revoir, Harry

FOOTSTEPS OF SERGEANT HAROLD LANTZ:

April 18th, 1915. Time has glided since my last entry with routines and the occasional spurts of work. We have been favored by frequent visits from Gen. Haig and many others of his staff. We have been having goose, salmon, veal, etc. which does not correspond with active service entant. I am having a change of help today, i.e. Clark instead of Bimms. Guess he will work alright. Have procured a few books and am trying to improve my time by some study. Have great weather now. Very little like a Sabbath today.

April 22nd, 1915. Still fine and quiet here. Some fighting around Ypres and other places. Lt. Berndectine is supposed to be suffering from appendicitis and may be operated on tomorrow. M.O.'s do not all agree on diagnosis. Have had two operations for same thing here lately, both doing well.

April 24th, 1915. Great excitement prevailed last night owing to reports French were driven back at Ypres with little resistance. Canadians checked advance. Recovered lost ground at cost of many lives. Today firing very heavy. Sights seen by our officers who were up today not soon forgotten. Germans are making very determined attack but are being stubbornly resisted. However, we had another concert tonight. Was given twice so as to accommodate all hands. Performers were a troupe of Pierots. National Anthem meant more to us than previously. Report says 2000 casualties at 12pm last nite.

April 25th, 1915. King George V sends appreciation to Canadian troops. Firing very heavy both in directions of La Basse and Ypres. Was downtown this evening. Rather an interesting old place. Plenty of injured soldiers, have a full houseful of patients but would still like to move up.

The dressing station is in chaos. I am assigned to a unit under Captain Downsley and Captain Stewart of Halifax. Nursing Sister Folliette and eleven other orderlies make up our unit at Hazebrouck to assist another British C.C.S. We are much closer to the fighting. The Canadian troops are in their first battle and inexperienced at trench fighting. There had been little training in trench warfare at the camp at Salisbury Plains; other than learning how to dig a trench. When the French deserted their line because of the first use of asphyxiating gas by the Germans, it left the Canadians well exposed to the fighting. In desperation, the 3rd Brigade tried to regroup and protect its exposed flank. The commanding officer, Brigadier-General Turner did an amazing job under heavy German bombardment but the cost was heavy in casualties. Soon our crowded dressing station was overflowing with injured soldiers to the point that many stood outside waiting to be treated.

Captain Downsley is desperate to get our field station organized and handle the flow of injured soldiers. It is apparent that many are gas victims who are blinded by the toxic fumes but otherwise not injured. He quickly assigns me to a section of the room where the gas victims are to be treated. I move among them as quickly as possible washing their eyes with a bicarbonate solution and then covering their eyes with bandages. Those that suffer lung damage from the chlorine gas can only be given a shot of morphine to help ease the pain. Although the casualties are great only a few have died from asphyxiation. Once they are treated, the blind soldiers are moved to another building to await transport to the Field Hospital in Vlamertinghe. Soon the building assigned to the walking wounded is full and I have treated over four hundred gas victims. With heavy bombardment in the trenches, more casualties arrive at the overcrowded dressing station. The ambulances cannot handle the huge numbers that need to be transported to the Field Hospital in nearby Vlameringhe. Stretcher bearers try desperately to reach the injured soldiers quickly but many are left to die in the trenches or in the dreaded No Man's-land. Shells are landing closer to the small village where our dressing station is located. Villagers are being killed and injured. It is chaos everywhere I go. Roads are being shelled making them almost impassable for the British Military to move heavy equipment to the front line to support the heavily bombarded troops.

Medical Officer Captain Stewart picks his way through the packed dressing station, stepping over injured troops who sit or lay on the floor as all the cots are full. He spots me in the far corner still washing chlorine residue out of the eyes of gassed soldiers. He is appalled at the sheer number of casualties knowing these soldiers will not be able to return to battle. As he reaches me, Captain Stewart puts his hand on my shoulder.

"A friend of yours is mortally wounded and is asking for you, Sergeant," he speaks in a low whisper so that the other soldiers cannot hear. "I have given him a good shot of morphine to ease the pain but he only has a short time left. He knows he is dying and asked for you. I am giving you permission to leave your duties and go to his side. Stay with him until the end; he is a hero and deserves this much, at least."

As I make my way over to the far side of the room. I say a silent prayer of thanks knowing my brothers are still in England. Orrin had explained in his last letter that his Battalion was still training at Shorncliffe and would be among the next shipment of fresh troops for the Western Front. The Medical Officer motions me to a bloodied soldier in the corner cot and then leaves. By now the sight of injuries are familiar to me but the cries of pain still jar my sensitive nerves. I will never become immune to the human suffering around me. As I approach the cot, I am shocked to see my dear friend, Ted Moir. The morphine has taken the edge off his pain but his eyes clearly show that he is suffering greatly. I quickly sit on the floor beside Ted and take his hand. It is cold and clammy and I involuntarily shudder. I am speechless as I glance at the mortal wounds in his side and stomach. They appear to be machine gun wounds which are the worst.

"Hey, buddy, taking a break from the trenches, I see." I smile but my heart is breaking. I hope my voice is strong as I am totally shaken up. "Do you want a smoke? I keep a few for special times."

"Thanks for coming, Harry. Thought the last face I would see was that ugly Captain. Can you stay with me for a while?" Ted's voice is barely a whisper. His life force is quickly leaving him. "Talk of the old days, Harry, before all this shit happened."

I start to say something but Ted moves his lips again to speak. "God, Harry, it was hell out there. We knew we didn't have a chance against the machine guns but they sent us over the top." He pauses until he has the strength to speak again. "Hadn't got very far when my friend got hit. I tried to get him back to the trenches until that goddamn officer ordered me to drop him and get back to the battle. They do shoot you, Harry, if you try to get back to the trenches. I saw it! Those battle police are worse than the Huns. Always wondered why they carry revolvers instead of rifles. Those bastards!" Ted pauses again and closes his eyes. His breathing is becoming more labored and I fear he will not open his eyes again. After a long moment, his lips move again.

"Remember the day we went to the Paradise Falls for a swim, Harry?" Ted tries to muster a smile but it is too great an effort. I know that Ted is near dying as the mind starts to review its stored memories before it shuts down forever. The old people would say "your life flashes before your eyes" to my father as he sat by the bedside of many a dying parishioner. I shake these thoughts away and look at my closest friend.

"You certainly knew how to make the girls scream, Ted." I want my dear friend to die with happy thoughts. As I watch the color leaving his face, I put a hand on his forehead. It is cold to touch. *Only a few more moments*, I think, and the tears start to stream down my face. Ted stirs again. His whisper is raspy.

"Harry, my good friend, don't go in the trenches. It is the worst hell!" I assure Ted that I will stay away from the trenches. Now the tears really flow and I take great gulps of air to regain my composure. I sit there for a long time; mixed emotions wash over me. I am locked into a state of disbelief. My dear friend who was so excited to go to war is now dead; his last words letting me know he cared. I sit there by his side for a very long time trying to pull my wits together. It is the chaplain whose kindly voice brings me back to reality.

"God has taken him, son. There is no pain where he has gone. May peace be with you." I look up at his kind face. "Now you have hundreds of heroes to attend to. This is a test of our faith, Harry. God has not forsaken us." A memory of my father rushes to the surface. My father would have used the same words of comfort. For a brief moment, I wonder why I am studying to be a minister. It is quite obvious there is little justification for this pain and suffering by the young Canadian soldiers. *I will rethink my choice of career when I return from the war as I cannot find God in this carnage,* I think.

****

It is decided I will take the walking wounded to the Field Hospital in Vlamertinghe. The Allied Forces has suffered terrible losses. Some battalions are completely wiped out; many of their officers killed or seriously wounded, never to return to the battlefield. The town Ypres is totally destroyed by shelling from the Germans hoping to hit the commanding officer's headquarters or the dressing stations. When I heard that the Princess Patricia Regiment suffered much devastation, I was not surprised that they proved their courage and determination by holding its line against the advancing enemy. When they were finally relieved, only one hundred and fifty men led by Lieutenant Niven carrying the Regiments' colors, marched back to the safety of the Menin road. Both their commanding officers had been severely wounded and had been taken to the Field Hospital. All other officers had been killed. Our boys lined the Menin road and cheered the brave soldiers but it was a disastrous blow for the Allied Forces. The Medical Officer conferred with Colonel Haig about the desperate situation. It was decided to send the remnants of the Princess Patricia Regiment along with the blinded soldiers to help with their transport. Colonel Haig, giving in to pressure from the Duke of Connaught, has granted the Regiment a month's leave away from the front to recover and rebuild its Regiment. On their way to the coast to catch a barge to England, they will assist me to transport the gassed soldiers to the Field Hospital where they can be assessed and then sent on to the Casualty Clearing Station. It is hoped that some of these gassed victims will regain their sight and return to battle; however, the majority will be sent home after months in a hospital in London.

Getting to the Field Hospital by foot is no easy task and I am frustrated with our slow pace. Not only do I have over four hundred blind soldiers but I have another fifty walking wounded with assorted injuries that make our progress extremely nerve racking. While the

Princess Pats' are wonderful in every way, we can only progress in pairs as the road is extremely busy with military traffic. A constant stream of motor and horse-drawn ambulances going in both directions, fresh troops being moved up to the frontlines and heavy guns being transported make it impossible for my group to make good progress. There is also the threat of an enemy shell landing in our midst so when we reach a point beyond that threat, I am so relieved that the beauty of the countryside calms me somewhat. My spirits improve and I push my pathetic group harder. The ten miles we have to cover stretches on forever. It is nightfall when we straggle into the small town thinking only of warm food and a clean bed for our weary bodies. What waits us is beyond belief.

Thousands of wounded soldiers are ahead of us. The more serious patients are on cots outside the converted schoolhouse, which is filled to capacity, and the lesser wounded wrapped in blankets lay or sit on the damp ground around the hospital. Doctors are frantically attending to the more seriously injured and when they spy my group, a wail of dismay is heard. Ambulances are leaving and arriving every ten minutes. It is the worst chaos I have ever thought to see and my spirits are dashed. One of the doctors breaks away from his duties and comes to meet me.

"My God, man, what have we here?" His voice is tired even though he tries a weak smile, the doctor knew what the bandaged soldiers meant. More work than he could ever hope to accomplish. He reaches out for the papers I am holding.

I am stunned and, for a moment, all words escape me. I had no idea the casualty count was so high. "How many injured do you have here, sir?" I finally ask.

"Well over three thousand and still counting. Word from the frontlines tells me there are another five thousand waiting for transport. Most of these patients are waiting for transport to England to hospitals. Ambulances and buses are overloaded. I see by these papers that most of your wounded are to be transported to the Clearing Station. Some may regain their sight? Where can I put you after this long walk here? I just don't have the staff to look after these men." He pauses as he looks over the pathetic group of blind soldiers. "Well, let's get started. No point wasting time here. I can make good use of these healthy soldiers you brought with you." The doctor waves me forward while shaking his head over this latest challenge

Lieutenant Niven finds me among the mass of wounded soldiers and complains about the lack of facilities for his men. "We are tired and hungry. Do you know when the next train is coming through? We just want to get to England for a rest." His eyes take in the impossible situation facing the Medical Corps. I hope he regrets the words he has just spoken. "Look, Sergeant Lantz, I don't mean to add to your problems. Perhaps we can ease this situation while we wait for a train. Let's see if there are any tents not being used. At least, it will shelter some of these poor souls from the weather."

Before darkness has fully descended, a hundred spare tents are set up and most of the wounded soldiers are moved in. A large tarp covers the ground in each tent to keep the moisture out. I am so thankful to the wearied Princess Pats. This opened up much needed space but it is soon overflowing as more wounded soldiers keep arriving. As I treat the blind soldiers that night, some report they can see once the bandages are removed. While the doctor inspects me washing their eyes, he insists they remain free of bandages. He is hopeful that many will regain their sight.

In the morning, before I catch a ride back to the frontlines with an empty ambulance, I check my patients. The improvement is remarkable and I feel good leaving them here. They will still have to go to the Clearing Station but some will recover in the Convalescent Depot and then return to the battlefield. What amazes me the most is the reluctance of the Canadians to be sent home before the war ends. Even the severely injured express their desire to come back and fight the Germans.

I have breakfast with Lieutenant Hugh Niven in a little French cafe close to the hospital. The Princess Patricia Regiment had found quarters in a small Inn and they are now prepared to catch the train to the coast. "Thanks for all the help you gave me, Hugh. I hope we meet in better circumstances next time." I am sincere with my praise as there were no words to express my gratitude. Lieutenant Niven stands up to shake my hand and promises to look me up when he returns from leave.

"We will be back to give those Fritz their due, Harry. We owe it to the comrades we left behind." With that comment, he salutes smartly and walks away. Any doubt I may have had about this remarkable regiment dissipates. They have earned their reputation as the finest fighting regiment through their courage and sacrifice on the battlefield.

****

I have been on the frontlines for four months. Mostly, I have been assigned to the Field Dressing Station behind the frontlines where I assist the medical staff. The smell of the wounded and dying has permeated my soul. I have forgotten the aromatic smell of the kitchen and the pride in preparing food for the officers. In the trenches, officers eat the same as the ranks; canned meat, biscuits, water…whatever and whenever they can. The war has stolen my pride and my emotions. The goal is to survive. Even recalling my mother's face eludes me. I don't keep a war diary now because the horrors that I witness need not be recorded. Instead I try to comfort the wounded but even that has become difficult. Not that it matters, most of the wounded that pass through here are too badly injured to concentrate on the words of a confused comrade. We patch them up and send them to the nearest Canadian Base Hospital. The severely wounded will be transferred to the Canadian Convalescent Homes in England before returning to Canada. No one wants to be sent back home until the war is ended. The Canadians' pride of their beloved country manifests into a fighting spirit that has perplexed the British commanders. I don't think they can complain about the Canadian soldiers anymore. We have proven our worth on the battlefield.

Night has fallen; another bombardment, another offensive push. I dread nighttime. Stretcher bearers risk their lives to bring in the wounded. The moans and screams fill the night air; no one wants to be missed. Sometimes the German snipers will silence a particular wail. In a way, it is a mercy kill but our boys consider it a cowardly act to kill a wounded comrade. To die alone in No-Man's Land is fear that one never speaks of. Soon the first wave of wounded soldiers arrives and I work feverishly as I know there will be too many for our limited staff. Those who are lightly wounded and can return to the trenches are patched up first. They come in on their own and are anxious to get back to their comrades in battle. Tonight I am working with one of the doctors on the more seriously wounded. I soon lose count as I cut away clothing to expose the wounds for the doctor. It is so regimented that I barely look at the brave soldier unless the wound is fatal. Then a cigarette is lit and offered, sometimes a tot of rum, a priest or minister is found and whatever comfort can be given to the fallen hero is offered. The courage displayed by these dying soldiers always amazes me; there is no crying or wailing, just a quiet acceptance. I am told by the doctor that most of them are in shock from their wounds but I find them quite coherent as they ask me to send messages home to their family. Tonight is especially busy for the priest as he is called from one cot to the next. I think about my younger brother Gordon who is assigned to a chaplain and will be exposed to this suffering and dying. Since he arrived on the frontlines, I have not heard from him. I hope he is holding up in this chaos. Fragments of the fighting pieced together the day's tragedies. It seems the 1st Canadian Division was detailed to secure the right flank of the 7th British Division which was attempting to breach a heavily fortified stronghold of the enemy known as "Stony Mountain". I have very little knowledge of the battlefield landmarks but I could piece together the battle from the soldiers I worked with tonight. It was a bloody and horrific day with most of our officers killed on the battlefield. Today is June 15, 1915. The Battle for Givenchy cost us many brave souls and the *Angel of Death* will visit many Canadian homes in the coming weeks.

It is close to midnight as I make my way to a billet. I have to push my feet to move; exhausted and spent, I hope to get a few hours of sleep. The guns are silent now; only a rifle crack from a sniper's gun is heard occasionally. *Another mercy killing. Perhaps they are doing our poor boys a favor by ending their suffering,* I think. As tired as I am, I still try to bring reason to this chaos I find myself in. It is pitch black, no moon tonight but the sky to the east is full of stars, sparkling in the dark void. I wonder how this war will end. I think of my brothers and offer a short prayer for their safety; at least, they were not among the wounded I tended tonight.

****

I am roughly shaken awake. In a sleep fog, my mind is lost in my dream of bloodied soldiers waiting to be bandaged.

"Sergeant, come quickly, sir!" A private is standing over me.

"What is it? I just got to sleep," I complain. I struggle to my feet. I now sleep in my uniform and greatcoat. Looking around I realize I am still in the Field Dressing Station. Slowly my mind recalls the events before I went off duty after working feverishly for sixteen hours. The station had been swamped with wounded soldiers from the fierce fighting. Everyone was called in to handle the tremendous workload. Totally spent from exhaustion, the orderlies find a place to grab a quick nap in the station rather than go back to our billets. Fighting is extreme in Festubert, Givenchy and Loos resulting in heavy casualties in the summer of 1915.

Captain Stewart is waiting for me as I make my way around the numerous cots filled with wounded Canadians. Many of them are too dazed from the recent fighting to feel the pain of their wounds. I find it hard to look at them. All are waiting for ambulances to take them to the Canadian Field Hospital in Boulogne where arms and legs will be amputated to save their lives. As I tread carefully through the maze of wounded soldiers, I know that many will die before the ambulances arrive.

"Sergeant Lantz, I am assigning you a very delicate mission. We have a situation that is top secret." Captain Stewart speaks quietly but his tired eyes never leave my face. I wonder what keeps this kind man on his feet for days at a time. "I am sending you and Nursing Sister Tremaine to a chateau a few miles away to care for a very important patient. Put together a kit to last a few days; there is a motorcar waiting to take you. Nurse Tremaine has been briefed and is waiting. I must ask you to say nothing of this to anyone. It is top secret." I don't even get to ask any questions as I am escorted out of the Field Dressing Station.

The road is lit up by the constant flashes of gunfire. Many of the shells land dangerously close to the motorcar as it makes its way around the obstacles on the road. Because any light will make us a target for the German guns, we are driving in the dark without headlights. I can make out shadows along the road and I wonder how the driver could see well enough to miss hitting anyone. Nursing Sister Vivian Tremaine sits beside me but other than a formal greeting, she offers no conversation. She is a timid creature and I wonder what possessed her to go to war. The suspense of finding the identity of the mystery patient keeps me on edge. *Who could be so important for all this fuss,* I wonder. As the miles pass slowly, the rough road and rocking motion of the car gradually soothes my anxious nerves. Suffering from lack of sleep, I am lulled into a deep sleep only to be jolted awake by a blast of the car's horn. Dawn is breaking, casting a pink glow over the countryside revealing fields and rolling hills. I recognize the landscape as being close to Aire where my unit had set up the 1st Canadian Convalescent Care Station in March.

A lovely chateau sits amid lofty trees and flower gardens. *There is no sign of a war here,* I think as I exit the motorcar. After four months of listening to the constant roar of shells exploding, the sound of the birds singing in the trees seems foreign to my ears. Breathing in the fresh country air, I look around the military structured chateau. Its beauty is marred only by the French soldiers guarding the entranceway. Flocks of small sheep are feeding on the grass alongside the driveway. Entering through the tall stone gate highlighted by carved scenes of Greek and Roman mythology over the entrance, I am most curious as to the important patient that I almost trip on the stairs leading into the foyer.

Inside the drawing room, General Haig paces the black and white tiled floor as he waits for the medical staff to arrive. He realizes that this situation is so imperative that it can alter the outcome of the war. Slapping the riding crop against his right thigh, he watches us enter the double paneled doors. I am ashamed of the rumpled state of my clothing and the fact I have not had a shower in a few days but I was not given a chance to clean up. I can't help but notice how clean and well pressed his uniform is.

"Welcome to Citadel of Lille and thank you for coming so quickly," he announces as he waves us to the chairs by the window. "This is a very unfortunate situation and the patient you will be caring for is extremely important to the outcome of the war." The General pauses and then announces, "His Majesty, King George V, was with me close to the frontlines last night when his horse spooked at an exploding shell nearby. It reared and fell, rolling on His Majesty. Now his injuries are not severe but the doctors feel he should have several days' bed rest before he can be safely escorted back to England. You may not be aware, being Canadians, but the British are very superstitious and should their King fall in battle, it is taken as a bad omen. In the old days, it meant defeat. Therefore, I cannot let the British Army know of this incident as it would affect the morale of the British troops. I am relying on you, who love our King dearly, for your excellent skills in nursing care. I, myself, have been cared for by your staff so I know how dedicated you are."

The General looks at us, taking in our tired and bedraggled appearance. His words have shocked us both and I feel myself sway a bit. I am having trouble grasping the significance of the situation. "I will see that you have a hot breakfast, followed by a hot bath, to freshen you from your expedient trip, before you are escorted to His Majesty. I regret the secrecy of this expedition but it is imperative that no one speaks of this little accident. Your quarters are ready and now if there are no questions, please allow yourselves to be escorted to the breakfast room where a hot breakfast awaits. The Medical Officer will join you at breakfast and brief you of your duties. The French government owns this lovely chateau and the two garrisons house French troops. Their staff will wait on your needs. The King greatly appreciates your services. Dismissed."

I watch the General briskly walk from the room leaving me stunned by the news. I glance at Sister Tremaine and note that she also appears shocked. It is the first time she looks me directly in the eyes and I notice she is quite pretty. The General's adjutant approaches to escort us to the

Breakfast Room. The table is laid out with a generous meal of eggs and ham, cheese and warm baked bread. The smell of freshly brewed coffee beckons us and I realize I have not eaten a proper meal in two days. Casting aside any doubt about the secret mission, I quickly fill my plate and sit down. Forgetting my manners, I pick up the solid silver fork and begin eating, savoring each delicious bite. I notice that Nursing Sister Tremaine is delicately picking at the small portions on her plate. This brings a smile to my face as I look around at the luxurious surroundings. *What a magnificent building and a perfect spot to hide a King,* I think.

Through the ornate wooden doors of the vestibule, the medical officer, Major McKinnon, appears. I immediately stand and salute.

"Stand down, Sergeant," orders the Major as he picks up a gold rimmed plate and proceeds to heap steaming food on it. "I advise you both to take advantage of this good food while you are here. This is a rare treat on the battlefield." As he sits down, he acknowledges the presence of Sister Tremaine who gives him a nervous smile. Major McKinnon is well known to both of us and is respected for his skill in surgery. He is in charge of the 1st Canadian Convalescent Hospital in Aire.

After a pleasant breakfast, tea is served by the staff. The Major launches into the routine that is expected in the care of His Majesty. While it will be intense, I feel that a daily walk around the grounds and a good bed to sleep in would more than offset the long hours expected of me. I am glad the King has not been severely injured and is only suffering from bruises and a sprained ankle.

My uniform has been cleaned and pressed while I had a short nap after a luxurious hot bath. I am escorted to the library to select some books for the King as I am responsible to see that His Majesty is kept entertained during his respite. His personal care will be administered by Nurse Termaine and she will sit with him during his sleeping hours. I look around the enormous library with its mahogany bookshelves filled with leather bound books. I cannot help myself as I lovingly run my hand along their spines feeling the richness of the leather. I have no idea what a King would read but having seen Buckingham Palace, I am sure there is a library there that rivals this one. My eyes fall on a chess board set up on a small ornate table by the window. I quickly move over to have a closer look. I had just learned how to play chess and I am completely fascinated with the intricate moves required. This chess board is quite spectacular with its exotic woods and carved figures. I decide I will take this with me and then I chose a thick book about the French royalty. Until I get to know the King's taste in literature, I felt this was a safe read. I brush aside my nerves as I enter the bedchambers. The French sentry outside the door carefully inspects everything I have brought with me before he allows me to enter the room. His Majesty is dwarfed by the huge canopied bed but his smile is encouraging as I approach. I must wait for him to speak to me before I am allowed to address him. But his voice is warm as he calls me forward and questions me about my family. He appears interested in my response and finally asks what I have suggested to keep him occupied for the next few days. I smile when he informs me he would rather be out hunting on his estate with his favorite hunting dogs. I present the intricately carved chessboard and assure him it will offer many hours of enjoyment. His reaction is lukewarm at first but sensing my enthusiasm, he confesses he has never had the privilege to learn this so-called fascinating game. I try to hide my surprise but I feel His Majesty is testing me so I set the game board up and proceed to explain the moves. At first, he is hesitant and asks me about every move before he makes it but I detect a slight smile as he looks at me while I explain. I suggest he consider the board a battlefield and the movement of his pawns would be his troops. His Majesty ponders this suggestion. I discover he has a splendid military mind as he becomes adept at the game. The afternoon passes so quickly that I am quite shocked when we are interrupted for dinner. Promising to return to the game later, I exit his chambers. *I am going to enjoy this mission,* I think as I make my way to the dining room.

I am a little dispirited when the motor ambulance pulls into the driveway of Citadel du Lille on the evening of the third day. The King has refused to stay in bed another day. No amount of coaxing by Major McKinnon can change His Majesty's mind. So I am given the task of disguising him as a wounded soldier which delights the King immensely. When his head is wrapped in bandages so just his eyes and mouth are visible, I have to smile at his childlike enjoyment. His ankle is tightly wrapped and a pair of crutches completes his disguise. I had been walking him in the gardens each day for exercise so he is quite familiar with the use of crutches. He and Nursing Sister Tremaine will leave for the train station where other wounded Canadians are waiting. They will board the train to La Harve where a hospital ship is waiting to sail to England. General Haig accompanies the King to ensure his safe return on the pretense of war issues to be discussed in London.

As I return to the frontlines, I regret I did not get to go to England with the nursing staff but understand the need for my return to the frontlines. Every available hand is needed to handle the massive number of casualties resulting from the ongoing battles. All I can do is dream about living in Buckingham Palace for several weeks. It is hard to hide my disappointment when General Haig announces his plans. To add further to my disappointment, I cannot share the amazing past few days with my friends. I cannot even write home about my time with His Majesty but I vow I will tell my sister as soon as the war is over. She will get great delight learning that her brother taught the King of England how to play chess.

Well rested and well fed, I watch the changing landscape as the motorcar returns me to the Field Dressing Station. Soon the quiet road is choked with troops marching to the front. We meet many ambulances carrying injured soldiers to the hospital in Aire. It is a sight I am very familiar with and the past few days with His Majesty slips into a memory that I will cherish.

****

75

FOOTSTEPS OF PRIVATE GORDON LANTZ:

I stand on French soil for the first time in the summer of 1915. Such a feeling of exhilaration courses through me; never have I been so excited since I was a little boy on Christmas morning. Finally I am on the Western Front and it has been a long, exhausting trip to get here. I arrive with a battalion from the 17th Reserves Highland Regiment, the very lads I had seen at the train station in Truro in 1914. With them is their chaplain and I am his Batman or, as I found out in England, a military term for a man servant. All high ranking officers have them. No matter my station, I have reached the battlefield. My older brother is already here and I hope to find him as soon as I get my bearings. We are close to a little village called Loos. The Western Front is not like I had pictured it. It seems too quiet for a war that is raging on around these small villages and towns.

I follow the chaplain everywhere. Keeping the Canon's clothes clean, neat and free of lice and polishing his boots until I can see my reflection is my first priority. *Cleanliness is godliness* is one of his favorite quotes and I have learned that he has a quote for every duty. Afraid to ride a horse, the Canon prefers motorcars or the sidecar of a motorcycle which I drive. When I ask him why he doesn't ride a horse like the other brass hats, he quickly comments, "God gave us two legs to use. Why burden those poor, dumb beasts with our simple needs?" He is one of the most fascinating men I ever met. For a man of the cloth, the Canon is unlike my father who believes the sins of man are the work of the devil. I asked the Canon one day after Sunday Mass what he thinks about man's sins.

"My son, God forgives all sins of man. But the devil, now that is a different matter." He shakes his head as he speaks.

The Canon is a Highlander, to be sure, as he drinks whiskey and curses in Gaelic. But he is such a caring and gentle man that he becomes more like a loving grandfather than a chaplain to the lads from Cape

Breton. After arriving in England from Canada in late 1914, I spent my time training how to administer to the spiritual needs of the dying and wounded soldiers. The proud young men from the Cape Breton Highlands were merged into the 17th Reserves Highland regiment. They were not too happy to lose their identity as a battalion but the British brass had plans for these brave young men.

Adjusting to life on the frontlines is challenging. Most of the time, we are in the field hospitals giving hope to the wounded. Every Sunday, regardless of weather or war activities, Colonel Canon O'Brien will hold Mass several times. Finding a suitable place to set up his makeshift altar is not easy; often times it is a barn or the rubble of a ruined church. Sometimes, we go to the trenches where the soldiers are. This is my favorite place as I am in the trenches with the brave soldiers ready to go over the top. They cannot leave their posts but that does not deter Colonel Canon O'Brien.

"God is everywhere," he tells me. "These wretched souls sitting here in the mud need our blessing."

At first, the sounds and sights of war disturb me. But as the weeks go by, I have learned not to jump every time the roar of a whizz-bang passes over our heads. I even learn to sleep through the sounds of heavy gunfire. The war has intensified around Loos in the last week or so. As yet our boys have not been in battle; they are busy training in the bull ring behind the lines. It is September, 1915 and the battle at Loos is in full swing.

Colonel Canon O'Brien shakes me awake. We have been especially busy this day, administering the burials of many fallen heroes. I am exhausted.

"Quickly, Gordon, a terrible tragedy has happened. We must hurry!" The Canon is clearly upset.

I dress quickly and join him in the kitchen of our billet. He passes me his kit and we leave without another word. Jumping on the motorcycle, I drive in the direction of the village of Loos. We are billeted in a small farm house just outside the village. The villagers had fled the onslaught of the German army many months ago. I had heard a lot of gunfire in the night and I knew there was heavy fighting by our boys. It is not unusual for the Canon to go out to the fighting but we usually have an escort. As we approach the village, a group of sentries stop us.

When they see it is the Canon, they wave us on. "The commanding officer is waiting for you, sir. One of the men will show you where to go."

We leave the motorcycle and proceed on foot. Such is our haste that I have little time to think of what this tragedy could be. Even in the dark, I can see groups of soldiers standing together. I find this unusual as normally they would be trying to sleep between their tours in the front trenches.

The commanding officer, Colonel Turner, comes forward and greets us. "Thank you for coming so quickly. A terrible tragedy! There are no words to describe it. But we need your services before we can proceed. Please steel yourself, sir. It is not a pleasant sight!"

He glances at me and then turns to lead the way. I follow them blindly; my mind going in all directions. As we come upon a large number of troops, I hear the wail of the bagpipes. My heart leaps to my throat. Now I know it is my battalion in trouble. This is their first battle – their *baptism of fire* as the seasoned veterans call it.

We stand on the edge of the trench and look down. Even in the dim light, I can make out the faces, twisted in agony, of the dead Highlanders. I find it hard to believe that those cheerful lads from Cape Breton are now a tangled mass of kilts and burnt bodies. I know most of them by name and, despite the twisted and tortured faces frozen in death, I recognize some of them. Many are my age, a mere eighteen years old. A chill sweeps over me and I clench my teeth to keep them from chattering. I step closer to the Colonel as he quickly explains what had happened; his voice cracking a bit as we are told of the massacre.

"They were called up from the Reserves to fight with the British who were desperately trying to break through the German line. This was their first encounter with the enemy and the battle was in full swing. In the confusion of the pit-head landscape of the mining district in the dark, they marched in the wrong direction. This brought them closer to the German line and the enemy would have clearly seen them," said the Colonel. "Thinking they were in position, they hunkered down in this shallow trench that had been vacated by the British the day before when they were driven back by the enemy. The rest of the division did not know they were here and by the time the commanding officer realized their mistake, it was too late. The Germans shot canisters of yellow cross into their shallow trench; the Highlanders had no protection. The Germans enfiladed while they were screaming in agony and trying to get out of the trench. Standing on the parapet, they shot the helpless and defenseless Highlanders without mercy. Then the Germans proceeded to push their way to the back of the Allied line only to be stopped by another Reserve Division which was moving up to the front. The Germans quickly retreated to the safety of their own trenches, leaving behind in their wake, hundreds of casualties including the slaughtered Highlanders." The Colonel pauses as he looks at us; he is having a hard time keeping his emotions under control. I am standing here stunned by all this and glance over at the Canon who has yet to say anything.

Looking at both of us carefully, he continues. "The trench is contaminated with mustard gas so we have to bury them here, Canon. We cannot even recover their ID tags or personal effects. We must bury them as they are and use our records to identify them. It is such a tragic loss of good men. But the Germans did them a favor by ending their suffering; at least their death was swift. Cruel as it may seem to shoot the wounded, dying from mustard gas poisoning means unspeakable suffering for many days. Will you say your prayers for the dead as we fill in the trench, sir?" he concludes.

Colonel Canon O'Brien stares at the twisted and tortured faces in the trench. Already the yellow cross is making ugly sores as it eats away at the exposed flesh. I watch the Canon cross himself and say a silent prayer. I know how hard this must be as he knew every one of these boys by name. We had been with them since they arrived at Quebec in 1914. The Canon had been by their side telling jokes to cheer them up when fear of the unknown would creep into their thoughts. He had been like a grandfather to these Highland lads and they had loved him dearly. The Canon looks around at the living soldiers ready to shovel the limestone soil over the victims, and then crossing himself again, starts the litany of prayers for the dead.

Not a gun is fired from the enemy lines as the somber task of burying the unfortunate highlanders and their pipes proceeds. The Highland Regiment from Toronto is playing the mournful laments while the chaplain's voice is barely heard over the noise made by the shovels. Slowly the tortured faces are covered; but they are forever etched in the memories of their comrades.

I walk beside the Canon as he sprinkles holy water in the trench and prays for their souls. When we reach the end of the trench, I feel such sadness that I am almost overcome with it. I look back over the filled-in trench and notice that stakes are being pushed into the soft ground. On each stake, a highlander field dress cap is placed instead of the usual helmet. The helmets, being contaminated by gas, could not be removed. For these poor souls, this will be their monument. Of course, there are not enough stakes for the number of dead but the sight is impressive. A long line of stakes topped with the colors of the Highlanders, the feathers and red *torries* move slightly in the soft breeze. We are all struck by the simplicity and beauty in such ugly surroundings. The urge to sing overcomes me as I have a good voice and often sing for the Canon during his Mass services. When I suggest this to the Canon, he simply says, "The angels are singing for these souls going to heaven this night."

When, at last, the mournful wail of the bagpipes end, a new and terrifying one begins. I jump straight up in the air. The hair on my head lifts a good inch and my heart skips a few beats. I look at Colonel Turner who is just as startled as we are. Turning to the Canon, I am about to ask him what is making such a spine-chilling noise when the mascot, a white goat named *Robert the Bruce*, walks up to the trench. It is giving off the most sorrowful bleats I have ever heard. Just where it came from is a mystery as it is usually with the pipers. But with the pipers dead in the trench, the goat must have been wandering around and came back to the sound of the bagpipes.

"There will be a few Germans changing their underwear tonight," remarks the Colonel before asking me to take the goat back to my billet. This white goat has a bad reputation for being cantankerous but as I look at it, bleating for its comrades, I almost cry. Walking over to where it is standing, I talk softly hoping it doesn't chase me as it is known to do. But it looks at me sadly before dropping its head, crowned with impressive curved horns, and meekly follows me back to the village. I could have sworn I saw tears in those big brown eyes of his but I keep that to myself. I don't think anyone would believe me, especially the chaplain who considers all animals dumb creatures.

I like to think that when the Germans look down from their trenches the next morning and see the colorful feathers on the khaki tam o'shanters nailed to the stakes waving softly in the breeze, they will fear the ghosts of the Highlanders. They must have felt something because their guns are quiet all the next day.

Somehow, I became the custodian of *Robert the Bruce*, the regiment's mascot. He is good company and we get along famously. He refuses to stay with the other livestock, and every night, he sleeps on the floor by my bed. He considers himself my watchdog and, more than once, chases anyone who dares enter my room. I am slightly pleased but the Canon is a little upset by this turn of events. During the day, he accompanies me everywhere. I hear more than one chuckle escape those who watch the Canon and I making our rounds among the wounded with our white goat following us like a dog. The wounded soldiers are delighted to see him and sneak cookies and tobacco to him when they think I am not looking.

The Canon says that *The Bruce* is the best medicine for the weary and suffering soldiers. "God has His Ways, son, even in this Hell."

I don't think the doctors agree as they keep a wary eye on us whenever we are in the hospital. I will hate to see him leave when the reserve units from England arrive to fill the 17th Reserves Highland Battalion losses. That old goat is so spoiled by all the attention it gets that I nickname him *The General* as he really has taken control of us all.

I am saddened when the 40th Battalion adopted *Robert the Bruce* as their mascot. His new home is now with the 40th Battalion Band and I often see him marching proudly beside the pipers in the parade square, still wearing his original colors of McKenzie tartan, and lending his own musical version in an amusing way. Sometimes I catch a fleeting look of far-off longing in the Canon's eyes as he watches the white goat proudly marching along, bleating its heart out. I discreetly look away.

The memories of that night in Loos still haunts the Canon as I hear him crying in the night after he thinks I have fallen asleep. I don't know how to comfort a man of the cloth but I pray hard every night that he will find peace to ease his grief.

****

PART TWO

The Great War: 1916 – 1917

FOOTSTEPS OF SERGEANT HAROLD LANTZ:

The Battle of Somme in 1916 is fought with valor by the Canadian and Newfoundland troops. The commanding officers cancelled all day passes as the casualties mounted. I have been working for eighteen hours without a break as the wounded pour into the Field Dressing Station. I ask the medical officer for a break when a brief lull came. Once outside, I find a quiet corner for a smoke. I only smoke when I am stressed; normally, I keep cigarettes to give to the wounded to alleviate their worry. My billet is too far away to snatch some sleep so I hunker down in the mud. I have not had time to read a letter that arrived in the morning mail from one of my nursing friends in Boulogne. But the light is poor so I left it in my pocket to read later. My brother Orrin is in the trenches with the 85th Battalion and I am worried about him. When he arrived at the front several months ago, he immediately found me at the Field Dressing Station. Although our reunion was brief, it was such a relief to see him again and hear all the news from home. We both worry about Gordon who does not stay in touch very often.

"Sergeant Lantz," calls the medical orderly, his urgent voice breaking into my thoughts.

I quickly go into the Station to see about the emergency. The medical officer is standing with a group of officers from one of the regiments. When he sees me enter, he waves me over. It is hard to assess the situation so I proceed to the group with a heavy heart. I feel something is wrong and I hope it is not bad news about Orrin. I notice the officers are with the Princess Patricia's Regiment and I knew they had taken quite a hit on the battlefield in the last few days.

I salute and ask the commanding officer if I can be of help. One glance at the concerned faces of the officers alert me to brace for bad news.

"Sergeant, we have a situation here that is serious and needs your help. It is unusual to go to the wounded in the field but we have to do it this time. As you are aware, the Pats had heavy casualties and these officers have just found out that a Colonel and two more officers are wounded and trapped in No-Man's Land." Captain Stewart is watching my reaction carefully. "These officers are badly wounded and need medical attention before transporting them back to the Dressing Stations. I want you to go with the stretcher-bearers and attend these officers' wounds. Prepare yourself a medical kit and include lots of morphine. You will leave in several hours as soon as it is dark"

My heart stops at the mention of No-Man's Land; it is my greatest fear. All the wounded soldiers I have attended spoke of their fear of the killing fields that separate the enemies' lines. My mind floods with the warnings and, as my heart pounds with fear, I obediently pack a medical kit. It never occurred to me that I would have to go out on the battlefield to tend the wounded. Picking up the cleanest greatcoat from the pile of discarded clothing from dead soldiers, I quickly make my way to the waiting stretcher-bearers. A young lieutenant has joined the group; I learn that he is our guide to find the shell hole where the wounded officers are hiding. As we are about to leave, one of the officers from the Princess Patricia's Regiment passes me a flask.

"This will come in handy, Sergeant. Nothing like whiskey to light the fire in your belly. Those officers will appreciate it." He gives me a smile as I slip it in my greatcoat inside pocket. By now, I have accepted that whiskey and rum are part of the daily rations of war.

The Lieutenant gathers us outside and starts instructing our small group. "No talking. Even a whisper carries on the wind. Single file and follow me. If I crawl on my belly, you crawl. The Germans have left the area but their snipers are out there covering the retreat. Sergeant Lantz, you come behind me and do everything I do." I glance around at the group whose faces are smeared with black oil; only the whites of their eyes could be seen in the dark. Quickly, a private comes up to smear my pale face with the oil. I have a terrible feeling about this mission but I push away the doubts that try to take over reason. *This would have to happen on my shift*, I mutter to myself as I follow the Lieutenant closely.

Leaving the safety of the trenches, we slowly make our way out into No-Man's Land. Our destination is Sanctuary Wood which is about three hundred yards away. It is pitch black and the ground we are crossing is pitted with shell holes and corpses. This battle, dubbed "The Big Push", has been raging for over three weeks. We reach a point where we have to crawl and the going is slow and treacherous. Trees that have been shattered by bombardments are now just sharp stumps but we crawl around them. Strangely, one tree stands alone and although its branches have been shot up, the trunk stands eerily like a guard over the decimated forest. But the pile of corpses here is unbelievable; in some places, they are piled on top of each other just as they fell. We have no choice but to crawl over the rotting corpses and the stench clogs my nostrils making me nauseated. I am glad it is too dark to see the mangled death masks of the Princess Patricia's regiment. We are close to the enemy line. I panic and bump into the lieutenant's boots. His harsh whisper gives me shivers. "You will get us all killed, Sergeant. Pay attention." I am in a perpetual state of fear. Sanctuary Wood is a living hell. We feel the enemy watching us but we push on. As soon as we had left the trenches, I was lost. I cannot tell what direction we are going or even what direction we had come from. Inch by inch, we move forward until the lieutenant stops. He points to a shell hole that I could hardly make out but I feel this is my destination. Quietly I slip into it and wait for my eyes to adjust to the darkness of the hole. There are two figures huddled in one corner; only their pale faces stand out from the dark wall of the shell hole. Inching forward, I whisper, "Medic here to help. Are you okay?" There is no response so I crawl closer.

The major whispers, "Bad shape. Need something for pain."

When I reach them, I realize that only one is alive. The Colonel had been too badly injured to survive. "Where's the other Colonel?" I ask the Major as I prepare a shot of morphine.

"Germans took him prisoner. We were too badly injured so they left us." The major's voice is cracking up. I can see he is badly injured and it will take my best efforts to get him in shape for the stretcher-bearers. The lieutenant slips noiselessly into the shell hole beside me.

"How are they, Sergeant, almost ready to transport?" he asks. Peering into the darkness, he looks at the dead Colonel. "Is he dead? Are we too late?"

"The Colonel didn't make it sir, and this one is in bad shape. If I bandage him, the white dressing will show in the darkness. He is bleeding heavily from that wound in his thigh and needs a tourniquet. I will do what I can but getting him back quickly is paramount." As I am speaking, I quickly cut away the leather boot and start dressing the wound making it as tight as I can to slow down the bleeding.

The lieutenant scans the darkness for the third officer. "They said there were three officers here. What happened to the other Colonel?" he whispers.

The major, slightly revived by the morphine, told him about the Germans checking the shell hole for their own survivors and had found them. He motions to the dead Colonel. "We were too far gone to be taken prisoners. They should have shot us rather than leave us to die like this." That comment sent shivers up my spine as I quickly finish the bandaging and pull the leg of the major's uniform down over the white dressing. I am anxious to get back to the safety of the dressing station.

The stretcher-bearers quickly lift him from the hole and quietly wait for the others to come up with the dead Colonel. Not a word is spoken and as I am the last to leave the shell hole, I find myself at the rear of the group. The lieutenant had already started the slow crawl back to the trenches and I had no choice but to follow blindly. Suddenly the sound of machine gun fire ruptures the stillness of the night. It sprays dirt and bits of flesh and bone into my face. I lay there with my face buried in the mud. With my heart beating so fast that I get a sharp pain in my chest, I think I am dying. I couldn't feel any pain anywhere else in my body so after ten minutes, I slowly start to crawl forward. The stretcher-bearers have been mutilated by the machine gun but by some strange twist of fate, the major is not hit. As I inch further forward, I come upon the dead lieutenant. I am riveted by this situation; I have no idea where to go and I still have a wounded officer to care for. To leave him in the field is certain court-martial. I inch backward to where the major is lying and whisper in his ear. "We need cover, sir. You have to help me get you to a shell hole." Not getting a reply, I slowly drag him by his cartridge belt until I come upon another shell hole and quietly slide into it.

I sit here as the reality of my situation penetrates my numbed brain. I try to guess how many hours of darkness are left for cover. I reason that it had been close to midnight when we had left the trenches, and I feel sure that we spent at least four hours out here. Soon the early dawn will be breaking over No-Man's Land. I realize I cannot risk trying to get back so I will have to spend the rest of the night in the shell hole. Surely someone will come looking for us when our group does not return. I wonder how much longer the major can stay alive. He has lost a lot of blood. I know he will sleep for a long time as I had given him a good dose of morphine. With that last thought, I pull my greatcoat up over my ears and hunker down in the soupy mud. Weary and exhausted, I soon fall asleep.

It is a noise close to my ear that awakes me. The sunlight streams into the shell hole so I figure it must be close to noon. With a jerk, I sit upright and see a giant rat scamper up the side of the mud wall. When I look at the major, I am horrified to see two more rats chewing on his hands. Quickly, I throw mud at them and watch them scamper away. They are the biggest rats I ever saw. Both the major's hands are bleeding profusely; his fingers chewed to the first knuckle. I quickly move over to see if the major is alive and am very surprised to find a weak pulse but he is unresponsive. Checking him carefully, I wash the wounds made by the rats and bind them tightly. *At least the rats cannot chew his fingers now,* I mutter to myself. So concerned with the major, I did not notice the drips of blood on my greatcoat until I feel something sticky on the side of my neck. When my hand comes back bloody, I realize I have been bitten as well. A new fear settles on me. We will be eaten alive by these huge rats unless we can get out of here soon. After I wash my wound, I try to figure out how to bandage it and finally wrap the dressing around both ears and my nose, just leaving my eyes and mouth uncovered. Now we are trapped because the white dressings will certainly show up at night and alert the snipers. *Crawling out of here is not an option even if I knew which way to go,* I say to myself and feeling great despair, I sit back in the mud.

It is late in the afternoon when I remember the unopened letter. The major has become semi-conscious and is having a lot of pain. I give him another dose of morphine to keep him quiet and now he is comatose again. I reach into my pocket and withdraw the letter. I knew it wasn't from Penny even though I have been expecting a reply to my last letter over a month ago.

3rd Canadian Hospital
Boulogne, France

Dear Harry:

I am the bearer of bad news but my heart tells me I have to write you. I do not know if the news has reached you yet of the sinking of the hospital ship last month. It was a terrible and unnecessary loss of life. As you know, the Germans have increased their control over the seas between France and England in the past six months and travel has become dangerous. One of our hospital ships carrying wounded soldiers and five nursing sisters struck a mine and sank off the coast of England near Folkstone. The escort destroyer tried to save any survivors but it too struck a mine and sank in fifteen minutes. Nurse Penny was on this ship travelling with the wounded soldiers. Some of them were going to Taplow. I know you were fond of our dear Penny as she was fond of you. I hope you can bear this sad news with a strong heart. This war has become very ugly and so many wonderful souls have departed before their time.

I wish you well and I hope you will visit me when your travels bring you this way.

Your kind friend

Elizabeth Pierce, Matron

At first my dazed mind does not grasp the contents and I read it twice. As the realization sunk in, a wail of despair froze on my lips. My precious Penny is dead. *A horrible death*, I groan, *her beautiful body lay at the bottom of the North Sea probably blown to bits.* My pain became unbearable. Memories of Penny's smile and dancing brown eyes flash before me. I bury my face in the mud to muffle my cries of anguish; my heart has been ripped in two. Never have I felt such pain. It is dark before I finally lift my head from the mud and look around. Now anger becomes my fuel to survive; I want out of this hole so I can kill some Germans. This is the first time I have the urge to kill the enemy. It is the major who stops me from climbing over the top.

Finally alert and suffering less pain, he is watching me groping around in the dark hole. Realizing I am going to abandon him, he barks an order. "Sergeant, get a hold of yourself! You have a wounded officer to look after."

At first I ignore the major as I am intent on leaving but a grain of sanity brings me back. I sink down in the mud trying to put the pieces of my life back in order. *They will come for us tonight,* I think, and reach for the flask in my greatcoat. I had forgotten it but I could feel it jamming against my chest. Having never had a drink of alcohol in my life, the first swallow of whiskey takes my breath away and catches on fire in my empty stomach. I cough and choke while my eyes water but I foolishly take another big swallow. This one nearly does me in. It burns all the way to my stomach and feels like hot coals. I almost lose my breath as I cough and choke violently.

"Hey, take it easy! No more now. We will need this to keep us going. Sergeant, give me the flask. I need you alert for the stretcher-bearers," the major says softly as he reaches over and takes the flask from my trembling hands. "Now you be ready to help get us out of here. We will take turns staying awake so the rats can't chew on us." He looks at me with concern; he can see that I am coming apart at the seams. The major had seen it before in battle; perfectly good soldiers become a bundle of weak nerves losing all sense of duty. Some even throw down their rifles and deliberately walk into the line of fire.

I look at him but I don't respond. Resentment is starting to build inside me. The whiskey has given me a warm glow as it spreads throughout my body. A feeling of euphoria settles in and my situation begins to look brighter. Life feels good as long as the flask is within reach. *I will wait for the major to fall asleep and drink what is left*, my confused mind reasons. It eases the pain in my heart but the memories are still there. *Good memories*, I think. I imagine I can even hear Penny's voice; so light and soft. I fall into a drunken stupor and when I awake, it is morning. The major has slumped over and is dead. *How did that happen?* I wonder. The ground around him is saturated with his blood. *Lord, the bandage must have slipped and he bled to death. Maybe he tried to get up while I was sleeping,* I reason as I try to figure out what to do. When I start to move, the pain in my head is so intense I have to shut my eyes against the light. "I can't take this," I cry and great sobs break the stillness. In my misery, I forget about the sniper.

It is late afternoon before I can lift my head without a searing pain bringing me to my knees. I have lost track of time and try to figure out how long I have been in the shell hole. I know I have to get out tonight or I will die along with the major. But when darkness comes, fear grabs me and I cannot force myself to crawl out. *Better to wait,* I think, *they will come.* Finally admitting defeat, I curl up in a ball making sure my hands are in the deep pockets of the greatcoat so the rats cannot chew them. *They will come,* I say over and over until I fall into a restless stupor.

****

FOOTSTEPS OF LIEUTENANT ORRIN LANTZ:

I make my way over wounded soldiers lying on the floor of the dressing station to where the Medical Officer is working. I am sure I will find my brother Harry working tonight. I had searched everywhere for him but with so many wounded soldiers crowding the station I know it will be quicker to speak to the doctor.

"Sir, I wonder if you can tell me where Sergeant Lantz is working tonight?" I ask the weary doctor. As he turns his bloodshot eyes on me, I am sure he can see a family resemblance.

"Corporal Lantz, your brother is missing. He is either a prisoner or he got pipped. We sent two details to assist but they could not find him. He went out four nights ago to Sanctuary Wood with a detail to assist with three wounded officers from the Princess Patricia's Regiment. The bodies of the stretcher bearers and one officer were found but there was no sign of Sergeant Lantz and the other two officers." The doctor's voice is strained with worry and fatigue.

I am stunned by the news. At first, the impact did not register but when I realize that Harry has been out in No-man's Land for four nights alone with wounded officers, my training takes over. "Can you get me a detail and I will go look. The Germans have left Sanctuary Wood so we can search in the daylight. Please, sir, I just need a few men to help me with the wounded officers."

The doctor shakes his head sadly. "All the stretcher-bearers are busy gathering up the wounded cavalry from today's battle. You probably heard that General Haig ordered the cavalry to charge the Germans. Horses and swords against machine guns, my God, what was he thinking? Twenty thousand dead and forty thousand wounded in a single day! All hands are helping the British. There is no one left, Corporal. I am sorry about your brother. He is a fine man and a good soldier. I keep praying he is still alive somewhere."

I stand outside the dressing station and smoke a cigarette. I need time to digest the news and make a plan. I am on four days rest so will not need permission to go look for Harry but I still have to let my commanding officer know. Maybe I can talk some of my buddies to come with me. Quickly I make my way back to my unit. Instinctively, I know I have to get to Sanctuary Wood as quickly as possible. My brother is waiting for a rescue and I know Harry is too sensitive to the horrors of war to survive for long on his own.

Once we leave the trenches, we start searching every shell hole within a two hundred yard radius. The burial details are busy burying the fallen heroes. I am glad I don't have that job; it is one of the toughest jobs we have to do. There are corpses everywhere; the Princess Pats bravely tried to hold the line against the German army. I look at the grim faces of their surviving comrades who are courageously gathering up their dead. At least, the fallen heroes receive the respect they deserve. We find Harry and the dead major in a shell hole about a hundred yards from the trenches. It is a pitiful sight. Harry is incoherent and does not recognize me. No amount of talking can break through his ranting as we carefully carry him back to the dressing station. The doctor takes one stunned look at Harry and announces that he is shell shocked.

"I'm sorry, Corporal. His mind is broken from the terrors he faced. Shell shock is a strange thing; sometimes rest and quiet away from the war heals the mind but sometimes it never heals. I will have him transported to the Canadian Convalescent Hospital in Boulogne for thirty days. Away from the noise and horror of the war, Harry might recover enough to come back. However, if he doesn't, he will have to go to England to convalescence before going home to Canada." The doctor shakes his head as he looks at my brother who is cowering on the floor. "God, he must have seen some terrible things out there for him to go dinko. And you found the major dead, you say? Did you bring him in? The Pats will want to claim his body; they are very protective of their own and will want to bury him themselves." As the doctor walks away to find a motor ambulance, I squat down on the floor by Harry and try to talk some sense in him. His eyes roll around wildly and he shrieks louder so I leave him. I decide I will have to go to Boulogne with him and I need to find my commanding officer to get permission.

Getting Harry to Boulogne is difficult; every little noise bothers him even though the doctor had sedated him for the trip. Even the motion of the swaying train seems to upset him as he keeps up a stream of chatter that makes no sense to me whatsoever. I try all the familiar names to no avail, Harry does not respond to anything. When we reach the hospital, the matron is shocked to see Harry's condition. She immediately finds a quiet room for him and orders a strong sedative as the effects of the other sedative had worn off. It is impossible to work with him in his frenzied state of mind. After one of the sisters bathes Harry and he is sleeping quietly, I ask to speak privately with the matron.

I sit in the sunroom of the 3rd Canadian Hospital with Matron Sister Elizabeth Pierce. I find her easy to talk with and learn that she has known my brother before all this tragedy was placed on him.

"What is this gibberish about the Germans making him loose a penny in the sea? It makes no sense at all but my brother has been saying this ever since we found him." I ask, clearly expressing my concern.

"Your brother had just received news of the death of a nurse he had become very fond of while he was at Taplow before coming over. Penny was her name and she was on the hospital ship taking wounded soldiers back to Taplow which the Germans sank. I am afraid that this news was too much for him to bear and then the ordeal in No-Man's Land broke him. Harry is such a sensitive man and the war is not kind to those who care about life. I was not aware that their relationship had deepened this much," she replied while watching me carefully.

I wonder what she sees in me that fascinates her so. Unlike Harry, I am already hardened to the cruelties of war. My bayonet has tasted the enemy's blood and I do not lose any sleep over it. But her news has stunned me. I stare at the walls of the sunroom for a long time before I speak again. "I did not know Harry had found a girl. He never mentioned it in his letters to me. My brother was studying to be a minister when he enlisted and he is a sensitive and caring man. If a girl stole his heart, she must have been very special to him. He would have taken the news badly, I am afraid. What are his chances of recovery, do you think?" I ask quietly.

"Well, I hope the peace and loving care he will get here will mend him. Sometimes it does in cases like this. But the Canadian hospital in Taplow will certainly be better for him. He loves that place and it will be a more peaceful setting for him. While the memories would be there, I think they might anchor him somewhat. I am going to see if I can get him over to Taplow as quickly as possible. So many wounded, you know, all hospitals are overcrowded but I have a little pull." Nurse Pierce smiles as she speaks. I find her quite charming in a matronly way. I know my brother will be in good hands here so I rise to make my departure to the railway station to catch the next train back to the frontlines.

Extending my hand to Matron Nurse Elizabeth Pierce, I offer my gratitude. "I regret I cannot stay longer but I promised my commanding officer I would return as soon as I delivered my brother safely. I will give you details to write me and keep me informed of Harry's progress. I hope I do not ask too much."

"No, Corporal Lantz, I most certainly will keep you informed. I found something of Harry's that might need your protection as it could be valuable to his recovery at home. He kept a small diary which many soldiers do and it may help Harry remember some of the happier times while he was in England. Sometimes shell shock wipes out memories, I have learned. Wait here and I will get it for you," said the matron as she disappears through the doorway.

My mind is bothered by conflicting thoughts. I hope Harry will be dismissed from duty and sent home when he is physically able but then I know my brother will consider it a failure not to return to the frontlines. As Matron Elizabeth Pierce returns and passes me the small red diary, she wishes me Godspeed. My blue-grey eyes betray a brief moment of longing as I look at the familiar handwriting in the small booklet but it passes over. I didn't know Harry kept a record of his days but then it is so like him. Harry will always be a scholar. I thank the kind Matron again and then turn and walk away.

On a train somewhere in France, 1916

Dear Father:

I am on my way back to the frontlines having just left Harry at the Canadian Hospital in Boulogne. It was hard to leave him but I was lucky to be able to come with him as he was in no state to look out for himself. You probably got a telegram from the War Office declaring Harry missing which he was for five days. I had a brief respite from fighting and went to the Field Dressing Station to visit him and learned that he had been abandoned in No-Man's Land. Details had gone looking but did not find him and figured he was taken by the Germans. Let me tell you about No-Man's Land. Every soldier fears and hates this strip of land between the enemy's line and ours; sometimes it is only fifty yards wide. This land is filled with rotting corpses that can't be recovered and there is no cover except holes made by mortar shells. These holes are half-filled with stagnant water and overrun by huge rats that feed off dead soldiers. Some of the holes are filled with dead soldiers and our burial detail will just fill them in and make a grave out of them. Needless to say, it is not the best place to bury our fallen heroes as the constant shelling will unearth the bodies and our troops have to advance over them during a charge. Well, I went searching for my brother and found him in one of these shell holes. He had gone mad, father, talking nonsense and scared of everything. The doctors call it shell shock and many soldiers suffer from it. I have seen a strong fighting man throw down his gun in battle and go dinko in a flash. War does that! It is the worse hell you can imagine. Harry had been sent out to attend badly wounded officers and got lost from his detail. At least, it looks that way since everyone else was killed by snipers, leaving him alone and lost. Anyway, I digress. I spoke with the matron of the hospital (a lovely woman from Alberta) and she is arranging for Harry to be transferred to a convalescent hospital in England. Apparently, Harry spent a few months there cooking for the officers before coming to France. It is a quiet and healing place, she says, for wounded soldiers. From there he will come home, I think.

They never send these soldiers recovering from shell shock back to the front; most come undone again. I am sending Harry's diary along for you to keep safe for him. He has carried this in his chest pocket since he left Quebec in 1914 so it is important to him. I cannot follow Harry's recovery because I am in the thick of the fighting but I left your address with the matron, Elizabeth Pierce. She promised to keep you informed. Please keep your kind letters coming as they are the only sane thing in this insane war."

Sincerely, Orrin

****

My boyhood friend, Lance/Corporal Ralph Borden, and I watch the arrival of seven tanks with great interest. It is late September 1916 and the Battle of Somme drags on since the summer months. The casualty count rises to a staggering figure. We have just arrived after a march of fifty miles from the south over hot, dusty roads. Our Allied forces have gathered for an assault on Courcelette and the famous German stronghold beyond, Regina Ridge. This is to be the battle that will finally break the exhausted Germans. We were informed that General Haig is confident that victory is imminent.

I have just been promoted to a Lieutenant's rank in the 85th Battalion and I now have a company of men to lead. As we watch the armed monsters roll into the square behind the Canadian line, I am the first to comment.

"So these are the Butcher's babies! This should stir up the Huns, eh, Ralph? Sure will make our job easier," I conclude as I appraise the huge machines that are now lined up for inspection by the commanding officers. The troops gather around and chat excitedly; the Australians and New Zealanders expressing regret they are being relieved before they can see the willies in action. Their casualty count has been extremely high and it grieves them to leave their fallen comrades behind.

"We have to name them," yell one of the Canadians as he jumps up on the huge tracked runners that can go over anything in its way. These land creepers are practically indestructible according to the War Office. General Haig has ordered another thousand from the Department of Munitions; this is the magic weapon he has been searching for. The call for names start a barrage of suggestions; *Cognac, Chablis, Créme de Menthe, Champagne, Cupid, Cordon Rouge.* Each name suggestion brings a cheer as the Canadian troops laugh and raise their helmets to salute the newly arrived tanks. But I watch the excitement quietly. *I will wait for their first battle before I salute these land creepers,* I say to myself.

Ralph and I grew up together and we share many childhood pranks. I was delighted when he joined my unit at Bramshott training camp in England. Now we both watch General Sir Arthur Currie walk around the parked tanks; he has a worried look on his face. I can tell his mind is fully occupied with the impossible task given our Canadian Corps now that all four divisions have finally arrived at the Canadian line. When we first arrived, we learn that taking Regina Ridge has nearly wiped out the British, Australian and New Zealander troops. The corpses still litter the killing fields although every effort has been made to recover and bury the dead respectfully. They have died a heroic death but the fierce fighting makes it impossible to reach all of them. So Haig has sent in tanks with orders to take Regina Trench if we have to fight to the last man. This is their first appearance on the battlefield. We have two weeks to prepare the men. Our General Currie knows the outcome of this war depends on our success in routing out the enemy. At the battle planning meeting, he expresses his concern about the use of the tanks.

"These tanks could be the key," the General inform us, "but I rely on my men. Machines are only machines; men fighting for survival are invincible. I pray that Haig is right on this one."

Snuffing out his cigar, he leaves for his headquarters to go over the battle plan one last time as he looks for any sign of failure. I like General Sir Arthur Currie who came up through the ranks to command the Canadians. He is an excellent battle planner and he often consults me about small details in the field. Some of the officers complain that he is aloof and doesn't have a caring bone in his body but I find him quite the opposite. His sole purpose in battle planning is to save as many lives as possible and I agree with some of his rather untraditional schemes to oust the enemy from their strongholds. We spend many hours in the bull ring practicing new maneuvers.

At dawn I stand with my men waiting to advance. Our target is the village of Courcelette. It is known to be a virtual stronghold of German defense and it stands between us and the Regina Trench. Once we capture the village, and three divisions have been given the task, then the 4th Division will move on to Regina Trench. With the tanks giving us cover from the enemy machine guns, I think the advance can be made with little loss of lives. My concern is the many hiding places the village houses offer the enemy. Willies are no good in tight places. Even though the citizens have left the village many months ago, the British failed to bombard the houses in its attempt to rout the enemy. I hate fighting invisible enemies but my men are well prepared for the task.

As the hour of the planned attack approach, our officers make their way through the troops. The fact that it has rained steadily for the past two weeks is a major setback. Four of the seven tanks will not start, leaving only one land creeper each for the three assaulting divisions. It is less cover than we planned and without a bombardment prior to the initial assault, I express my concern to my commanding officer.

"This just leaves us with Mills bombs and Lewis guns against their machine guns, sir. I consider that one-sided fire power. At least, let us take the tank into the village and level a few hotspots," I say to Major Ralston.

"Lieutenant Lantz, in the field, you are in charge. To our knowledge, there are no civilians in the town so do what is necessary to take the village. It is our only access to Regina Trench. Don't let us down!" And Major Ralston walks away.

Our tank, *Créme de Menthe,* is the only land creeper to reach its objective. The other two are blown up by German shells. The Germans who appear startled at their first sight of the tanks soon recover, and bring out their big guns. It was a horrible death for the gearsmen in the tanks. They are burned alive. *So much for indestructible,* I think as I watch in horror. My division reaches Courcelette within a half hour of leaving the Canadian line. Our willie gave us adequate cover and destroyed the machine guns in its path. My battalion along with the French Canadians arrive in the village to find it deserted; not an enemy in sight. As we push through the streets and throw our bombs into various houses along the way, not a single German emerges. My battle senses are on high alert; I know something is afoot. I consult my men and decide to push further out from the town. We have only progressed a hundred yards when firing begins behind us. There is little cover but we flatten ourselves on the ground. The tank is still in the town with the battalion from New Brunswick. We are trapped between the Regina Trench and the village. Lying on the ground, I try to sort out the enemy's strategy. They let us through not knowing there was another battalion behind us so I figure their plan was to ambush us from behind. I could see why so many British troops had been killed here. These Germans are brilliant battle planners. I hope our troops in the town will keep them occupied long enough for me to get my company back to safety.

The battle rages for two days in Courcelette with our boys fighting off eleven counterattacks. It is house to house fighting; even as the troops storm a house, the Germans are still in basements and tunnels below. We bomb the tunnel entrances so fresh recruits cannot come from the German held trenches beyond. I find it the hardest fighting I have encountered thus far; hand to hand combat with bayonets when we stumble onto a nest of hidden Germans. There is not a chance of relief, and after two days, most of us are so exhausted we can hardly stand.

I kneel beside the bullet ridden body of my boyhood friend. I lost three men in the last assault when a German machine gunner opened fire from the cover of an underground tunnel beneath the rubble of a house. We pull our wounded into a house protected by a stone wall. I am filled with rage; we are sitting ducks as I realize how efficient the German defenses are. I wonder why the British had not demolished the town with shells but then I reason they were all killed before they got this far. My decision is swift and without emotion. We will employ the willie and systematically destroy the village.

"What the hell are you doing, Lieutenant?" yells the Captain of the New Brunswick battalion when he sees the tank coming forward.

"Let's just say we are lowering the odds, Captain," I reply coldly. "I will not lose any more men to those Huns. They want to play dirty so let's give them a taste of dirty fighting."

The Captain looks at me before speaking. "What about prisoners, sir? The Colonel will want prisoners, don't you think?"

"What Turner wants is this town secure for the 4th Division to move in. Besides, the rats in the basements will escape through the tunnels they dug. If you don't like it, take your men and walk away. Perhaps you will find a kind German on the other side of town that will shake your hand and ask to be a prisoner." I can hardly contain my anger but I keep my voice steady as I wave to the gearsman operating the willie to proceed. My mind is still filled with the sight of Ralph being shot down by the hidden snipers.

It is hard on the men listening to the screams of the trapped Germans as the tank pulverized the houses but eventually, the enemy surrender brought a respite in the bitter fighting. The 2nd Division has achieved its objective; Courcelette is now in our hands. The way has been cleared for an attack on Regina Trench. I hope the Germans will remember this battle and give us a little more respect in the next one. Knowing that the town is secure, we allow ourselves to rest before the 4th Division will join us and proceed on to capture Regina Trench. Although I am totally chin-strapped, I cannot sleep. My mind is filled with the image of the bullet ridden body of my boyhood friend. We had joined the war effort at the same time and have been fighting together since 1915. We never think about rest camp when we are in battle. The thought of getting killed is overshadowed by the adrenalin surging through our veins. Grief is on the very edge, threatening to overtake my senses. I fight it down shutting off any emotions that I feel.

I will have to write his mother to tell her how courageous Ralph was and that he died a hero. God, I hate this war! I put my head in my hands and try to shut out the ugly images that threaten my sanity. Only the memory of my brother Harry huddled in the shell hole keeps me from stepping off the edge.

The Regina Trench nearly broke us; Currie used his now famous tactics of creeping barrage but our losses are staggering. The German

Marines held the Trench against everything we threw at them; even the land creepers could not give us the edge. Our Battalion, which had captured Courcelette, is reduced to seventy-four men by the time we reach the wire enclosing the German held trench. Not having enough men to continue, I order the men to gather any wounded that can still fight and retire to the destroyed village. Attempts are repeated again and again until we finally capture and take control of the Regina Trench on November 10, 1916.

The day after we captured Regina Trench, all is quiet; the guns are silenced. The Germans had retreated to another trench not too far away. They did not surrender much to General Currie's surprise. We are busy gathering up our wounded and burying our dead comrades. Our hearts break at the sight of our fallen pipers. At the height of the fighting, they had laid down their bagpipes and drums and picked up stretchers. They could not stand back and watch their comrades suffering in the field. The Germans killed every one of our stretcher bearers and our pipers. It is a sad day for the Canadians; our victory has no glory.

When a German officer appears waving a white cloth attached to his rifle, I go over to meet him. I want to riddle him with bullets. To my mind, one live German is too many. He requests permission, in perfect English, to gather up their dead comrades and their wounded. It is a courtesy I find hard to grant but agree as the rules of war are quite clear. I look at this strange sight; enemies working together to gather up fallen comrades. It is the first time in this godless war that I see a bit of humanity surface.

The relief units arrive later that day, and we march off the field to the ruined village to wait for Colonel Borden. When he arrives on horseback, with a brass band, we muster strength to stand to. Major Ralston stands with the medical doctor, Colonel Hayes, and the chaplain, Father Ronald MacDonald, and takes the salute. Only sixty-nine men with voices strong and steady answer the roll call.

"Where are the rest of your men?" The Colonel asks our commanding officer.

I am proud of Major Ralston as he stood straighter and with a proud voice says, "This is what is left of the 85th, sir!"

I watch the shock settle on the Colonel's face as he looks at our assembled troops. *Take a good look, Colonel. We reached our objective and held it but it cost us five hundred comrades.* Without another word, he turns his horse and rides away. Unsure what to do, the brass band follows but we stand where we are. There is no joy in our victory this day. We will not celebrate a battle that cost us so much and gave back so little. We will relive the horrors of Regina Trench for many days until another big battle pushes us into a killing machine.

****

FOOTSTEPS OF LIEUTENANT ORRIN LANTZ:

The Canadian Corps capture and hold Vimy Ridge on a snowy Easter Day in 1917. It is a remarkable feat that the French and British had failed to accomplish. Unknown to me, my brother Private Gordon Lantz was floundering about in No-man's Land looking for the rest of his battalion while my platoon is mopping-up after the Infantry had chased the Germans off the Ridge. Mopping-up is messy and dangerous; clearing the captured trenches of enemies requires a cool head and a quick trigger finger. The War Office refer to it as *neutralizing the enemy*, I call it cold-blooded murder. My motto, "The only good German is a dead German", steels me for the task. Whenever I feel any remorse about the job, I recall the slaughter of the 17th Highland Regiment in 1915. Then my resolve strengthens; all emotions tightly locked inside.

I am shocked to see the wonderful trenches the Germans had made; planked floors and no standing water, walls plastered with a thin layer of concrete, electricity and water. All I could think about as I wander through the empty network of trenches are the rat-infested, water-filled trenches the Canadians are forced to use. More than half the Canadians suffer from trench foot. Such a contrast makes it surreal; the Germans lived in luxury. My mind pictures the smug, arrogant Germans sitting here shooting our Canadian troops in their miserable trenches; shelling the hell out of us while the German soldiers ate proper food and were warm and clean. I shake off the thought and enter another tunnel much the same as the previous one. Private Ralph Henshaw follows close behind; the rest of the platoon has broken up in pairs and are inspecting the endless tunnels. As yet we have not encountered any live Germans which I find disturbing. Suddenly the hair on the back of my neck stand up and goose bumps are raised on my arms. I make the signal to stop; something is out of place but all I can see are a few pieces of furniture along a wall. It is unnaturally quiet; all the red flags are going off in my head. We are in a small room and as I survey the walls, my trained eye notices a shadow behind a table that had been dragged away from the wall at an angle. The unmistakable soft click of the safety being removed on a revolver is barely heard. I make a motion to get down as I quietly creep closer to the shadow. The light is poor and I can barely distinguish the outline of a door but I know there is a room off this one and there is someone in there waiting for us. As there are only the two of us, and not knowing how many Germans are hiding, I decide to bluff it.

"Hey, boys, we got a live one!" I shout, hoping that whoever is there will think a whole platoon is outside the door. "Throw out that Luger and any other guns you have and come out. We won't shoot if you surrender."

The seconds tick by. I start to fidget. Then the door slowly opens a crack and a gun is thrown out but no-one attempts to come out. This does not fool me; I have seen all the tricks the Fritz pull on surrendering. "What about the rest of your arms? I know you got more. Throw them out now!" I know only officers carry lugers so he must have a few others with him.

"Kamerad! We come. Don't shoot!" The door opens wider and two rifles are thrown out. A grey uniformed private steps out, followed by a high ranking German officer. They have their hands held behind their heads and as they step over the guns, one glances back over his shoulder. I sense something is wrong with this scene. Since these two are out, my bluff will not work if there are others left in the room. I motion the officer and his private to move to the further wall. The room is smaller than I would have liked but I wave Private Henshaw to retrieve the weapons.

"Ah, General. If you want to live to see your family after the War, call out the rest of your men. I will shoot you first!" I am pulling at straws; this is a tight situation. *Stay calm*, I tell myself. Reaching down, I pick up the Luger that Ralph had kicked toward me. Without hesitation, I quickly fire a warning shot above the General's head hoping to scare those in the hidden room or, at least, some of my men might hear it and come running. What happens next is pure reflex and years of training as a soldier. The door flies open when another officer jumps through firing his revolver at where he thought we were standing. I had dropped to the floor after firing the Luger to retrieve my rifle and the shots went over my head but they struck Ralph in the chest.

Without another thought, I turn the rifle on the Germans and fire continuously until I am out of shells. I know Ralph has been hit as I heard that familiar thud when a bullet hits flesh but I make sure the enemies are dead before checking my friend. The rest of the platoon heard the gunfire and burst into the tunnel to see what had happened. They are stunned by what they see; three enemy dead, one a high ranking officer, and Private Henshaw clinging to my arm in death throes. I quickly give the order to search the hidden room for other Germans while I hold my boyhood friend in my arms.

"Christ, man, stay with me! I'll get a medic here." But even as I speak, I know it is too late for that. "Ralph, say something. What can I do for you?"

"Te..ll my mo..th..er I lo..ve h..er." They are his last words. I hold him close to my chest and fight back the tears. I never thought I would lose another friend so quickly. I should have seen the danger sooner. I am filled with remorse.

"Sir...Sir!" Corporal Burnett watches the dying scene and hates to cut in but all our safety is at risk in this tunnel. "We found another tunnel off that room and it looks like it goes back quite a fair ways. It's narrow and only allows single file. We think there might be more Huns hiding there."

I gently lay my dead friend on the cold floor and stand up. I only have nine men with me, not enough to carry out a full search. "Corporal, go find the other platoon. I think we stumbled onto something big here. You never find a General without a full company of men. There has to be more and I wonder why the General did not escape unless he had something too big to carry."

When I enter the hidden room, my eyes cannot believe what I see. It appears to be a headquarters of some sort with papers and maps laid out on the round table. I know the commanding officer will want to see this so I dispatch another man to find him. I post a guard at the entrance to the dark tunnel with orders to throw in a grenade to blow it up if he is rushed by the enemy. Meanwhile I go to check out my dead prisoners. After searching them carefully, all I can find are IDs. *Very typical of war, no private information for the enemy,* I think. They were high ranking officers and I wish I could have taken them alive. The other platoon arrives, followed shortly by my company's commanding officer. After being briefed on the situation, Colonel Brutinel praises me on my discovery.

"Only a sharp eye would have found this hidden room, Lieutenant Lantz. It is the headquarters of Colonel-General Falkenhausen, Commander of the Sixth Army. Too bad he didn't surrender quietly but I heard he was a stubborn old bastard! He left us a gold mine of information. I'm going to bring in my troops to explore this tunnel. First thing we need is light so let's secure this place until my troops arrive and then you are relieved to continue your work. Sorry about your loss, Lieutenant, I understand he was a friend as well as a good soldier. See that he gets a deep burial; that's the best we can do for him now."

Later that evening, I stand on the concrete parapet of Vimy Ridge looking east where the German Army fled. It is a pretty scene with green grass and the trees starting to show budding leaves. In the Douai Valley, thousands of fires glow from the German Army's hastily made camps just out of gun range. There are no shell holes or craters, no sign of a war at all. It is like a mirage after the two years of mud and shelled villages that have been the only scenes that I have witnessed. As I smoke my last cigarette, my thoughts drift to another green valley and a little white church where I had spent happy hours as a child. Thoughts of my family and the childhood joys that were so carefree and precious fill me with a strange sadness. *Will I ever see my family again,* I wonder, *or will I die as quickly and unexpectedly as my friend.* I remember the day we left home and how proud we were as we stood on the platform waiting for the troop train in 1914. When the train pulled to a stop, Ralph's mother took a gold locket from her neck and gave it to her favorite son. "To keep you safe," she said as she watched her four sons leave for the war. I have been away from home for three years now and a strong longing to hear my father's voice envelopes me. I finger his mother's locket in my pocket as my thoughts drift back to our happy childhood. *I will write his mother and tell her how you died a hero and return her locket. Maybe that will give her some peace.* I know this melancholy is brought on by my friend's death but its grip is smothering me. A voice calls to me in the fading light of dusk breaking the spell, and I turn to finish one last task for the day. The burial detail is waiting for me to say a final farewell to my boyhood friend. I turn back to take another look at the scene spread out in the Douai Valley below. *I am coming for you, you bloody Huns,* I vow.

****

FOOTSTEPS OF PRIVATE GORDON LANTZ:

Colonel Canon O'Brien and I are with the 85th Battalion during the siege on Vimy Ridge on Easter morning in 1917. He is preparing for an Easter Mass for the Battalion which comprises of the surviving veterans of the 17th Highland Regiment that had been massacred by the Germans in 1915 and the 40th Battalion to bring the Regiment up to standards. The highlanders from Nova Scotia will not wear kilts nor will they take pipers into battle. Known by the other battalions as the *highlanders without kilts;* Lieutenant-Colonel Borden, commanding officer of the Nova Scotia battalion, did not want the Germans to know the Highlanders were back in battle. As yet, the 85th had not been in battle since arriving in France; they had been kept busy digging trenches and constructing roads. However, the Battalion was seeking revenge on the Germans and was anxious to meet them face to face. Many of the fresh recruits were younger brothers of the slain 17th Battalion. The Canon was especially protective of these young men. When the order came to exchange their shovels for rifles, it was met with a fierce war cry.

Company D from Cape Breton and Company C from Halifax are assigned the task. They had less than an hour to get in position to storm Hill 145. It seemed an impossible task as the Germans were well situated and had lots of gun power. It had already cost our Allies many lives in several attempts; their corpses were two-tier deep in No-Man's Land. And every shell hole was filled with injured soldiers waiting for stretcher-bearers. This was the only place to hide and many died or drowned in these shell holes that could be as deep as eight feet. So when the order was given to "Take the Hill at all costs" seasoned veterans knew exactly what they were up against.

Colonel Canon O'Brien hastily packs up his Mass kit so he can be ready to leave with the troops and he looks around for me. He needs a few things from his billet and the most important were combat boots for the water logged trenches. His well-polished high leather boots were of little use in this terrain. I had proved to be a good batman; always there when he needed me, getting him meals or giving him privacy when he asked. But I longed for a taste of the battle and this worried the Canon. He could see the longing in my eyes when other troops marched off to the fighting trenches. This time, he would take me to the trenches so I could see the horrors of war hoping to appease my longing but I wanted my *baptism of fire* that seemed to excite every soldier I talked to.

As the battalion slugged through the water filled trenches, I could hardly contain my excitement. Finally, a firsthand look at the battle; as of yet, I had not even seen the enemy despite being on the Front for two years. I spent most of my time in hospitals and dressing stations with the Chaplain or in the billets preparing meals or doing laundry. Whenever the Canon went to the front trenches, I was left behind to do some chore that could have been done later. I knew that Colonel O'Brien had been deliberately keeping me in safe places but this just fueled my desire to get into the action. Now I was going to get a real taste of the war. *I might even get to fire my rifle,* I thought as I labored through the mire behind the Chaplain. My head was full of silly thoughts of killing the enemy and how I would feel the true excitement of war. Little did I know, I would actually get to play out these desires. The Canon had decided to go to Hill 145 with the troops. He explained his plan to me as we waited for the order to go over the top. "These lads need us to administer to their wounded and dying. We should be safe enough if we stay behind the main assault." The Canon looks at me for a reaction; I did not disappoint him as I realize this is my *baptism of fire* finally.

It had been snowing all day and No-Man's Land was white. At first glance, I failed to see the white humps as they blended into the bright snow. It is still snowing and Hill 145 could not be seen from the jumping-off trenches as the Highlanders stand in waist-high water. The melting snow added to the woes of water-filled trenches. The water is freezing cold and I cannot keep from shivering. Suddenly the sun broke through the clouds; it blinded the Germans and the Highlanders jumped out of the trenches and swarmed across No-man's Land. It took me by complete surprise as I had not heard the whistle that was their signal to charge. It was mayhem; bullets were flying everywhere and men were falling wounded or dead. I was frozen with wonder as I witnessed Captain Crowell, leading the Cape Breton Highlanders, get shot in the shoulder while climbing over broken wire, bits of wood and corpses, and yet he kept going. The Highlanders rush forward; their war cries echo across the frozen landscape. I watch as the Germans throw down their rifles and flee. I had been told that the Highlanders' ancient war cry puts fear in the strongest of men. No wonder the Germans feared *The Ladies from Hell*. It certainly made the chills go up my spine. I am so absorbed in this scene that the Canon has to shake me. He is getting ready to go over the top with the last of the battalion. We must move fast to keep up but neither one of us is trained for this. The Colonel, unhindered, could move fast but I was weighed down with his haversack and my rifle. I soon fall behind and, in a panic, I run without looking down. I trip over a frozen corpse hidden in the snow. My rifle flies from my hands and my face hits the hard ground as I lay sprawled on the snow covered ground. Bullets are whizzing all around me and for a moment, I think I am hit. I look around and see Colonel O'Brien looking back at me but then he turns and follows the rest of the troops leaving me stranded. Somewhere in the back of my mind, I remember one of the rules of combat. *Don't stop for fallen comrades, keep moving!*

When I realize I am not shot, I quickly scramble to my feet. Looking around, I find myself alone. The troops have disappeared and only the moans and cries of the wounded in their wake can be seen and heard. Now panic sets in, and I experience fear for the first time. I can see my rifle a few yards to the left and I run to retrieve it. Bullets are hitting the ground around me, and as I run, I realize I don't even know where I am going. I trip over another snow covered corpse and fall headlong into a shell hole half filled with partially frozen water. As I regain my feet, I realize I am standing in two feet of water in a deep shell hole. I have lost my rifle again and I am staring at two dead soldiers. They must have been wounded that morning on the advance to Vimy Ridge by the Canadian Corps and died waiting for rescue. I think I am going to be sick as I look at them. One soldier has half his face blown off and the other one is slumped over with his stomach contents floating in the water. I had seen these sights in the field dressing stations so, while I am shocked, I can keep myself from throwing up. But it is a grisly sight and I frantically try to scramble up the side of the shell hole. To my horror, I fall back into the blood stained water. I realize there is no way to get up that slick mud wall and I am trapped.

"Got a grubber, private?" speaks a voice from the other side of the crater. I swing around and see an officer sitting in water up to his chest. One arm has been badly mangled by machine gun fire. Although his face is ashen, his voice still carries strong.

"Sir, how bad hurt are you?" I cry.

He sizes me up as I stand there looking like an idiot. "Are you a medic, private? If you are, my luck has changed. I am Major Daniel Ormond. What company are you with?"

I know the man must be in terrible pain. He would have been here all day sitting in this water filled hole. "No, sir, Batman to the chaplain for the Highlanders," I answer and taking the Canon's silver flask out of my jacket pocket, I pass it to the Major. "I think the chaplain would want you to have this, sir. He swears by it!"

A look of surprise crosses his face as he takes the flask. "Highlanders? Are they out there ousting the Germans?"

I can tell the whiskey hit the Major's empty stomach like a whizz-bang making every nerve in his body come alive. The British often gave credit to the amber colored liquid as a lifesaving tool. I sneaked a small swallow once when the Canon wasn't around and it almost knocked me over. I never tried it again but it always amazed me how the officers can finish off a flask and still stand up.

"Yes sir! We got called out about three hours ago to take Hill 145. Seems all other attempts had failed. But the Highlanders will push the Germans off that Hill, sir." I know I am boasting as if I was a soldier that knew about these things but I am proud of the 85th Battalion.

"What happened to you, private? How did you lose your battalion? And while you are figuring that one out, start getting us out of here. I can't stand because my hip and leg have been shot up. Start using that grubber in your pack, private!" The whiskey has revived the Major, and with the shooting out of range, he wants out of this stinking hole.

"Maybe you can make some kind of steps in the mud; anything that will get us out."

Digging in the limestone soil is hard work but eventually, I make several steps. I glance at the Major and realize I will never be able to get him out alone. Not only is he severely wounded but he is a sturdy man. "Don't know where the goddam stretcher-bearers are. I have been sitting here all day in this stinking water." He grumbles as I keep digging until I am satisfied I can get up the side of the crater.

As I am about to climb up the Major yells at me, "Wait, private! Those snipers will love a head to shoot at. Take your helmet and put it on your rifle and stick it above ground. If it gets shot at, we are stuck here. Where is your goddam rifle? Whatever did they teach you in training camp?" I know it is the whiskey making the Major querulous so I reach over and take away the flask.

"Save the rest for another time, sir. I lost my rifle when I fell into the hole. Where is yours?" I am getting nervous; I want to get out of here as I am missing the battle. I am not sure what to do with the Major but I do know I can't leave a wounded officer in the field. I remember that much from my training manual.

"Mine! No goddam way! Take one from that dead hero over there. He won't need it, poor bugger." With that remark, the Major made an effort to move which brought on a new spasm of pain and he fell back against the cold muddy wall.

Wrenching the rifle from the stiff fingers of the dead soldier, I check to see if it is loaded and then proceed to stick it above the crater wall with my helmet on the bayonet. I hold it there for what seems like a long time but no shots are fired. Feeling safe, I climb up the wall which is a bit tricky because I have no handgrips. I stick my head carefully above the top and just as quickly I jump back into the hole.

"Germans sir! Half a dozen grey coats coming this way! We are sitting ducks." I wail. At first, the Major appears confused by my revelation. I suppose the whiskey has made him a bit fuzzy but he quickly recovers.

"Get back up there, private. Now tell me what you see!" He orders. I am glad I didn't hear the rest of his comments as I scramble up the crude steps. Five Germans are advancing with their hands over their heads and carrying a wounded Highlander. Prisoners! Relief washes over me as I quickly relay the message to the Major who is still muttering about my lack of training.

"Quick, private! Climb out and intercept them. They will get me out of this hell hole. What embarrassment to be carried into camp by German prisoners." He mutters to himself.

"Sir, I can't speak German." I blurt out the first thing that comes to my mind. This is my first encounter with the enemy. I look back at the Major whose face is turning scarlet with rage. My instincts take over and I climb up the wall of the crater as fast as I can. I am thinking the Germans are a better option than dealing with an outraged officer. To my surprise, the Germans stop when they see me emerge from the shell hole.

"Don't shoot! Don't shoot!" cries the officer in front of the group. "Prisoners! We surrender!"

I wave my rifle toward the shell hole and hope I look threatening to them. I finally get to see a live German. "I have a wounded officer that needs help. Two of you go get him." I mimic the Major's voice hoping they don't notice my trembling but the gun is shaking like a leaf on a tree branch in the wind.

The German officer looks at me; his blue-grey eyes are like steel which sends shivers up my spine. I am taken back for a moment as his eyes remind me of my father's eyes. "I don't take orders from a private. You bring him out," he barks at me.

A bellow from the hole catches the officer's attention and he walks over to the crater's edge and peers down. When the Major sees him, he waves his good arm and yells, "You stinking Germans! You are our prisoners and if I send my private up with orders, you will obey. Now get some of your men down here and get me out or I will shoot the lot of you," And with that, he waves his rifle at the German officer. This Major totally amazes me. He must know he is not in any shape to shoot anyone but apparently the Germans think he is as they quickly retrieve him from the shell hole.

We are weary and bedraggled as we stagger into camp later that evening. The Major has to be carried as he is so weak that his good leg couldn't support him. Because of his weight, the German prisoners have to keep changing and that slows us down. The Highlander is unconscious by the time we arrive because he lost so much blood. I hope he makes it but the doctors are skeptical. I became an instant hero; bringing in prisoners and two wounded officers.

By the time we reach the Field Dressing Station, the Major is in a better frame of mind. He thanks the Germans and makes sure they have a hot meal before being processed and sent away to a holding cell. He even expresses gratitude to me, telling me I will make a fine soldier after a few more cracks at the enemy. "But my advice, son, is stick close to the chaplain if he survived the battle to take Hill 145. His work is much more satisfying than killing Huns. Now go find your chaplain, private, before he wears out his knees saying *Hail Marys'* for your wretched soul."

I am too ashamed to admit I have no idea where to look. It is too dark to try and find Hill 145. I give a helpless shrug. "I'll stay with you, sir, until the ambulance comes. Did the morphine help?" I ask the Major.

"I'll be alright, private. I think the Canon will be in the Main Dressing Station with the wounded unless he is injured himself. You could try there or the Officer's Mess. Fighting works up quite an appetite. Oh, by the way, private, you better trade that water logged rifle for one that works. Now off you go. I am on my way to the big hospital in England, son! I've earned me a Blighty One! This bloody war is over for me." Major Ormond gives a big sigh and closes his eyes. I was saddened to later learn that the Major died of his wounds and never made it to England.

I am exhausted. I have searched in vain for the chaplain. I did not find him in the Field Dressing Station behind the old Canadian line, so I went to the Office's Mess. No one had seen Colonel Canon O'Brien since the battle ended several hours ago. Having no other places to look, I make my way back to our billet. At least I had a decent meal at the Officer's Mess. While I was eating, I listen to the officers talking about the victory of Hill 145.

It seems the Highlanders took Hill 145 in an hour. Their only regret was that they were not wearing their traditional battle kilts and that the bagpipes were not playing. I think they were happy they had extracted their revenge on the Germans as many would be prisoners were shot before they could surrender. I was told that Colonel Canon O'Brien was there to help them celebrate their victory and bless the wounded that had fallen during the assault. One of the officers told me the Canon was concerned about me and went to find me as he was quite convinced I had died a hero and he would have to send a long sad letter to my father. When I asked if they knew where he had gone, they were sure he was out on the battlefield looking for my body. This news grieves me but I am too tired to go back out on the battlefield. Now that I know the chaplain survived the assault, I can return to the billet for a much needed rest.

I am covered in mud and filth; it has been a difficult day. The shock of the horrors I had witnessed on the battlefield is overtaking my tired mind. I gratefully drop my kit and rifle on a chair and make my way to the bedrooms. *I should have a hot bath,* I think but exhaustion is taking over my body and my legs are feeling like rubber. Seeing a light under the chaplain's door surprises me. Slowly I push it aside as it is not tightly closed. Colonel O'Brien looks up from his prayers; exhaustion and grief showing on his muddied face.

"By the Lord's Mercy, I cannot believe my tired eyes!" The chaplain jumps to his feet and rushes toward me. I am unprepared and shocked; we both fall to the floor clutching each other. "This is a miracle! I saw you get hit. How can it be? I was sure you were dead."

It takes a few moments for the Canon to recover from his shock as he patiently listens to my exploits in No-Man's Land. We are having tea in the kitchen and sharing our day's adventures. As exhaustion finally takes over, we both go to our beds. I fall asleep before my head hits the pillow. I am fully clothed and caked in mud and blood. My last thought is my *baptism of fire.* I found it a big disappointment. There was no glory in going over the top.

In the morning, Colonel O'Brien has a serious talk with me. He tells me he is going to request a transfer to the Canadian Hospital in

London. "Christians killing Christians is too much for my sensitivity. I cannot take much more of this carnage. God's work for me is in the hospitals giving hope to the wounded men until they go home to an uncertain future," he tells me sadly. The chaplain gives a great sigh. "I will request you go with me; leaving you here would not be my choice."

I am shocked by his comments. The thought of working in a hospital in London does not sound very exciting. I try to hide my disappointment from the Canon but I think I failed as his eyes get a little misty.

After he leaves for the Command Post to make his request to the Commanding Officer, I sit at the kitchen table for a long time. I know he is making this decision for my benefit but I don't want to leave my comrades. The Canon told me that he relived the horrors of the battle all night. His mind could not let go of the cries of pain, the shattered bones and faceless dead soldiers cast down in the mud. Hill 145 was the first time he actually went with the troops in battle and saw firsthand how brave and courageous they are. "These men run toward certain death; machine guns mow them down but they jump over fallen comrades and keep going until they reach their objective, whether it is the enemy or death. God Bless their fearless hearts as only one in ten reached that German stronghold. The rest are left, wounded or dead, in the wake of the onslaught." He shakes his head sadly. "I can still do God's Work in this Great War but England will give me a better sense of peace. I hope you can understand this, Gordon."

I will miss the excitement of the war but I know my first duty is a batman to Colonel Canon O'Brien who has protected me for the past two years. I can see the wisdom in his decision. The Canon would be lost if he didn't have me looking after him. I smile as I try to picture the Canon doing his laundry or preparing a meal on an old stove. I realize I have become quite fond of the chaplain. He is forever giving me bits of wisdom with his daily quotes. Going to London will be new excitement and I start to warm up to this new adventure the war is offering me. My brother Harry is already in England in a convalescent hospital and I will be able to visit him. But I will miss my other brother Orrin who will remain here on the Western Front fighting the enemy. Thinking of Orrin, I decide to go find him and tell him the news. Now that Vimy Ridge is in our hands, he should be on a few days rest from his hard fighting. He will enjoy hearing about my *baptism of fire*.

****

FOOTSTEPS OF LIEUTENANT ORRIN LANTZ:

The spray from the North Atlantic washes my face. I love the smell and taste of the salt water; a reminder of the small fishing villages at home. As I stand on the deck of the hospital ship, my mind reviews the last few days. A letter from the matron of the Canadian General Hospital in Boulogne started this latest chain of events. She had promised me she would stay in touch and now she writes to say that Harry is being sent home in two weeks. The doctors at Taplow decide his mental health too fragile to return to active duty so he is being medically discharged from the Corps. Harry wants to see me before he leaves so the matron has arranged for me to accompany wounded soldiers to England. I took my fourteen day leave, the first since I came to France, to visit both Harry and Gordon. Now that Gordon is working in the hospitals in London with the chaplain, my concern for his safety has lessened.

As I gaze out over the green ocean waters, all I can see are British destroyers. Not only do they flank the ship on both sides, but they sit within sight of each other all across the channel. The Naval war has heated up considerably since I had crossed in 1915. The Germans are determined to disrupt the transporting of our Allied forces across the channel. Quite often, a hospital ship will strike a mine and sink; such is the tragedy of war. I feel better fighting on land as I reflect on my part in the war; at least I have a chance for survival. Out here on the water, there is little opportunity for survival, I think. I decide to go below and talk to some of the wounded soldiers who are headed to the Red Cross Convalescent Hospital where my brother is a patient.

Getting off the ship at Portsmouth, I take a few moments to look around. This is where my adventures had started three years ago. Somehow the town looks different to me. The docks are empty of cheering crowds to greet us; even the dock workers barely glance our way as we depart the ship. The motor ambulances are waiting to take us to the train station and I follow along. It feels strange to be back on English soil again. My thoughts turn to my bother Harry who will soon be stepping on Canadian soil. This is daunting to think about and I can't help but wonder how strange it will feel to go home after we have seen and done so much in this war.

I find the atmosphere at the Red Cross Hospital casual and very comfortable. The patients' rooms are filled with light from the many windows; everything smells fresh and clean. The surrounding gardens outside hold promise of many different flowers but it is winter in England so I cannot enjoy the full beauty it offers. I can see why this is called a healing hospital. The nurses are young and pretty and they cater to the wounded patients every need. I find Harry in the solarium engaged in an animated conversation with a well-dressed woman. As I approach, Harry rises from his chair and embraces me. He has been expecting me as our friend, Elizabeth Pierce, had written him advising of my visit.

"Orrin, please meet Lady Astor, our benefactress," he says with pride.

Taking the extended hand of Lady Astor, I bow low but keep my eyes on the beautiful face in front of me. "This is indeed a pleasure, your Ladyship. I have heard good comments of your hospitality," I say.

"The pleasure is mine, Lieutenant Lantz. Harry has told me so much that I feel I know you already," she responds. "I will leave you with your brother who has anxiously awaited your arrival. You will stay here, of course. Officers are lodged on the first floor of Taplow Lodge. Harry will show you around as he knows the place quite well." With those remarks, she quietly withdraws like a soft summer breeze.

Harry is the first to speak. Laughing, he says, "Take heart brother, she has that effect on everyone. When I first met her, I couldn't breathe for a full five minutes."

"Who is the lucky Lord?" I ask as I turn back to my brother and sit down. "I did not know her Ladyship is so young and pretty. You have been holding out on me, Harry." I reach over and playfully slap his arm. It felt good to see Harry again.

"Lord Astor is a wonderful chap, Orrin, and a military man. You will get to meet him tomorrow night as we have been invited to dine at the mansion. It is good to see you, Orrin. I hear the fighting is very heavy on the front. How did you get time off?" Harry asks.

I look closely at my brother before I answer. I am greatly surprised to see Harry looking and acting so normal. Only his eyes give away his suffering. "Well, that was easy. I was owed a fourteen day leave since I haven't had one in two years on the front. It has been steady fighting now for months; I really needed this break. But let's talk about you, Harry. By Jove, you look good! Are you all better now? And they tell me you are going home. How lucky can you get?"

A shadow falls across Harry's face and I regret my words. I had been prepped by Matron Pierce. So sensitive, she had said, and I had been warned to be careful with my words. But Harry recovers quickly and when he speaks his voice is steady. "Not quite better yet, Orrin. I have night terrors still and it makes it a living hell for anyone within earshot. I even have my own room so as not to disturb the other patients, and a nurse sits with me all night. I cannot go back, Orrin, even though I want to. The doctors agree my nerves are not completely healed." His sigh is deep with regret and his eyes mist slightly.

We both fall silent, each absorbed in our own thoughts for a moment. For some strange reason, I think of my mother who used to collapse on the kitchen floor with her epilepsy seizures. As children, we learned to adjust to her sudden collapses and now I wonder if Harry might be prone to these attacks. He breaks through my thoughts as he suddenly stands up. "Come, Orrin. I will show you around and where you will eat and sleep. Promise to stay off the nurses' floor, though. I should warn you that they have a guard stationed there in case you get any ideas." Harry laughs and throws his arm around my shoulders. I wonder if he notices that my shoulders are broader since I have become a soldier. Carrying an eighty pound pack and a heavy rifle every day is a great muscle builder. *We have changed in so many ways. Life will never be the same for any of us*, I think as I follow my brother.

That night as I lay between clean sheets that smell slightly of lavender, I try to figure out what is different about my brother. While he talked and laughed like the old Harry, there was something missing. I notice it mostly in his eyes; something has changed in him. As I am falling asleep, it comes to me. *Of course,* I think, *I have seen it before in my own soldiers. The fight has gone out of him. He has left his soul back in that shell hole from many months ago.* Sadly I roll over and fall into a troubled sleep.

Dinner with the Astors is a delightful event. Lady Astor chose the morning room instead of the massive dining hall. She explains that it makes for a more informal and intimate occasion as she has the three oldest of their four children joining us. Normally, the children ate in their wing of the mansion with the governess, she explained, but as they are fond of Harry, she wanted them to have one last special time with him. She is hoping to soften the sadness the children will feel when Harry leaves for Canada. I am a bit surprised how fond everyone is of my brother.

The main course is wild game killed on the estate which is modest fare for the Astors but to Harry and I, it is extravagant. The children are delighted to be with us and chatter happily. I notice they are extremely well mannered and beautiful children.

"Is that handsome pony in the stable getting enough exercise, Master William?" I ask their ten year old son. William is a beautiful child with his mother's eyes and smile. His eight year old sister, Nancy Phyllis, who is the spitting image of her father, answers instead.

"I ride him more than William. William likes to read, doesn't he, father?" she turns to her father with a bright smile complimented with dimples and adoring eyes.

"Now Nancy Phyllis, what have you been told? You must not answer your brother's questions. Please apologize to the kind officer!" responds Lord Astor but a smile appears in the corners of his mouth that suggest how pleased he is with his daughter's winsome ways. I am so caught up in her coquettish beauty that I almost miss her brother's response.

William speaks with a slight tremor, "I do ride, sir, but not as much as my sister. I will soon give him to Nancy Phyllis when I get real horse." A glance at his mother confirms his wish and he drops his gaze to his plate. I notice he has barely eaten any meat but has finished all the vegetables.

Lord Astor quietly speaks to his oldest children. "Say goodnight, children, and go up to your rooms. The governess will have dessert with you, as usual. Your mother and I will be up to say your prayers before you go to sleep."

After the parting of the children, a quiet lull settles around the table. I notice a slight discord between their parents and hope I am not responsible. But we soon retire to the drawing room where whiskey and tea are ready to be served. Lord Astor draws me over to overstuffed chairs by the fireplace while Lady Astor and Harry retreat to a private corner where they engage in a conversation on holistic healing. I wonder if this seating arrangement had been planned as I sink into the comfortable chair with pleasure.

"Tell me, Lieutenant Lantz, what is the latest news on the frontlines?" asks Lord Astor, a major in the British Army. His heart condition keeps him from combat duty and tied to a desk in London, he explains to me, but he is keen on being part of the war.

I take a generous swallow of the best whiskey I have ever tasted. Closing my eyes to better savor the smoky taste of peat from the Scottish Highlands with a hint of burnt sugar, I am aware that Lord Astor is watching me closely. "The Scots have the secrets to a good malt whiskey," he comments as he waits for my answer.

"I am sure you are up to the minute on the latest battles, your Lordship." I respond as a warm glow starts to build in my belly. "It seems we have gained on the enemy but the sacrifices are still too high. Of course, I am only aware of what is happening in my own unit. I have to read the papers to catch up on the war as a whole."

"I would be interested in your opinion of General Haig. Now that your Corps has a Canadian Commander, have you noticed a difference in the fighting?" he asks while watching me carefully. I am still enjoying the incredible beauty of this whiskey. I never drank before I came to France but I now appreciate the amazing power of this deep gold liquid the British Army hands out freely.

"To be honest your Lordship," I reply, "I only met the British General once. He was with King George V when our General Currie who, at the time was a Colonel, was knighted on the battlefield. I was just one of more than a thousand soldiers watching. But General Haig was impressive to me. I didn't get to speak to him but he did mingle with some of our officers and chatted freely."

"Yes, but your General Currie is having relatively better success on the battlefield, is he not?" Lord Astor persists. "It is my understanding that the Canadians have not lost a battle."

I had read in the London papers that with the high casualty count of British soldiers and the dismal failures in the field, certain government corners were questioning the British General's efficiency. While it is never spoken out loud, many of the members of the House of Commons are calling for his resignation.

My battle senses are on high alert as I finish my glass of whiskey. "Yes, the tanks have been a great help. They have cut our losses to a great extent but even one life lost is too many. But you must know that the Germans have higher ground, and deeper trenches. Our greatest obstacle is the pulverized mud we have to cross to get to them. Carrying eighty pounds on your back and sinking in cement-like mud up to your knees is an impossible situation. When that limestone soil gets shot up from bombardments, it can pull you down. Men drown in it. It even swallows horses. When we are advancing, and fall on our face in the mud, it is impossible to get up. I have seen men leave their boots in the mud and continue fighting in their socks. Even the tanks get mired down which reduces our cover. It's the same for all troops, British or Canadian, your Lordship. Once we get the Germans on a full retreat, the fighting will shift to better conditions for ground cover, I would think."

Lord Astor appears impressed with my comments. He thanks me for my candor and honest comments.

I rise as Lady Astor approaches us. "I hope you are enjoying your stay with us, Lieutenant?" she asks and, without waiting for a response, adds, "It is time for Harry to return to the hospital. Rest is most important in his recovery. I have been told that you are taking Harry to

London tomorrow to meet your younger brother. I must caution you not to overtire him. He has made tremendous progress here and, of course, he will be leaving in five days to sail to Canada."

I thank Lady Astor for her concern and assure her that I will not overdo the trip to London. After making our farewells, Harry and I walk back to Taplow Lodge. It has been a pleasant and informative evening for both of us.

The train ride to London is uneventful. Harry is very quiet and seems absorbed in the scenery as the train speeds along on its tracks to Paddington Station. It is his first outing since he came to England many months ago. As my brother reflects on different events in his life, I strike up a conversation with a well-appointed lady sitting in the next seat. She is a gracious lady and our lively conversation keeps me occupied but I still glance occasionally at Harry. I learn that she is on her way to visit her husband in a London hospital. He was badly injured in the war and doesn't want to live with the loss of a leg. I sympathize with her as her turmoil is quite evident.

When we depart at the station, I wish her well. Harry and I register at the Union Jack Club on Waterloo Street where we will spend the next two nights. We then proceed to the Y.M.C.A. to meet our younger brother. It has been three years since we have been together and the reunion proves to be marvelous.

My youngest brother is overjoyed when he sees us; his excitement overcomes his awkwardness and soon we fall into a vigorous conversation. After remarking on how good we both look, Gordon's first question to me is about the welfare of the Battalion's white goat. I assure him *Robert the Bruce* is alive and well. He laughs at some of the antics I relate to him about the goat as I knew he had become quite fond of him when he was with the 17th Highlanders.

"He is a constant source of amusement, Gordon. One of my favorite stories, and I had to write home and tell our little brother about it, was the kidnapping of *The Bruce* by some of the boys in another battalion." I glance at Gordon's excited face as he listens intently. "It started as a bet at a drinking party but when the boys had succeeded in luring the goat away from its guardian, they were hard-pressed what to do with a cantankerous and not too co-operative goat. So they smuggled him out of camp and gave him to a French famer who thought he had struck it rich. A nice fat goat for his herd was more than he could accept so he offered money for him. Now the boys felt very guilty by now but they didn't know how to get out of the situation. There was no way to sneak him back to his stall as everyone was looking for the mascot." Gordon burst into the conversation with concern. I put up my hand to stop his questions. "Wait, Gordon, until I finish. It is quite a story. Three days later, a farmer appeared at the commanding officer's door begging him to take back the goat. He told Major Ralston that the goat wrecked his gardens and chased him back into the house every time he tried to catch him." This brought a gale of laughter from both Harry and Gordon. I continue on with the story. "The Major knew that something was afoot and finally got the whole story out of the farmer, paid him back the money he gave to the culprits and then called in our bandmaster. Old Dan went back with the farmer and was so happy to see his beloved goat, no worse for wear after his adventure, he actually kissed it. Needless to say, he is well guarded now. Our boys haven't discovered yet who actually did the nasty deed but trust me, they will and I would not want to be them." I didn't tell Gordon that I knew the culprits but the Major decided it should be kept a secret. He didn't want any fights between battalions.

Gordon gleefully tells us of his amusing adventures at the Canadian Hospital in London and entertains us for hours. I had to caution him several times about Harry's delicate state but Harry seems amused by our younger brother's adventures.

After dinner, Gordon left to return to his duties. He did not have any leave owing him but had been granted several hours to join us. He explained that the chaplain would have liked to extend his time off but military life is strict and rules must be abided. We were sad to see Gordon leave but relieved that he was no longer on the frontlines.

Noticing that Harry appears weary, I suggest we return to the Union Jack Club for an early turn in. Harry begs me to leave him there and go out with other soldiers for a bit of entertainment. But I insist on staying so we have a quiet talk about the family and how things have changed since we had left in 1914.

"You will find such a difference when you get home, Harry. Have you thought about it?" I ask as I take off my jacket and sit in a chair by my bed. We are sharing a room with twin beds; much the same as army life except the beds are more comfortable.

"Not too much, Orrin. The letters from home have been a wonderful help; Hazel has kept me up on all the news. You knew Everett and Lenley have been recruited and are in training camps here. Do you write our sister often?" he queries.

"Not as much as I write father. You were always closer to our sister. But she sends me letters once in a while. My unit is on the move so much that mail doesn't always catch up with me. She did send me a picture several months ago of our two younger brothers. Beecher has certainly grown a lot. He can't remember me and wanted a picture. I should do that while I am in London. What do you think?" I glance at my brother. "Of course, I will have to shave off this moustache. I look too much like father. I did know that our older brothers had been recruited but I had no idea where they were." I conclude.

My light sleep has been conditioned over the years as a seasoned soldier. While I grab a few hours wherever I can, I never let myself sleep soundly. After we had retired for several hours, a slight sound alerts my senses. I glance over at my brother's bed and find it empty. Reaching for the light, I see Harry huddled in a corner of the room, sobbing quietly. It is a sight I have seen many times on the battlefield. Battered by the horrors of war, soldiers withdraw into themselves, locked into their own battle of the wits. Usually a tot of rum and a good talk will bring them back to reality but Harry is battling ghosts that will not go away. Quickly, I jump out of bed and grab a sheet to wrap myself in as I am sleeping in army skivvies. Harry, of course, is wearing his hospital pajamas but he looks chilled so I get a sheet off his bed to wrap around him, as well.

As I sit on the floor beside my brother, I ask gently, "What troubles you, Harry? Why are you so sad?"

Harry spoke without looking up. "I have failed everyone, Buck. Even you."

At first I am stunned as our mother used to call me Buck when I was young. She had favorite pet names for all of us; it was a term of endearment she used to soften our strict upbringing by our Baptist father. No one has called me by my pet name for years and the fact Harry used it shocked me.

"Harry, how could you have failed me? You have not failed anyone." I say. "Tell me why you think this."

Between sobs, Harry blurts out that he has failed our father in protecting his younger brothers. "How can I go home like this," he cries softly. "You know Father will not understand how I failed. I can't even find God anymore even though I have tried hard. Oh, how I have tried to pray but the words are lost to me. Buck, what will he think?"

I now have a better understanding of what is troubling Harry. At first, I thought it was the terrors of the war but now I understand his fear. His fear of our father's censor has a grip on him. I knew I could write to our father and warn him in advance so a confrontation could be avoided. As children, we were all afraid of our father; he set high ideals that he expected us to meet. His wrath, in any of our failings, was something to fear, I remembered. I suppose it had to do with his ministry. But I had outgrown that childish fear and had assumed my brothers had as well.

When I spoke, I kept my voice as gentle as possible. "Harry, Father will understand. Trust me, I will write to him and instruct him on your condition. He will not be angry or upset. He will be happy to have you home again. Now come back to bed before you catch a chill off the cold floor. Everything will be fine, I promise you."

After I tuck Harry warmly back in bed, I return to my own. Getting back to sleep now is impossible. I regret that I cannot see Harry safely home but I realize it is time for him to take control of his life again. After a short prayer, I fall back into a restless sleep. I dream of our childhood; we are playing in the field by the brook. When I go too close and fall in, Harry jumps in to pull me to safety. Returning home in wet clothes, our mother secretly sends us to our room to change.

"Your father will be very upset to see you boys like this," she says. "You must never upset your father! He will not understand." I sit up in bed, bathed in sweat. I remember now how afraid we had been as young children of our father's anger. Every Sunday, we sat in the front row of the church and listened to his sermon. Our father spoke of '*evil doings*' and '*God's wrath*'. We were too young to understand the meanings of these sermons. Our mother sat with the youngest children but always glanced at us older boys to make sure we sat still and straight. But when our father's eyes happened to fall on any of us during his sermons, the fear was firmly implanted into our young minds. I put my head in my hands and groaned. The impact of Harry's fear was now clear to me. Now I knew what was holding my brother back from a full recovery. I will write our father and tell him everything. He has mellowed since our early childhood and is more understanding. It is all I can do for my brother.

Two days later, I nervously stand in the foyer of the Astor's impressive mansion. I have requested an audience with Lady Astor before going to the train station. After hours of worrying what to do about Harry, I reach a decision.

"Lieutenant, this is a pleasant surprise! Please come into the drawing room." The soft voice of Lady Astor rings out and as I enter the drawing room, I hear her order tea. Lady Astor smiles at me as she asks me to sit by the window. "I trust all went well in London," she inquires as she sits next to me.

Dressed in a beautiful blue dress, her eyes are even more enchanting. The fragrance of lilies and winter roses wafts around me. I focus on my mission but I cannot help but stare in admiration. Sitting this close to her arouses senses that have lain dormant for the past few years.

"Thank you for seeing me on such short notice, your Ladyship. It is about Harry, as you may have guessed," I say. Just then the tea arrives and Lady Astor fusses over the pouring before dismissing the maid. While we drink our tea, I relate the experience in the hotel room and then I fill her in on Harry's childhood. While she appears calm, there are times during the course of our conversation that she seems quite surprised. She looks at me with such intensity that I am afraid I have overstepped my bounds. *She is a lady that is used to a pampered world,* I remind myself. The intimacy of my situation is more than my physical endurance level can handle. For the past three years I have only been exposed to battle hardened soldiers. I find that sitting here in a luxurious room having tea with this beautiful creature is quite bizarre.

"I apologize, your Ladyship, if I have upset you in any way. You see, I think Harry should return to the frontlines and take up his duties again. Is this possible?" I ask.

Lady Astor speaks firmly but softly, "I am afraid that is not possible. He has been relieved from military duties and must return to Canada in a few days. I do not believe I can help you but I do see your point quite clearly. If only this news had come to light sooner, I might have been able to do something about it. My poor dear Harry, what will become of him living with such fear? Perhaps he will turn to God and resume his ministry. Do you think that is possible? Many great and wonderful people have found refuge in the church." She studies me with soft grey eyes which unnerve me quicker than any enemy ever could.

"My lady, he was only studying ministry because of our father. Harry never wanted to be a minister; it is our father's desire to have his sons follow him in ministry. None of us were brave enough to refuse. But this is a family matter and I do not wish to burden you with it. I was hoping to bring Harry back to the frontlines now that we know it is not the war he is afraid of. I think my plan might have worked but I am too late. I did not know he was given his ticket." The heady fragrance of lilies, mingled with the tantalizing sweet scent of winter roses, toys with my imagination. It pulls me into a surreal image that is breaking down my resolve. My senses are conditioned to the smell of the battlefield but now my body is awakening to the feminine scents that surround me. I had forgotten how alluring the female scent was. *I have walked into danger,* I caution myself.

Abruptly I stand; every nerve in my body is on fire. I thank Lady Astor for her time and the tea. I do not dare linger any longer.

"I have to catch the train to Southampton, your Ladyship. My ship leaves for France tonight. It has been a pleasure meeting you, your husband and beautiful children. I wish you all good health. Good day."

Lady Astor watches me as I swiftly cross the room. When I reach the doorway in the foyer, I look back at her seated in her gold brocade chair. It is a sight that steals my breath. I hold her gaze for a moment and then bowing low, my eyes never leave hers. I want to take this vision with me. She is the most beautiful woman I have ever met. Our eyes are locked as an electric shock travels through my veins. It is but a brief second but the impact is felt with such ferocity that the world seems to stand still; all thoughts of Harry are forgotten. I get a pain in my chest from its intensity and from holding my breath. Her eyes widen with surprise and a blush comes to her flawless cheeks. Quickly I turn, rushing through the door and down the steps. I almost forget my kit which I had left outside the door. *That was stupid of me and totally ill-mannered.* I scold myself as I run down the road trying to get as much distance from the mansion as I can.

Later that day, I sit at the bar in a pub in Southampton trying to erase the shame I have brought on myself. Several soldiers join me but I am not in the mood for conversation. I need to nurse my wounded ego. After another glass of cheap watered whiskey, I make my excuses and leave for the ship. I am sorely in need of a fight to vent my frustrations but it will not be one with my fellow soldiers even if they are Australians. I have a couple of days to get over this humiliation before I reach my men in Northern France. By then, my poor excuse for manners will be just another bad memory.

****

FOOTSTEPS OF REVEREND GEORGE LANTZ:

I pace the kitchen floor. The dreaded letter has arrived with the morning's mail and it caused such turmoil, I sent the children out of the house so I could think. I miss not having my daughter, Hazel, running the household but I knew it was selfish to keep her from making a life for herself. She has been contributing to the household finances with the pitiful wages she makes in the old folks home but she likes her job. With the war taking all the young men in the community, her chances of finding a suitable husband are greatly diminished. It is a sad time to be living but as the pastor I must keep the community together. Now I have another challenge facing me. When the Prime Minister had first introduced a conscription bill to Parliament in May 1917, the country was appalled. Canada had already sent four hundred thousand volunteer troops to the Western Front but as the war dragged on, the casualties kept mounting. The number of young Canadians volunteering had dropped dramatically but Britain called for more recruits as the Allied Forces desperately tried to defeat the German invasion. I was hoping my oldest son, Everett, would be missed by the Conscription Law as he was living in the United States. He was happy working in the woods and at thirty-two years of age, he had no desire to fight in this war. But now the letter with orders to report to the nearest recruiting station as soon as possible has arrived.

As I sit at my writing desk and pen a letter to my oldest son, I urge him to heed the call to uniform. My other two older sons, Havelock and Lenley, have been called up to wear the uniform as well and have already left for Halifax to be recruited. This will put six of my sons in this terrible war; no father should be asked to sacrifice so much. I pray for their souls every night. We are a God-fearing family and this war is testing our faith. Ever since Conscription became law in Canada, all able bodied men between the ages of 20 to 45 years who were bachelors or widowers without children, are required to sign up. The radio reports that thousands of conscripts, particularly French speaking ones, refuse to be sent to the Front and went into hiding. Federal agents comb the countryside looking for them. Riots are breaking out in Montreal. I am disturbed at this current state of affairs. The war is tearing this young country apart. There is little choice left for my oldest son. Everett has to join his brothers and fight in the Great War. Everett's twin, Ewart, is married and has a family, so he will be spared the call to uniform. I can find comfort in that news at least.

I look up from my letter writing as my daughter Hazel enters the room. She is hoping for a letter from one of her brothers in France. I smile as she sorts through the mail. "Father, Harry has written me another letter. He must be feeling better now that he is in England," she comments.

"Hazel, can you look after the boys for a while? I must visit Mrs. Henshaw to make arrangements for the service on Sunday. The Henshaw family has lost its third son in the war. He and Orrin were inseparable as children." I study my daughter's face. I knew she had feelings for this young man but a father can only do so much to prevent hardship to his children.

I harness my old mare and drive down the road to the small farm of the Henshaws. It is a bit run down of late as four of their five sons have been in France since 1914. Their youngest son Percy is still home but he will soon be old enough to join. They keep sheep and Mrs. Henshaw cards and spins the wool into yarn. She has been knitting wool socks for the boys from the community who are in the war. It is a very kind gesture and my sons were very grateful to get a pair of her wool socks. The Henshaws live a simple, God-fearing life. They are the salt of the earth, I think, and they sit in my church every Sunday despite their hardships. This will be a difficult visit for me as our children have been close friends since elementary school.

The door to their farmhouse is open and I am ushered into the parlor. Mrs. Henshaw, an ample woman, busies herself with making tea. Her husband is not present as I am sure he is busy somewhere on the farm.

"Reverend Lantz, thank you so much for coming," she gushes as she passes me her best bone china cup brimming with hot tea. "It is so good to see you looking well. Your poor Elsie, God rest her soul, would be pleased how you have managed your large family after her passing."

I thank her kindly and smile. She says this each time we meet. My late wife who passed away ten years ago had been one of her closest friends.

"I am sorry my visit is one of sorrow," I reply. "Your son Ralph was like one of my sons to me. You have suffered so much in this terrible war. Losing three sons to the madness in France is most unfortunate."

She looks away for a moment and then busies herself with the freshly baked biscuits that she has put on a plate for me. Mrs. Henshaw is an excellent cook and her pies fetch a dollar at our church suppers. I know it is hard for any mother to talk about the loss of a beloved child and Ralph was her favorite. My late wife never recovered from the loss of our three year old son, Irwin, who was killed in an unfortunate accident in the mill.

"He is with the Lord now, Mrs. Henshaw. All the pain and suffering are gone. We must be thankful for that," I say as I reach out to take her trembling hand.

"I only have one left over there, Reverend. The war has taken three of my dear sons. How does one cope with such a loss. This has broken their Pa. He sits in his chair at night and never says a word. If only our son Milledge can come home to us, we would be so grateful to God." Her voice betrays her broken heart and I pat her hand in comfort.

"Now, Mrs. Henshaw, we will pray together for your son's safe return. I listen to the news every night on the radio and they say this war will end soon." I hope this will help her deal with her sorrow.

She looks at me with her sad eyes and then quickly gets up from her chair. "I got a nice letter from your son Orrin. He was with my Ralph when he died a hero, he said. And to think he died on Easter Sunday! Those Germans must be heathens to make our poor boys fight on such a holy day. It being the anniversary of Christ's resurrection and all! I must let you read it. You know, Orrin wrote such wonderful words of comfort. I do believe he has the Calling, Reverend."

As I leave her place an hour later, I remember her comments about Orrin. I read his letter of condolence and was quite moved by his words. If he is destined to be a man of the cloth, then surely God will bring him safely back to me after this war ends. I am grateful that my three sons in France are safe even if Harry is taken ill from its horrors. At least he is still alive and can come home. Now I have three more sons going to France and I worry what their fate will be in this dangerous war.

After posting the letter to Everett, I make my way home. I stop at my beloved church and pray for the safe return of all my sons. Then I make my way to the quiet cemetery on the hill behind the church. It offers me a measure of relief to come to this quiet, undisturbed place where the birds sing in the trees. It feels sacred; the glistening tombstones stand as sentinels over the graves of loved ones. I sit beside my late wife's gravesite and pour out my heart. Here is where I escape the chaos of life's problems. Among the dead, there is peace and comfort. I watch a squirrel run across the nearest grave and scamper up the granite tombstone. There it sits, chattering at me, totally unafraid of my presence. I don't have to read the lettering on the headstone. It is the family burial plot for my neighbor and dear friend, the Henshaws. Even a servant of God has to have his faith restored sometimes and this scene gives me a measure of relief that God has not forgotten his Children.

****

FOOTSTEPS OF SERGEANT HAROLD LANTZ:

When I step off the train in the small town close to my home in Nova Scotia, I am overcome with emotion. It has been a long and arduous journey from England. The crossing in rough seas was especially hard and many of the wounded soldiers became sea sick. I worked in the hospital on the ship in an effort to relieve the overworked orderlies and doctors. It kept me occupied throughout the long sea voyage and my mind off the upcoming meeting with my father. When the hospital ship finally docked in Halifax, I was glad to see the end of the voyage. It took several days to go through the demobilization routine but now I am just a citizen again with a new set of clothes. Sometimes I wonder how I survived three years in the war. It now seems so far away.

I look at my family gathered on the station platform waiting for me. They are expecting me to be in uniform and when I approach my father in my new suit, I am not surprised to see the shock and disappointment register on his face.

"Father, it is good to see you." I reach out to clasp his hand but my voice lacks its usual cheerfulness. "The boys have grown a lot in three years. And Hazel, you are now a beautiful young lady."

My father soon recovers from his momentary shock and studies me carefully as he takes my hand in a firm grip. The shock of seeing me so aged and wearied clearly shows on his face but he smiles and says, "Come Harry, we are glad to have you back. Beecher has been driving us crazy waiting for the train."

I look at the youngest member of our family noting that he resembles our father, and smile, "You have grown into a fine young man, Beecher. Or should I call you George? Have you outgrown your pet name yet?"

Twelve year old Beecher looks at me curiously. "Where are your medals?" He asks. "Don't all soldiers get medals?"

Hazel quickly shushes the young boy and sadly glances at me with concern. She saw the pained look in my eyes before I could hide it.

"Beecher, where are your manners? Your brother has been wounded and spent the last six months in a hospital." My father gives his youngest son a stern reprimand.

Beecher looks down at his well-worn and handed down shoes and mumbles an apology. "I am sorry, Harry, but the kids at school said you would have a lot of medals 'cause you were in the war."

I feel sorry for my younger brother's confusion. "Medals are for the soldiers who fight in the trenches, Beecher. I looked after the wounded soldiers and we don't get medals for that. Perhaps Orrin will come home after the war ends with a few medals to show you. But I have lots of good stories to tell you about England. I met the King and saw where he lived." I look at my father who is staring off into space. I knew this would be awkward after being away for so long but the tension in my father is tearing me apart.

Satisfied with my explanation, Beecher smiles at me and reaches for my hand. "I have some things to show you at home," he says. "I know where there is a rabbit's hole with babies in it."

I smile as I remember when I was his age and I explored the woods and streams around our home. As we climb into the wagon, I notice the mare is the same one the family had before I left for the war. "I see old Mary is still able to haul us around, father."

"Some things never change around here, Harry, which is a good thing. But she is getting old and will soon be put out to pasture to live out her last years. I will need your help with the mill since I lost Lenley and Havelock to the war effort. It's been tough these last few months, Harry." My father keeps his eyes straight ahead but I hear a deep sigh as he slaps the reins on Mary's back to urge her into a trot.

"I heard that Lenley went overseas Father but what about Havelock? Why didn't he go to France?" I ask. The fast trot and weight in the wagon has the mare blowing hard so my father slows her to a walk.

Glancing at me before answering, his voice is hushed. "Havelock is posted in Halifax he tells me. I get a letter from him once a month. He didn't want to go overseas and who can blame him. He is still serving his King and country. Everett and Lenley are in France now. Everett writes once in a while but I never hear from Lenley. Gordon keeps in touch regularly and he is still in England. Orrin used to write often but I guess the fighting has increased and he is in the thick of it. I haven't heard from him for some time. I will be happy when this war has ended and all my sons are home again." I sneak a peek at my father while he is speaking and see the pride in his face. I am glad my father does not know the horrors I had seen on the frontlines and that my brothers are in great danger every moment of the war. There is so much I cannot speak about.

The familiar countryside passes by as the mare slowly trots down the dirt road to our home. I am happy to be back with the family but a part of me regrets I never went back to my duties in France. My mind drifts to the crowded field dressing stations and the bloodied soldiers I had cared for. *Perhaps I should have gone back; maybe my night terrors would stop if I had faced my fears.* I will miss the sweet counsel of Lady Astor. Without her constant support, I never would have made it through this nightmare. I must write her as soon as I get settled and let her know I arrived home safely. I will keep her memory bright despite the ocean between us.

Later that evening, we sit down to a wonderful chicken dinner which my sister carefully prepared. After the usual blessing, it is quiet as we pass the steaming dishes around the table. I start to tell Hazel of my experiences cooking for the officers. I hope it will lighten the tension that I am feeling. It seems so strange to be back in a civilized environment again where the war is hardly spoken of.

While I am telling Hazel about the incident with the live turkey, Beecher pipes up and asks, "How many Germans did you shoot, Harry?"

All eyes turn to my youngest brother who sits there quite innocently expecting my response. Our father clears his throat before he speaks. "You will apologize to your brother, George Warren, and then excuse yourself and go to your room! There will be no talk of war at the dinner table."

I am not offended by his question. It is normal for a twelve year old to be curious about the war but I am shocked by our father's strict reprimand. I look at my defiant youngest brother and his eyes shoot daggers at me while saying he is sorry. After he leaves the room, an uneasy silence descends on us. Hazel is on the verge of tears as she keeps her head bowed over her plate.

"Father, I am sorry for this confusion. But Beecher's curiosity is quite normal." I felt I should say something to break the tension.

My father stands up and looks at me strangely. "Thank you for a wonderful dinner, daughter. Harry, I will see you in my study to discuss this after you finish your dinner. Please excuse me children, I have some work to do."

I watch him as he leaves the room. His back is ramrod straight. There is no question in my mind that three years has not changed my father and memories of my childhood flood back weakening my resolve. After our father leaves, Hazel breaks down in tears and quickly runs to the kitchen. Now I am confused as what I should do. This only leaves my fourteen year old brother, James who is on his third serving of potatoes, and me sitting at the table staring at each other. My appetite is completely gone and the delicious chicken dinner is sitting like a hard rock in my stomach. I can't force myself to continue eating the rich food.

"Well, James, if you will excuse me, I will go see what father expects of me." I offer a smile but James does not appear to be sympathetic to this turn of events as he continues to eat heartily.

I find my father sitting at his desk in the study surrounded by books and papers. He casually waves his hand toward the only other chair in the room but does not look up from his papers. This study brings me unpleasant memories of the many times as a child, I have been reprimanded here. But I am not a child now and I confidentially stride to the chair and sit down determined to stand my ground.

"Harry, I apologize for the scene at the dinner table on your first night home. I had hoped to ease you slowly into our life so the changes would not disturb you," he raises his hand to silence me as I am about to protest. "Beecher needs a firm hand, Harry. His curiosity, as you put it, has led him into bad situations. I have to curb his natural instinct for his own good. I will ask that you respect my choice of rules. I know you have seen many things while you were gone and your view of life is different from when you left here. But our life has not changed and you must respect that. While you live under my roof, my rules are not to be questioned. The burden of this large family fell on my shoulders after your dear mother passed away. I trust you agree with me on this subject, Harry," he concludes.

I am at a loss for a decent reply so I simply nod in agreement. *He would have made a good general for the enemy. Those Germans were just as cold and heartless,* I think as I hold back an improper retort.

"What are your plans, Harry? I need you to help me with the mill as all the older boys have gone to war. It will be good for you to have manual labor again, I would think. Have you thought about returning to your studies for the ministry? That would be my choice for you, Harry, but you are a man now so the final decision is yours to make. I just want to let you know that I support you in your decisions." This revelation is startling. But it is quite obvious that my return has prompted my father to give it considerable thought.

I clear my throat which has seized up with emotion despite my best efforts to stay strong, "Father, I will help you with the mill, of course. I have always enjoyed working with you. As to my studies, I have decided against the ministry. I saw and endured too much on the battlefield to resume my studies just now. I want to contribute to your financial situation as I know it has been hard for you. Now that my army pay has stopped, helping you with the mill will be the best thing for me." I look at him carefully but his face does not change while I am talking.

"Well, that is a wise decision for you right now. I need your help desperately. James is fourteen but still at school so I try not to burden him too much. You will notice that the millwork has slowed considerably since this war began. But there is still enough work to support the family," he replies. "I have a special service to prepare for on Sunday. You may not be aware that Ralph Henshaw was killed in action on Easter Sunday and the family has asked for a service to honor his memory. This is the third son they have lost in this war. These are good people and lifelong friends of our family. If you noticed your sister a little upset at the table, it was because she was sweet on him. They had planned to marry after the war although it was never spoken of. Talk of war in this household does not bring any joy. We have lived with its aftermath of death for three years now." He pauses and looks at me carefully. I know my father's heart is in the right place and as the pastor of this small community many burdens are his to carry. I regret I had judged him harshly and vow to be a better son. He has aged prematurely since my mother's death. Her absence as the main caregiver to the children has placed a great burden on his shoulders. I often wondered why my father never remarried even though I knew he was exceptionally fond of my mother. I shake off these silly thoughts and return to the present.

"No, father, I did not know about Ralph. I have been away from the news of the frontlines for some time. I do not want to place any more burden on you as you are a busy man. I will try to console Hazel, if that is alright with you. Now I must say goodnight as you have a lot of work to do and I am in need of sleep." The weariness of the long day has gripped me. I want to find Hazel and offer her my support. She reminds me so much of my mother that a deep longing overcomes me. This is not the homecoming I had expected but I will help my family as much as I can. How the war was affecting the families back home never entered my mind as I thought they were in a safe place. Now I know I was wrong. Our letters home were so carefully void of any war news thinking we were shielding our loved ones of disturbing news. But of course the shocking death of their sons and daughters would bring the war right to their doorsteps. I decide there is no safe place in this Great War.

****

The days stretched into weeks as I spend my time working in the mill with my father. All the young men had gone to France to fight in the war so there was no one my age to socialize with. I am the first wounded soldier to return home to this small community. When I walk to town to meet with some friends, the old people wave at me from their porches as they sit in the shade or from their fields where they are working. The women run to meet me by the roadside with baked cookies or bread.

They always ask the same question, "Did you see my boy when you were across the pond?" I am a bit of a celebrity but I still feel a failure as all my comrades are still in France. Slowly I am adjusting to my old way of life prior to the war.

The night terrors return much to my dismay. I work long hours just to tire myself to the point of exhaustion but my mind will not sleep. My cries of torment ring out through the night making everyone's life miserable. Hazel comes to my room and gently talks to me until I fall silent. Her experience in the nursing home makes her valuable to me. She tells me that father prays half the night for my tortured soul and poor Beecher is convinced that I killed so many Germans that it makes me distraught. I cannot relieve his mind as I am forbidden to discuss the war experience with him. So I am not surprised that he makes up stories of my imagined bloody battles to impress his friends at school. I learned this one day when his teacher met me on the road as I was going to town. I explained to her that I did not kill any enemy but spent my time in hospitals caring for wounded soldiers. When she inquired about my injuries, I felt quite silly telling her that I was shell-shocked from the horrors of the war and not physically injured. I had to further explain that my father forbid me to talk to Beecher about my war experience so my brother is forced to make up these stories which are not true. I ask her to talk to my father about this so they can come to an agreement about Beecher's war tales at school. A few days later, Beecher comes home from school with a black eye but refuses to talk about it. I assume the teacher had made him stand in front of his class and tell the truth about me. If my father knew anything, he kept it to himself. He sends Beecher to bed without any supper explaining that hitting another person in anger is an unforgiveable sin. I feel very sorry for my youngest brother coping with his growing pains but telling untrue stories about me is very wrong. A few days after the black eye incident, our father gives Beecher a puppy.

The next day while we are working at the mill, I ask my father about the puppy. "It is hard for a boy to grow up without his mother's love and counsel. He was only three years old when the Good Lord took his mother. I hope the puppy will give him something real to love and talk about. He has a lot of rules to live by but I did bend the rules when I let him take the puppy to his room at night," he explains. There is no doubt in my mind that the youngest son is the favorite in my father's eyes and punishing him must be pure torture for my father. I do hope this plan works for my over imaginative brother. His delight in his new puppy is evident as they romp together every day after school. While his choice of name for the black and white ball of fluff is odd, no one questions him except our father. Beecher calls his puppy *Bullet* and stands firm on his choice of names despite our father's suggestion of a more suitable name. I am saddened that the war has affected my little brother so much and it will leave a permanent imprint in his mind.

More wounded soldiers are returning from the war. After working in the mill all day, I walk the five miles to town where we meet in the only restaurant and talk of the war. I discover we all feel the same shame in coming home before the war ends. There is very little work in our small town and communities especially for those with only one arm or one leg. These men were once strong and healthy destined to be farmers or woodsmen. They are now a burden to their family and very unhappy. Jokes are offered about wooden limbs but I know, having worked in many field hospitals, that their injuries are a real hardship. We all talk of going out West to find jobs. It is a fantasy that gives us hope for a future where we will feel whole again.

****

FOOTSTEPS OF CORPORAL
HAVELOCK LANTZ:

My brother Lenley and I arrive in Halifax to report to the recruiting station. We had been caught by the new Conscription Law passed by the government to meet its quota for recruits that the British General still demands. Lenley is excited as he served in the 69th Reserve Canadian Military for several years in New Ross so he felt he was already trained to go straight to the front trenches in France. I am not happy about this change in my life. I am quite happy working with my father in his mill. Going to war did not appeal to me and I hope I will fail the medical exam. I am twenty-seven years old and although I am single, going to France holds no excitement for me. When the medical officer appraises my muscular physique, my heart sinks.

Lenley asks the recruiting officer for the quickest way to get to the Western Front where our brothers are fighting. "Well, we need railways bad," replies the recruiting officer. "Right now, we are forming a battalion to leave here in two weeks. Are you interested?" Without any hesitation, Lenley is assigned to the 256th Overseas Railway Construction Battalion. Two weeks later, he boards a troop ship and sails for England.

When asked if I am interested in the same opportunity, I decline. Seeing my hesitation to go to war, I am assigned to the 4th Company, 1st Regiment Canadian Garrison Artillery at Fort Charlotte on Georges Island in Halifax Harbor. Here I will spend the remainder of the war years but I am quite satisfied even if I miss my brother Lenley. It is the first time I am alone without any of my brothers. I find it a strange feeling to be on my own but my days are filled with duties and time passes quickly.

It is early December and I am on my way to report to the Commanding Officer at Headquarters. I returned late last night after escorting the last prisoners of war to the new camp in Amherst. I felt sorry for these immigrated Germans who are being locked up during the war as most of them were born here. I could relate to them because my own family had ancestors from the early German settlers in Lunenburg. However, if Headquarters found reason to doubt the loyalty of these prisoners, then I agree it is best to put them under lock and key. These prisoners work on large government farms that supply food to the military so I think their confinement must be endurable. I was quite impressed with the new facility in Amherst. There were comfortable quarters for the prisoners and lots of land to cultivate for gardens. Even though they were confined, they had lots of outdoor space. I thought it was as comfortable as these immigrants could expect under the circumstances.

Intent on delivering my report to the commanding officer as my first duty of the day, I check my watch and realize it is early. It is only 08:45 hours. I am curious to see the troop ships so I climb the hill to get a view of the busy harbor. It is filled with ships of all sizes but my attention is drawn to the two troop ships and their escort destroyers from the Royal Navy that is leaving for England today. It is an impressive sight. Hearing a flurry of ships' whistles, I watch as large ships jockey for right of way to get through the Narrows of Bedford Basin. Not only was the outgoing traffic heavy this morning but several big ships were entering the port. Few ports are open in winter but Halifax Harbor will remain ice free making it valuable to the war effort. The Royal Navy is situated here and with the war increasing in intensity, the port of Halifax is under their protection. While the German U-boats hover, on occasion, around the waters outside the port, underwater nets keep them at bay. Once a day the gates in the nets are opened for sea travelers to leave or enter, closely monitored by the garrisons situated on the islands at the head of the harbor. Realizing I am going to be late for my appointment, I quickly descend to the Parade Square.

As I enter the Command Headquarters, the Colonel's adjutant waves me through. "Make it brief, Corporal. This is a busy day for the Colonel," he says as he bends over a telegraph machine.

I salute smartly as I step through the door of the office. It is obvious the Colonel is agitated as his face is flushed when he reaches for my reports.

"Any problems with the prisoners, Corporal?" he asks as he quickly scans the pages.

"No sir, everything went as planned. They have a fine facility in Amherst." I reply.

"Good…good. At least that is one problem off my plate. Now if I can get the troop ships out of the harbor today without any delays, I will…" A loud boom shook the building. The glass in the small window shatters and falls to the floor. A look of shock and horror registers on the Colonel's face. "Lord Almighty! The Germans got through the gate!"

The Colonel is out the door grabbing his hat on the way before I could even figure out what has happened. I follow the Colonel as he runs from the building and climbs the hill to look down at the harbor. Everyone is streaming out of headquarters in a panic. To the north end of the harbor, a huge white cloud billows thousands of feet above the city. Several ships that are close to the Narrows are on fire. All the activity seems to be near Pier 6 and the convoy ships are close by. All the recruits had been boarded the day before from the Pier 6 and their ships now are anchored only a short distance away. A hospital ship that had come into the port several days ago with wounded soldiers from France is also sitting close by. It is returning to England under the safety of the convoy. I stare in horror as sailors jump overboard from a burning ship amid the confusion of boats trying to get away from the burning pier. Looking at the north end of the city, I can see that all the buildings within a two mile radius of Pier 6 have been demolished by the force of the blast. Fires are breaking out everywhere and people are screaming with injuries from flying glass and debris. Halifax Harbor is in total chaos. Within minutes of the blast, a huge tidal wave washes ashore sweeping dazed survivors into the harbor where they drown amid all the confusion. I am mesmerized by the horrific scene unfolding before my eyes.

The Colonel grabs my arm and pulls me along with him. There is no doubt in our minds that Halifax is being attacked by the enemy. He barks out an order to his adjutant to follow. "Get on the telegraph to all the garrisons. We are under attack. We need to mobilize quickly.

I am headed to Fort McNab. Whoever let those German U-boats in will pay dearly."

Leading the way to a parked jeep, the Colonel indicates that I drive. Suddenly a military jeep roars into the Parade Square blocking our way and two officers jump out. The Colonel leaves his jeep and runs to meet them.

"Sir, two ships collided in the harbor. One of them was a French ship loaded with munitions. It caught fire and then exploded. You will not believe the destruction. It is beyond anyone's imagination!" Lieutenant Baker is breathless. He had managed to get ashore from the naval ship but a lot of sailors are dead or badly injured.

The Colonel is shocked to hear of the naval accident. "So it is not an invasion by the Germans. Thank God for that but where was the pilot on the ship to have allowed this to happen? Did the French ship have a warning flag of its cargo?"

"No sir. It came in without any warning flags but the ship that struck it, a Belgian relief ship, was in the wrong channel leaving the port for New York without any cargo. Many military have been killed or wounded. What can be done, sir?" asks the lieutenant.

The Colonel has to make a quick decision. "We look after our own first, Lieutenant. If the hospital ship *Old Colony* has been undamaged, gather as many men as you need from any garrison and get our injured to the ship. What about the Barracks?"

"I hear it was badly damaged as well as the naval base," replies the lieutenant. "In fact, there is very little left of the north end. That was the most damaged area but I suspect there are a lot of injured survivors under the rubble. Streets are impassable and lots of areas on fire, sir."

I watch the Colonel shake his head in dismay as he listens to the news of the damage. "Organize rescue parties from every available garrison and ship, Lieutenant. Once we have all the wounded military on the hospital ship or in hospitals, we will turn our attention to the civilians. I have to advise the Minister of Militia of this devastating event. You can be sure someone will pay! What happened to the crew on the French ship? Did they survive, do you know?"

The lieutenant replies, "As far as I know, sir. They jumped ship before it blew up but I don't know what happened to them."

The Colonel waves to me. I am still behind the wheel of the jeep. He turns to the lieutenant, "Take the corporal with you and get search parties organized from the ships. I will update the garrisons and get search parties organized from land. Whatever you need to rescue our men from this disaster, you have permission to seize it. Let's hope the troops on those ships are still in some kind of shape to get to England. The British general will not be happy with this news."

That night a blizzard swept over Halifax covering everything with thirteen inches of snow. The unexpected storm added to the woes of the injured waiting to be rescued and to the search parties frantically searching for survivors. It covered the dangers of broken glass and twisted steel as frantic civilians and soldiers searched the ruins for survivors. After a careful assessment of the two troop ships, there are enough recruits uninjured to fill one ship. It hastily leaves the harbor with its escort of convoy ships. I watch the grey ships leave. They look like ghost ships disappearing into the snow fog. The whole harbor has taken on a ghostly appearance with smoke and snow covering everything a ghastly pale grey. We soon have the hospital ship overflowing with injured soldiers and *Old Colony* moves into safer waters away from the center of the disaster. A newly built Camp Hill Hospital for Veterans which had just been completed takes the remainder of the injured soldiers. By now, all the hospitals in Halifax are overflowing with patients. A train is on its way to the city to transport injured civilians to a hospital in Windsor. It is the closest town to the disaster but trains are departing from other towns to assist with the tremendous task of finding survivors. Nearly half the city has been destroyed by the explosion and thousands are killed and injured.

The next day I am assigned several soldiers from Fort Hugonin to start looking for injured civilians in the rubble of their destroyed homes. I am not happy with the assignment as it is not a pretty sight. We have to dig through the smoldering rubble to look for survivors that might be saved. The snow has dispensed most of the fires but the rubble is still hot and smoldering. I gingerly step over the damaged boards of houses and turn over charred bodies, calling out for any sign of life. Mostly we find the bodies burned beyond recognition. It is a chilling sight and hard on our nerves. One young soldier is extremely agitated by the charred and mangled bodies we are finding. I take him aside and ask the young soldier why he is so upset. I guess him to be about seventeen or eighteen years old but he looks even younger. Gunner Percy Swinimer replies softly, "My father was killed in a sawmill explosion when I was five years old. I can still see him laid out on the kitchen table all burnt and screaming with pain. He lived three days before he died. It was a horrible death but, at least, these people died quickly, sir."

"Why did you join so young? Surely your mother would have needed you." I asked the young soldier who I learned was from New Ross where I was born. I could not help but feel a strong bond with him.

"I wanted to go to war so I lied about my age when I volunteered. When I went home to tell my mother, she was terribly upset. She immediately went to the recruiting station and told them my real age." He smiled as he related the events of 1916 to me. "It kept me from going to the battlefields but I could not get out of the army. So here I am, guarding the gates of Halifax Harbor and hoping to get a look at one German boat, at least."

I am about to assure him that his posting here is important to the war effort when a baby's cry is heard above the howling wind. It startles every one including me. We had uncovered the dead bodies of a man, woman and a young boy and were about to leave. Once we placed the corpses outside on the street to be picked up later, I had returned to the ruins as my map indicated four persons living in this house. We are using the last census as a guide to the occupants. Private Henneberry is closest to the baby's cries and looking under the kitchen stove, he is shocked to see a young child very much alive. Her dress indicates the child is a girl. She had been blown under the stove by the force of the blast. She was lying on the warm ash pan which probably had kept the child from freezing to death in the night. She must have been playing on the floor when the blast occurred. Quickly Private Henneberry gets down on his knees and carefully pulls the child out from under the stove. She is tightly wedged in but finally he extracts the little girl who appears to be about two years old. The cold air takes away her breath which strangles her cries and the child looks at her rescuer with big, blue eyes. She is covered with soot and ashes and has soiled herself during her twenty-six hour ordeal. I quickly remove my greatcoat and wrap the child snugly so that just the tip of her nose is peaking out. "Take her to the nearest hospital, private. Her family is dead but maybe someone will recognize her. There are going to be a lot of orphans after this day, I think." I am concerned she might freeze before she gets to warm shelter. We are on foot as the streets are impassable for vehicles. Quickly I write down the street and house number on a piece of paper and pin it to her dress so she can be identified at the hospital. That is how I was instructed to send injured victims to the hospital but she is the first one I have found alive. I shiver without the protection my greatcoat had offered as the wind swirls snow around anyone foolish enough to out in the elements. Making a motion to the young soldier beside me, I move to the next pile of rubble that had once been a happy home. On the street, dead bodies are stacked like cordwood to be picked up and taken to the morgue. Their only identification is a piece of paper with the street and house number pinned to their burnt clothing. It is hoped that a relative will come and claim the body for burial.

We search for bodies for over a month after the explosion. The Dartmouth side of the harbor has not been extensively damaged but one report indicates a small village of Mi'Mmaq in Tufts Cove has vanished without a trace from the tidal wave following the explosion. When I hear that this village had been slated to be relocated the day before the disaster, I feel very sad for the people who have disappeared completely. The tidal surge probably swept them to their death.

A month after the terrible explosion, I sit in the commanding officer's office and give my report on finding survivors in the destroyed homes. He needs to make a report of the civilian victims we recovered. He has been informed that the city officials are unhappy that the military had assumed control of the situation without consulting them. I could tell the Colonel was a very unhappy man. Not only was he furious with the needless waste of countless lives, he is appalled at the damage to the military establishments in the city. Wellington

Barracks, which houses military men and their families, has suffered heavy damage, as well as the naval school and the military hospital at Admiralty House. The dockyard has been demolished and the naval base suffered extensive damage as well. Many sailors on the ships close to the explosion has been killed or badly injured. It is a major blow to the recruiting and movement of troops for the war in Europe and the War Office is now considering using the Montreal port for the mass movement of troops. I watch the Colonel puff on his cigar, his face red from frustration, as he sifts through the pages of reports. "Losing this port for the military will make a huge impact on the war effort," he declares. "The Minister of Militia is on his way to inspect the port, Corporal. Let's hope we can pacify the city officials before he gets here. The Halifax Relief Committee has complained about our handling of the civilian survivors. After all, our quick efforts saved thousands of lives. When you add money to the mix, you get discontent. Britain was very generous with its' million dollar donation and even the King threw in five thousand dollars of his personal money. But I am more concerned about pleasing the Minister of Militia. I need you to take me to the naval base for an inspection. Report back here in an hour, Corporal."

I stand on top of Citadel Hill and look out at the ruined harbor. There are few ships lying in port as the cleanup efforts are still going on. Only military vessels are allowed in port while other ships wait outside the gates. When I look to the north end of the harbor, the flattened landscape indicates the major damage done by the careless actions of the captains of the two ships involved. Neither captain will take responsibility for the collision so it is a court matter. *If one explosion could wipe out half this city, the battle-torn cities in France must look twice this bad,* I wonder. I shudder at the thought that my brothers are in the middle of this cursed war. I hear a whistle below to let me know the Colonel is ready to inspect the damaged naval base. Sadly I turn from the once proud and prosperous Halifax Harbor, and descend to the Parade Square where the Colonel waits.

****

PART THREE

The Great War:
1918 – 1919

FOOTSTEPS OF LIEUTENANT ORRIN LANTZ:

I sit with my fellow troops in a small house in the village of Bourlon. We are waiting for the call to advance; the German Army is retreating and we are close behind them. Our troops are elated that the great German Army is not only losing ground but losing heart in this war.

Our Canadian Corps' Commander, General Sir Arthur Currie, carefully planned the attack to take the Canal du Nord which is a strategic stronghold of the German Army. We attacked at night taking the enemy by surprise and therefore made a significant gain for our Allies.

I am tired; we have been fighting non-stop since August but with the Germans in retreat, our Allies cannot stop its offensive. Freeing the villages in Northern France from the German occupation is rewarding but many of us are shocked by the conditions forced on the civilians. I am always stunned by the horrible conditions imposed by the enemy; starvation and cruelty, burned out homes forcing the residents to live in barns or cellars. When our Allies enter these villages, the residents rush to meet us with flowers. But I quickly realize that the old men and women, and the young children are badly traumatized by the four years of German occupation. What really makes my blood boil is the rape of girls as young as twelve; they only have their grandparents to protect them. The young men who would be their fathers are in the French Republic Army; many of whom would have been killed or wounded. Their mothers and older sisters have been taken by the Germans to work in mines or factories in Germany. The hardest sight is the fourteen year old girls with babies on their hips; pretty, dark-haired French girls with blond, German fathered babies. When a thirteen year old girl approaches me with a grotesque swollen belly offering me a wild flower, I can hardly contain the rage inside me. I look into her eyes and see death. How could this child possibly survive; it gives me nightmares. While we are neutralizing the villages, German soldiers that had been hiding are swiftly shot. As far as I am concerned, it is too good a death. It hardly compensates the poor French villagers who suffered four long years of German cruelty.

Right now we are on the outskirts of the town of Valenciennes; it is November 1, 1918. There is a lot of talk around camp that the Germans are close to surrender. Austria-Hungary surrendered in August. The Germans are in a slump; their soldiers want to go home and even though they are on the defense, the Huns still fight hard and dirty. They are buying time to get to their fatherland.

Our Canadian Corps has lost a lot of soldiers to snipers and nests of machine guns left behind to cover the Germans' retreat. General Currie is trying a new strategy to eliminate so many losses. Reconnaissance troops are sent ahead of the main Infantry to find and destroy enemy strongholds. My mop-up company is now what is commonly referred to as shock troops. We search buildings and ruins for snipers and machine gunner nests. It is dangerous and tiring work but it saves the lives of many Canadian soldiers. There are still a few villagers left despite their hardships and, being the cowards they are, we find most of the snipers holed up close to these poor citizens.

We work in groups of ten men and move swiftly through the streets searching for the enemy. When the Reconnaissance troops clear a town, the main Canadian Corps with a brass and pipes band will then make a grand entrance. My men are seasoned fighters and close comrades, we know our job and carry out our work without any hesitation. We have been fighting together for many months and a close friendship is shared among us.

We are hunkered down on the outskirts of the city; the Germans had flooded the north and west approaches forcing us to take the south entrance. I caution my men carefully and my final message is "use your grenades at any movement even if you can't see the enemy". We are using the moonless night to sneak into the city and once we clear the gate, we split up in small groups and disappear into the many streets and alleys. The darkness covers our stealth and we quietly find cover to await the dawn. Knowing there will be a nest of machine gunners close to the entrance, my group finds shelter in a burned out building that is still smoldering. We feel the heat through the soles of our combat boots but we hold that position until the sky turns pink with the beginning of dawn. Every nerve in my body tingles. I can feel the tension in my men but I know they will wait for orders from me.

Ten pairs of eyes scan the rubble strewn streets around the gate looking for a sniper. Only a minor movement betrays the German machine gunner and I spot him. He is well concealed and would have done serious damage to our Corps if left undiscovered. I motion the soldier with the Lewis gun forward and point in the direction of the enemy. We travel light without kits; our pockets are stuffed with grenades and ammunition. While the haze caused from the smoke-filled building offer us some protection, I am relieved to see that the gunner is pointed toward the entrance waiting for the main Canadian Corps. Private Duncan inches forward until he can see the enemy; the gun's weight of 28 pounds is easily handled by one soldier. Normally we only carry Lee-Enfield rifles and grenades but the commanding officer insisted on us taking a Lewis machine gun. He knew the German resistance would be fierce. The gun Private Duncan has been issued is a Model 1917 and is a .303 British caliber. It is a nasty machine that can take out a nest of machine gunners in a flash. Our boys often call it the Belgian rattlesnake because its bite is deadly. After neutralizing the sniper at the gate, I move my troops out into the street. I can hear sporadic gunfire in other parts of the town as the other platoons encounter enemy resistance.

We search the length of the street and turn the corner to cross to the next street when a single shot rings out. We scatter for cover except for Private Duncan who falls in the street with a bullet between his eyes. His Lewis gun has made him the sniper's target. Two of my men and I are inside a brick building but our view is limited; the rest of my men are across the street in another building with a better view of the sniper's hole. I yell across "where" and receive a quick response "3rd floor brick building ahead". We are trapped! It is certain suicide to get access to the sniper. As I sink to the floor of the building, I glance out at the Lewis gun still in the dead soldier's grip. *Poor Duncan, damn, he never had a chance.* There is no way to get the gun without getting shot so I have to come up with a plan. Looking around, I notice a door on the other side of the room leading to the street behind us.

"Hey, Mill." I call out. "Can the Fritzie see the street behind us?"

"No, this is a dead end street, sir," he replies.

"What does the building look like...apartments, offices? What do you think?"

Lance/Corporal Milledge Henshaw looks out at the building making sure he is well protected. "Looks like some kind of barracks. Lots of little windows facing the street. Maybe a prison or something like that."

"Hey, Mill, what else do you see, any churches close by or schools?" I wish I could see myself so I could draw up a battle plan.

"No," came the reply, "just a few houses and shops not damaged. There is a fence in front and a sign on the gate but I can't read it. Too far off, sir!"

I turn to the two comrades with me. "What do you think, boys? Shall we try the other street and give the Fritz a Canadian hello." They smile; they are quite familiar with my *Hellos* to the enemy.

I yell back to Milledge, "When you hear shooting, get over here and use the street behind us. We are going to storm the building. Come as fast as you can! Grab that Belgian rattlesnake if you can."

I wasn't sure my plan would work but as I check the street behind us, I can clearly see to the end. There has been little damage to the buildings and that worries me. So we dart from one doorway to the next until we are almost at the end. At the last house, I force the door open and carefully look in. *Too quiet,* I think but I wave my comrades to follow. We check the rooms and then move upstairs. The house is well furnished and has been empty for some time. I avoid the windows facing the brick building but I can see it clearly. I decide it is a school of some kind which means it has a lot of rooms for Germans to hide. I definitely need more men for this job. Looking around for stairs to the attic, I caution my men to stand guard. The steps are steep and narrow but there is enough light from the window for me to see. Cautiously, I raise my head above the stairs and find it is empty which amazes me. I crawl on my belly toward the small, dirty window which is at the same height as the third floor of the brick building. The sniper is in throwing distance of a Mills bomb but how to do it is the problem. Any activity will attract the sniper's fire. I crawl back to the stairs and look around the dusty attic. As my eyes survey the room, I notice a hatch in the roof where the chimney protrudes; *probably used for chimney cleaners,* I surmise but it's a way to the roof. *I can use the chimney for cover and lob a grenade over to the sniper's nest,* I plan; *not the best way to do the job but it might work.* At least the distraction will allow the rest of my men to catch up. I whisper my plan to Private George Price and then instruct him to guard the door at the street.

"No noise," I caution. "And be on the lookout for the rest of the men. There is no telling how many Fritzies will tumble out once these bombs explode."

It is a tight fit but I manage to squeeze through the small hatch by the chimney. The fact that the roof is quite slanted is a problem. I know I am a sitting duck if there are any other snipers in the buildings around me. I pull the pins on two Mills bombs and then throw them, one after the other, in quick succession. They both land in the open window and blow a huge hole in the side of the building. I know I got the sniper but I don't know how many more Germans are with him. Several windows are smashed open and rifles are stuck out firing in my direction. It is apparent to me they don't know exactly where I am. I lie down and use the peak of the roof for cover. My men are below on the street but I cannot see what is happening,

"Take cover across the street, boys!" I yell. "Mill, bring me up the Lewis so I can let those bastards know we have arrived!" The noise from the enemy fire covers my voice.

Lance/Corporal Henshaw sticks the Lewis gun up through the hatch beside me. "What do you want us to do, sir?" he asks.

I grab the gun and quickly get it in position by the chimney. "Once I start firing this Belgian rattlesnake, those Fritzies will pepper this place with bullets! Get the men across the street in a safe house. Check for snipers or hidden soldiers carefully. If I don't make it outta here, find the rest of the troops and join up with them. But stay on guard and when any Germans escape the brick building, shoot them. No prisoners today. Let the Infantry take prisoners if they find any."

With the Lewis gun, I spray the third floor of the brick building with .303 bullets. Smashing windows and killing Germans, I am amazed at the power of the Lewis gun. *What a killing machine! Too bad it gets so hot,* I think. Now that I have given away my position, I have to move fast. When the Lewis is out of bullets, I jump down through the hatch, a drop of five feet, and run down the stairs for the back door. As I step out on the street, the Germans are streaming out of their building and running in all directions. My men are heavily engaged and I start firing at the retreating German soldiers. Some get away but most are killed or wounded. My men spread out covering the area around the building which had been a school. Inside the school, we count over forty dead Germans which I find amazing. The enemy usually leaves only a half a dozen snipers behind to cover their retreat. I decide it was a well laid out plan to ambush our Canadian Corps that has been averted. General Currie never fails to impress me with his instincts on the enemies' battle plans. Sending in advance troops saved hundreds of lives. I send one of my men back to get the Lewis gun off the roof; it proved to be too valuable to leave behind. While it cost Private Duncan his life, it saved the rest of my men.

My section of the town is clean so my men take a well-deserved rest. "Hey boys, I guess the Fritzies know the Canadians have arrived!" I grin as I light a cigarette.

Private Price has been sent out to count the wounded and dead Germans. He returns with a wounded officer. I scowl at him and shout, "What is this, Private?"

"He is demanding his rights, sir! Wants medical treatment," reply the Private, noting my mood.

"Well now! *His* rights!" I growl. "What about the rights of those little French girls? Hey Fritzie! What about those old men and women you beat? What about their rights?" I glare at the German officer who doesn't waver. "Well, your bad luck today. We don't have a medic with us so I guess you will have to bleed to death!"

"Take me to your commanding officer, Lieutenant!" demands the German officer in perfect English. It always amazes me that they know our language so well. "As your prisoner, I have a right to medical care."

I look more carefully at the German and note he is bleeding quite severely from a shoulder wound; without a blood transfusion, he probably wouldn't make it. "Very well, Fritzie! It's a bit of a hike and you will have to walk it. We are the advance troops; we do not have medics or stretcher bearers. One of my men will take you back to the line."

I walk a few yards away and motion Milledge to follow. In low tones, I tell him to take the prisoner as far as the sentry at the gate. From there, a runner will take him to the First Aid Station. "Keep a close eye on this one, Mill, he's still got some fight in him. Stay behind him all the time and keep your gun ready. Don't let him trick you. He has lost a lot of blood and will drag ass before he gets to a medic. Tell the sentry to take a message to the commanding officer about our progress. The town will be ready for the main corps tomorrow morning. Hurry back and if you can find some rations for us, the boys will owe you a few beers."

Late in the afternoon, Lance/Corporal Henshaw returns with fifty troops and much needed rations. "Hey Buddy, what do we have here?" I ask as I look at the extra men.

"These are compliments of the commanding officer, sir! When he heard of the extent of resistance, he felt we were understaffed. Gave us two more companies! That German officer sang like a bird when questioned. He told us of another nest of forty or so Fritzies. These men will help us clean it out," reports Milledge. I found out one thing about the German soldiers, they don't like to die. No matter how hard they fight in the field, once captured, they willingly give valuable information if it means they will survive the war. Only the highest ranking officers clam up; they want to die a glorious death for their beloved Kaiser.

I quickly organize my new teams. We know exactly where to go but now the risk is not to get shot by mistake by our own troops who are already in the area. When we reach the location of the sniper's nest, we find it is too late. The bodies of the Canadians are strewn in the street around the nest of the machine gunners. They had been ambushed. Now that we had three Lewis guns I knew cleaning out the hated Germans would be easy. The building was accessible without revealing our presence and when everyone was in place, we open fire and completely demolish the hiding place. Parts of bodies of the hidden Germans are flung into the air and while there is sporadic return fire, it does no damage to us. With the Lewis guns too hot to fire any more shells, I wave the new troops to enter the damaged building. Scouting the back of the building, they come across several wounded Germans trying to escape and quickly round them up.

"What now, sir?" asks Milledge.

"Let's go find the rest of our troops. I think we have neutralized this fair town, Mill. Then we eat those rations you brought back. I bet that bully beef will taste like steak! Tomorrow we drink beer and celebrate." It has been a long day and weariness is slowly taking hold. With my men, I make our way back through the deserted streets to the meeting place area by the gate.

Dawn breaks over the shattered landscape and casts a pinkish glow to the ruins in Valenciennes. A band can be heard in the distance; the 3rd Canadian Division has begun its march to free the town. I stretch my aching muscles as I wake up my men. Sleeping on a hard floor with no blankets to shake off the night chill has become familiar to us. We have forgotten the comforts of beds and hot meals. Before the Canadian Corps reaches the town, hundreds of refugees flood back, filling the narrow road to the entrance gate. Old men and women push wheel carts or pull wagons piled high with their valuables. Small children run around, their faces expressing their joy. It always amazes me how quickly these wretched citizens know the hated Germans have been sacked. It seems like they appear out of thin air.

That evening President Poincareé of France thanks us for our bravery. We are gathered in the town square surrounded by the city ruins and accept the praise of the French President. In appreciation, he singles out General Sir Arthur Currie along with me and several other officers and presents us with the country's highest medal, Croix de Guerre, which France awards its own troops for gallantry. To receive this honor, a soldier is mentioned in a dispatch from his commanding officer recognizing his action performed. I am very surprised to be among the soldiers called up to receive this award and while I am embarrassed to be singled out, I am very humbled to receive such a prestigious award. The town citizens, who had returned gather around us, give us flowers and candy. The Canadian Corps band plays the National Anthem of France and this brings tears to many French eyes. My troops cheer and sing *For He's a Jolly Good Fellow.*

I stare at the medal supported by a green ribbon with seven narrow red stripes pinned to my chest. I find it quite pretty; the bronze medal is a cross with two swords crossed and a center portrait of a young woman wearing a Phrygian cap encircled with the words *République Francaise. I wonder which battle earned me this little trinket.* I marvel at this unexpected reward.

General Currie shakes my hand and thanks me for a job well done. I am overwhelmed with the praise but I wish I could join my comrades for a beer. Then the French President comes over to shake my hand and thanks me again while expressing his concern for the welfare of the villagers. "Buildings can be replaced, Lieutenant, but what about the poor citizens? They have been ravaged by those brutes!"

"What will happen to those little girls that they raped, sir? I saw so many of them in the villages we liberated. It is a hard sight to forget." My sleep is still haunted by the little girl who had approached me several weeks ago.

"Ah, yes, the damaged ones," sighs the President, fully aware of the situation. He looks at me carefully wondering if my interest is coming from real concern for his people. "I see this has disturbed you. Rest assured the government will take good care of them. If it is safe to do so, we will terminate the pregnancies. I am sure God will forgive us for this act. These poor children are now in the custody of the State until their fathers, God bless those who survive this war, return. France will be scarred in many ways for a long time, sir! The sacrifices made by the Canadians to rid us of those heathens will not be forgotten. It is one promise we can make!"

I join the rest of my company and endure much back slapping. We are given a few days leave to rest and relax before joining up with the main Canadian Corps to further pursue the hated Germans back to their own country. General Sir Arthur Currie is empathetic in issuing orders to rest and relax. "Sleep in a real bed and eat real food," he says. "I am sure these citizens will be most kind to you. I don't have to remind you that you are a guest of the President of France. Report to duty on November 5th; we should be close to the outskirts of Mons by then. I thank you again for a job well done."

****

France, Nov. 1st, 1918

Dear Harry:

We are sitting in our company headquarters, a very decent little French village, where not many days ago the enemy held full sway. For the present time there is not very much to do. The mail has just been brought up but there was nothing for me except a nice box of candy from some friends of mine on Blighty. Was expecting some mail from home. Had a nice letter from Millie C. a few days ago, telling me the home news. Also had your letter with the one enclosed from Florence Hicks. Was only glad to get the news.

You will have a very good idea of what part of France we are in just now, by reading the papers. A few days ago we had the extreme pleasure of being amongst the first troops to enter a fairly large town which a few hours previously had been held by enemy troops. By Jove! Harry, the reception that we got from the liberated French people amply repaid us for some of days we have spent under conditions which were not nearly so congenial. The streets were lined with old men and women, and little kiddies who went nearly beside themselves with joy. When our band entered the town playing the National Anthem of France, the people went fairly wild, two young women rushed out; one from each side of the street carrying a large bouquet of flowers which they gave to the bandmaster. Then together they embraced poor old Dan (bandmaster) who nearly collapsed with confusion while the others thoroughly enjoyed the performance.

I am enclosing a couple of German bank notes which are valueless except by the date and the signature they bear.

I just received word last evening that the French Republic had seen fit to reward my small services by decorating me with the Croix de Guerre.

Well I hope you are all in as good health as I am present.

Very sincerely, Orrin

****

I sit in the rain and read my orders. I am not happy with another night attack, especially in new territory where the men are not familiar with the terrain. The objective of the 85th Battalion is to capture the town of Quievrechain and the bridgeheads across the river Honnelle. My battalion has just arrived at Quarouble where the headquarters are set up. We have marched in the rain for two days from Valenciennes. As the transports are bogged down on muddy roads, we have to carry all we need, from spare ammunition, grenades and rations. Close to the Belgium border, the countryside has changed to hills and dense forests. There are rapid streams and hedges with lots of hiding places for the enemy to trap us. A planned night attack in this terrain and weather to chase Germans in fast retreat clearly upsets me. I have a bad feeling about this place.

Lieutenant Ernest sits down beside me and passes me a cup of hot tea laced with rum. "This gunfire will perk you up. I'm taking a patrol out tonight to get behind enemy lines," he says as he lights up a cigarette. "The Colonel wants another Hun."

I look at my friend before answering, "Take every precaution, David. These Huns are Germany's finest and they are desperate. How many men are you taking?"

"I've picked ten of my best men. We have both pulled black hand gangs, Orrin, so the dangers are known to us," he replies. "What are your orders? You don't look too happy about them."

"I'm not happy about night attacks in strange territory. We don't know where the snipers or machine gun nests are. I don't think this plan has been well thought out by the Colonel. I guess you might help with that problem if you can capture a willing Hun. My company is the left flank in the push to take Quievrechain. Look like a fair size town. At least the maps are well detailed," I comment.

"Well, Orrin, some of the advance patrols reports strong Hun presence in the small farms, and Fosse 2 is considered a nest of machine guns. Be careful, and don't get too far ahead of the right flank or you will get trapped," replies Lieutenant Ernest. He rises to leave, and looking back at me, smiles and says, "Meet you for a tankard of ale in Quievrechain after we oust the Huns from their easy living!" I agree and wave him on, wishing he had my back on this mission. We have been friends since first arriving in England but our paths only cross once in a while on the battlefield. Now that we have the Germans in full retreat, the General has all four divisions of the Canadian Corps together in battle.

It is after midnight when my men start on its mission. Our goal is to take the bridgehead at Fosse 2. We have quite a stretch of small farms to cross which prove hazardous as the snipers are well concealed. After clearing out the small farms along the way which cost my company dearly including some of my best men, we follow the Honnelle river bank. I have lost contact with A Company on our right flank so I have no idea where they are. According to my map, we are in the right position. My biggest concern is the woods on my left where heavy machine gunfire is keeping us pinned down with little cover. Behind us is the river, and with two engineers supporting my company, we have access to cork bridges for escape. Right now my attention is on the heavily fortified bridgehead which I expect the enemy will blow up rather than let us take it. They have their orders and we have ours; the bridgehead is vital to our success.

Sergeant O'Connell crawls over to where I am taking cover beside a tall thick hedge which runs alongside the embankment of the river. I consider him the company's best rifle-grenadier.

"What do you think, sir?" he asks me. "I might be in range of the bridgehead to cover our assault but that is a guess."

I look at the Sergeant before replying, "Well, this is a ticklish situation. Until we clear the bridgehead, we are stuck here. And the machine guns in the woods are picking us off like flies. This bridgehead will be booby-trapped, I am sure. The Huns will blow it before they will leave it. They did the same thing two weeks ago when we captured the bridge at Canal du Nord. We were lucky to escape with our lives that day. What we need is heavy artillery fire to make an assault," I conclude. This situation is a challenge and I wish I had more backup. I already lost more men to snipers than I initially had thought I would. We are pinned down so badly that I cannot risk a runner to go back to Headquarters to let the company commander know my situation and send in reinforcements. I check my watch. 06:45 hours and I have not reached my objective. Already behind schedule, I have to make a decision soon or the right flank will move forward without my protection on the left.

"How far do you estimate to the bridgehead, Sergeant?" I ask.

In the dark, Sergeant O'Connell can only guess. "Their machine guns can't reach us yet, so I would say about two hundred yards. The rifle-grenade has a range of one hundred-fifty or a bit beyond. We need to get a little closer for a sure hit. If I use this hedge for cover, I might make it another fifty yards closer."

I run all the scenarios through my mind. I can see a small company of men sneaking closer while we still have the cover of darkness. It is risky and putting my men in great danger as we will be outnumbered but then sitting here with little cover and waiting for daylight is suicide. Quickly I pick twelve men and with Sergeant O'Connell, we start to crawl along the embankment. Our only firepower other than our Lee-Enfield rifles is two Lewis guns and the rifle-grenade. I left the machine guns with the remainder of the company in case we have to make a hasty retreat.

As we inch our way forward, the sky starts to lighten with pre-dawn. The terrain along the embankment is hard to crawl through and already some of the men have minor injuries from scrub bushes and bruising stones. One of the men stuck a sharp stick in his eye so I left him with orders to quietly go back with the rest of the men. Finally, when I can hear the distinct voices of the enemies, I halt the procession. I know we are well within range and to go any further is certain death. I watch as Sergeant O'Connell gets his gun in position; my men know what to do and are prepared for the assault.

This better work or we are all dead men, I think as the first grenade sails through the air and lands in the middle of the enemies who are clustered around a campfire for breakfast. It is evident that they are totally unaware we are so close. Sergeant O'Connell quickly reloads and fires again. We have to kill as many of the enemy as we can but the camp comes alive with the first rocket. I know the Huns have better firepower so an assault has to be made while they are confused. My men break cover and run toward the bridgehead as quickly as the swampy ground allows. The marshy ground is soft from the recent rains and the assault is slower than I had anticipated. I can see the chaos at the campsite but there are more Huns there than I initially thought to be. We only have the cover of one more grenade before we reach the edge of the bridgehead.

Firing the Belgian rattlesnakes from their hips, the 85th surges forward, mowing down the enemy in front of them. It looks like a victory and, as I raise my arm to slow the forward advance, the bridge blows up. The huge explosion sends bodies flying through the air as far as my eyes can see. I feel myself lifted high in the air as a ball of orange fire flies past me. I fall back on the ground; all feeling leaves my body. Panic is clouding my thoughts. *Where are my men? They should be here by now.*

After the explosion of the bridgehead, I wait for the remaining company that had stayed back on my orders to rush forward to help us. Their minds will be haunted for the rest of their lives at the grisly sight waiting for them. I did not know that bodies had been thrown as far as fifty feet and all my men are dead or mortally wounded. There are parts of bodies floating in the river and some bodies hang off the shattered wooden trusses of the damaged bridge. All the Germans are dead, either from the assault or the explosion. They find me face down in the crater left by the huge blast, still alive, but badly wounded. I am told that Sergeant O'Connell lay dead beside me still holding the rifle-grenade, the last grenade still in its chamber. I was unaware that he moved forward with the assault and stayed beside me.

I am barely conscious and dazed as Sergeant Baker kneels beside me. I try to focus but everything is a blur. "Sergeant, take the men and wounded and get the hell out of here. Use sections of the cork bridges and float down the river. Don't wait for relief or the snipers in the woods will finish us off." I break off in a coughing spell which brings blood up from my internal wounds. The force of the explosion has literally broken all my bones. I am amazed I can still think clearly.

As the rest of my company get ready to leave, the men file past me, touching me and offering words of encouragement. They cannot believe I am so badly injured; I had come through so many close calls in previous battles without a scratch. I am fighting off their efforts to take me with them. "I am a dead man. The relief platoon will take care of the dead when they get here. I am ordering you to go without me." My voice is barely a whisper. Each word brings up more blood than I can spit out. It threatens to choke me. I cannot feel my body and my head weighs a ton. Blood is pouring from my ears and nose. As my vision starts to get fuzzy, I take a last look at my men. I am so proud of them but they appear to have two heads and I can't tell one from the other. I know my injuries are fatal. The blast has smashed me up inside. I want my men to get out of here alive and beg them to go without me.

A sensation of being lifted and carried down the riverbank startles me. When I try to protest, one of my men say, "Where we go, you go, sir. *Siol Na Fear Fearail-Breed of Manly Men.*" The motto of the 85th which has kept my men together in the toughest of situations gives them the courage to continue.

"You are carrying a dead man, private." My voice is weak. My vision is now so cloudy I cannot see who is walking beside me even though the private's head is only inches from mine. Six of my men have hoisted me on their shoulders to carry me to the raft. While they notice my body is like that of a rag doll, no one voices their thoughts.

"Sir, we are carrying a fallen hero! We will all die with you before we will leave you." Private Saunders is glad I cannot see the tears streaming down his face.

They gently lay me on a section of the cork bridge. Then climbing on with me, they paddle along the bank of the river using the butts of their rifles. It is a slow and somber procession.

I stir from a semi-comatose state. I have no idea where I am but I seem to be floating on air. The light around me is so bright that it blinds me. A female figure, shrouded in veils, emerges from the light and holds out her hands to me.

"Come with me, son. I have been waiting for you."

I recognize the familiar voice.

"Mother," I whisper. *"I am coming."* I reach out a bloody hand to touch hers. We run through meadows filled with flowers. I am a little boy again and my heart is filled with joy.

"Don't look back, son," her voice floats back to me and, and as my mother ran, the veils billow out around her like wings.

But I do look back and I can see the battlefield and the corpses of my comrades.

"Mother, wait for me," I call but she has disappeared into the Light. I am alone but I still run after her. *"Wait for me, I am coming,"* I cry.

Private Joudrey leans over my inert body. "He's gone west, boys. We have lost him. I was sure he would make it; the lieutenant was one of the finest men we will ever have to lead us into battle." The men on the makeshift raft stare in silence at the body of their cherished leader.

My company is the last group to straggle into headquarters that day and more than one comrade shed a tear as the news of my death became known. I was well liked among the ranks as well as the officers. Company Commander, Lt. Colonel Ralston, is visibly shaken. "I thought he was invincible," he comments as he listens to the tale of D Company's ordeal at Fosse 2. The commander realizes he had sent us out on an impossible mission with too few men and insufficient firepower. The loss of one of his best officers and half a company will be noticed by the General. Fear of being called on the mat, he carefully reviews his battle plans again to see what went wrong.

Lieutenant Ernest stares at the two tankards of ale but his mind is miles away. It is the custom for the officers of the division to gather and pay tribute to their fallen heroes after a battle. Glasses of whiskey are filled many times over as praise is bestowed on friends and comrades who have fallen in battle. Lieutenant Ernest sits alone absorbed in his own thoughts. The news of my death hit him hard. Slowly he reaches for the first tankard of ale and quietly says to no one in particular, "To the best chap I ever met." He drinks its contents without stopping to breathe. After a moment, he raises the second tankard and murmurs, "To my brother in arms, rest in peace." When he finishes the ale, he stands up and leaves the room seeking a quieter place to grieve. He had been told that the Colonel awarded me the coveted Military Cross for my last act of bravery. *What a crock! A trinket to hang on someone's wall while a good man rots in a shallow grave.* As he leaves the room his thoughts drift to his last conversation with me. *I think you knew this was your last mission. You must have sensed it as I have never known you to question a mission before this one.*

Deep in thought, Lieutenant Ernest walks through the dark night to my newly dug grave. He stares at my helmet nailed to the stake. *What happened out there, old chap? You could read a battlefield better than most of us.* Lieutenant Ernest's thoughts drift to the first time he had met me. We were both at Bramshott Camp in England three years ago training in the coveted Nova Scotia Rifles Regiment. The British officer who was training us for trench warfare had noticed that both of us were crack shots. We were almost singled out to be snipers but we both had another outstanding talent. We could read a battlefield with great accuracy; this brought the two of us together. Lieutenant Ernest smiles as the memories flood his grieved mind. *We became brothers in war – a bond stronger than blood.*

For a long time he sits here. He finds it hard to leave my gravesite. Lieutenant Ernest wonders if the French will remember the sacrifices of our men who are buried everywhere on their land. *What will happen to all the graves that dot the landscape,* he wonders, *the fallen heroes, our comrades in arms, left behind in a foreign land when this war ends.* He gets up from the cold, wet ground and throws away the empty silver flask. *What a bloody waste of life,* he concludes, *and for what? One crazy Kaiser's obsession for power!* He wonders if the rumors of the Kaiser and his son, the Crown Prince, escaping to Holland are true. *The handwriting is on the wall. This war is over and Orrin sacrificed his life for nothing.* Lieutenant Ernest walks off into the dark night without a backward glance. Tomorrow will bring another battle as the Allied Forces push the defeated Germans closer to their own fatherland. A deep longing for home creeps into his thoughts. *I will look up Orrin's family when I get back. They deserve to know that he died a hero.*

****

FOOTSTEPS OF PRIVATE EVERETT LANTZ:

I am nervous as I wait for the General's adjutant to return. My head is whirling with all the activity of the last twelve hours. The war has ended and everyone is crowded in the streets to celebrate our victory. Trying to find my brother Orrin in the celebrations going on in the streets of Mons is futile. Thousands of soldiers are milling around and the drinking is out of control. I finally find several soldiers from the 85th Battalion who take me to see their commanding officer. We find him quite indisposed from the celebrating and when I mention my brother's name, he immediately broke down. "Go see the General, son! He's got all my reports!" Then he dismisses me without another word. I am starting to worry. I am sure Orrin would be here celebrating with his battalion.

General Sir Arthur Currie sits at his desk in his new headquarters in Mons. Having been congratulated by the King of Belgium during the Armistice celebrations, he is now retired to the privacy of his rooms. His heart is heavy with the burdens the war has placed on him. His biggest disappointment that the war ended in a railway car with signatures on a treaty instead of the defeat of the Germany Army in the field weighs on his mind. *We sacrificed so many of our boys to get here,* he thinks, *and the Germans robbed us of the pleasure of their surrendering on the battlefield. Even the last shot fired in this war was by a German and it killed a Canadian soldier.* The fact that the whole German Army was camped on the outskirts of Mons when the Canadian Corps reached the city disturbed the General. *They were within gun range all night while we sat here waiting for the damn treaty to come into effect,* he fumes to himself.

In his hands are the reports from the burial detail, listing the November casualties. *So many fallen heroes in eleven days,* he realizes as he reads through the pages. Suddenly a name jumps out of the list of soldiers, *Lieutenant Orrin Lantz,* and the General reaches for his glass of whiskey. At first he thinks it is a mistake as he remembers the last time he spoke with the lieutenant in Valenciennes when the French President had decorated him with the *Croix de Guerre* for his outstanding gallantry in battle at Passchendaele. General Currie remembers how modest and humble this young officer was as he accepted the medal. *And he was killed five days later,* he groans and slumps in his chair. *Did I fail these young brave boys? He is only 25 years old. My God, this war has robbed Canada of it finest young men.* Frantically the General rifles through the stack of reports on his desk scattering papers everywhere. *Where the hell is his commanding officer's report? He has some explaining to do!* He grumbles.

A knock interrupts his search. His adjutant sticks his head through the half opened door. "Begging your pardon, sir. A soldier wishes to see you. Says he is looking for his brother, sir!" Corporal O'Hara views the papers scattered all over the floor and the General's flushed face.

"Tell him to go see the soldier's company commanding officer, Corporal. What do I know of this?" barks the General as he tries to straighten the papers on his desk.

"Says he is Lieutenant Lantz's brother, sir!" advises the adjutant watching the color drain from the General's face. "Can I help you find a report, sir?"

General Sir Arthur Curie rose unsteadily to his feet. He is a tall man but he pulls himself into a stiff stance and glares at the adjutant. "Give me a minute, Corporal. And then show the young man in." As soon as the door closes, the General scoops up the papers off the floor and piles them on his desk. His hands shake as he pours himself a generous glass of whisky.

The adjutant returns to the outer office and motions me to the General's office. I enter the room and smartly salute. "Thank you, sir! Private Everett Lantz, sir! I was hoping to find my brother before I leave with my regiment to go to Germany. The last I heard, my brother was fighting in this area."

The General is staring hard at me and I shiver a bit. I have heard about this great soldier and his victories in battle but this is the first time I have been in his presence. Orrin brags about his great battle plans in his letters to me so I stare back in wonder.

"Sit down, Private. Tell me what unit you are with? How long have you been on the Front?" As he is speaking, he pours a glass of whiskey and hands it to me.

I accept the glass of whiskey but I don't drink as I am offering my reply. "Sir, I am attached to the 7th Royal Newfoundland Regiment. I came over in July 1917." I take a quick swallow of the whiskey which burns all the way to my empty stomach. I manage to stifle a cough.

"July 1917, you say? Script or volunteer?" The General knew the Conscription Law was hated in Canada and caused a lot of turmoil.

"I was 'scripted, sir. Three of my brothers were already here at the Front and I felt my duty was to my father at home. But my father felt I should do my patriotic duty and fight for King and country. Two more of my brothers were 'scripted in 1917 as well." I catch myself from babbling by taking another drink of whiskey.

"Six brothers! Here on the frontlines? I wasn't aware of this. Why the Newfoundland Regiment? I thought Lieutenant Lantz was from Nova Scotia," asks the General.

"Well, sir, they needed replacement recruits after that disastrous battle in 1916 at Beaumont-Hamel that wiped out eighty percent of the regiment. Hard fighting lads, they are, sir! When I arrived in England in 1917, all Nova Scotia recruits were sent to bring the Newfoundland Regiment up to standard. Newfoundland had exhausted its supply of recruits. It is just a small island, sir. I handle the big guns making sure they are cleaned and ready to fire properly. We have been selected by the King to go to Germany for the duration of the Allied Occupation. That is quite an honor, sir." I am starting to squirm under this intense questioning. "You see I wanted to find my brother and say goodbye before I leave. I haven't seen him in four years."

"You said you had four more brothers here on the front line. Where are they, Private?" questions the General.

"My youngest brother is batman to the chaplain of the 85th Battalion and he is in England now. He was here on the Front for two years. One of my brothers was on the frontline until late 1916 when he was wounded. Shell shock, sir! He is home now. Another brother who enlisted in 1917 is either here or somewhere in England, I am not sure.

And one brother stayed in Halifax at the Garrisons there." I reply. "I am sorry to take your time, sir, but if you could tell me where my brother Orrin is camped, I will be on my way. His commanding officer said you had the reports."

"I always have time for one of my troops, Private. Of course, the Newfoundland Regiment is attached to the British Army but I consider all Canadian soldiers under my command. Now I must tell you the bad news. Your brother was killed liberating a town from the Germans a few days ago. He was capturing a line along a river and the Germans blew up a bridgehead that wiped out half his company. Lieutenant Lantz had just been awarded the *Croix de Guerre* medal a week before for bravery in a previous battle. It is an honor to have such a courageous and brave man under my command. He will be awarded the Military Cross for his bravery in his final battle. I am sorry to have to tell you this sad news, especially on such a day as this. If anyone deserved to celebrate the end of the war, it was your brother. One of my best officers," concludes the General as he watches me carefully.

The news hit me hard. At first I thought I misunderstood as the General kept talking about Orrin but then the realization struck me, and I start to shake. I am glad I am sitting down because all feeling has left me. The General gently takes the glass from my shaky hand and refills it. I try to pull myself together but I am having trouble breathing. Gratefully I accept the second glass of whiskey and take a big swallow. I am not a big drinker but my time with the Newfoundland Regiment taught me many things and drinking whiskey was first on their list. "Laddie, a gud man can 'old 'is w'iskey", they would say passing the bottle around freely. As the hot liquid warms my belly and the room stops swirling, I look at the General.

"No one told me this, sir! I need to find my regiment." I try to stand but my legs are shaking so hard, I sit down again. Putting my head in my hands, I can't suppress the sob that shakes me. "I am sorry, sir. This is a great shock."

The General goes to the door and calls in his adjutant. "I want you to escort this fine soldier back to the 7th Royal Newfoundland Regiment and give this note to the company commander." He puts his hand on my shoulder and kindly says, "My man will take you back safely. Again, I am sorry for the loss of your brother."

In the confusion, I forget to salute before I take my leave. I have to force my legs to move as I follow the adjutant out of the office. My head is still swirling with the news of Orin's death. I find it hard to believe that Orrin will not come home after the war.

Several days later a message arrives from the General. He has arranged for me to visit Orrin's gravesite on the outskirts of Valenciennes. The General hopes this will give me a sense of peace with my brother's sacrifice. Later that day, I stand beside a fresh mound of earth that was dug just a week ago as I look at a stake with my brother's helmet nailed to it. I touch his helmet lovingly knowing it was a part of his daily life for the past four years. It is the only tangible thing left and I regret I had not seen him in his uniform. I am tempted to tear it off the stake and hold it close to my heart. *You were such a risk taker, Orrin. I have had to climb more than one tall tree to get you down from your daring boyish acts.* I let the memories flood my numbed brain. I will probably be the only brother to visit Orrin's final resting place and I am grateful for the General's kind gesture. I can tell our father about the cemetery and Orrin's final heroic battle in the war. I look at the freshly dug graves around my brother's grave and realize these must have been his men that died with him during that ill-fated battle. A beer tankard filled with poppies has been left by the stake. *You had a brother in arms, Orrin, but that does not surprise me. Everyone loved you.* I find this a great comfort. *Brother, we will not forget you. Rest in peace, you have earned it.* I take a final look at the surrounding green fields with wild poppies growing everywhere. It is peaceful here. The guns are silenced now but traces of terrific battles are clearly visible.

I know I will never pass this way again as I leave my brother's final resting place. *I will write a letter home tonight and tell the family. My father will be torn apart by this news and Harry will blame himself. To die five days before the war ends is so tragic and it robbed my brother of his victory,* I think as I walk toward the waiting car. My regiment leaves tomorrow for the long march through Belgium to Germany. I am not happy about going. I wish I was staying behind with some of the other regiments to help clean up the battlefields of the debris left from the Great War. Forcing the defeated Germans to be constantly reminded of their defeat does not sit well with me. I know it was part of their agreement to surrender but I can't help but wonder what our troops will think as we carry out these demeaning duties. Everyone I spoke to was anxious to get back to Canada and I hope the next six months passes quickly.

****

FOOTSTEPS OF PRIVATE GORDON LANTZ:

I am so excited I can hardly concentrate on my duties at the hospital. The Canon left me to entertain some of the patients while he went to the Chapel. The chaplain's duties will keep him there most of the day. At the 11th hour on November 11, 1918, Big Ben starts its bells; they had been silent for four years. As bells ring out all over the city, my mind is filled with the joy of the war being over. One of the patients asks me to take him to the solarium so he can be with some of his buddies to watch the festivities on the street. I quickly make my way back to the ward where I am working today. I glance over to my two favorite patients in the far corner of the room and wonder what mischief they are planning today. Hardly a day goes by without them scheming to get out of their beds. When the Canon and I first arrived here over a year ago, these two soldiers who were badly wounded were so despondent the medical staff had almost given up on them. For some reason, probably because they were highlanders from Cape Breton, Canon O'Brien began spending every waking moment with them. When he finally made a breakthrough, I was elated as I had become very fond of them too. They were not much older than me and they faced so many obstacles to get back their health, I wondered if all our prayers brought about divine intervention. Now they faced another huge obstacle in the war ending as soon they will be shipped home.

Sergeant Ian McPhearson lay in his hospital bed and listens to the sounds of celebration on the London streets. For many months, Ian lay between life and death in the Canadian hospital in London. Both his legs had been brutally amputated in a field hospital in France after a shell exploded in the billet he was sharing with his comrades. He often wished he had joined them in death; his anguish and pain had been so unbearable. Now the war was over and he would return home, a burden to his family. His father's lobster boat would always leave port without him.

But the sounds of celebration from the streets outside the hospital window stir emotions he had long thought dead. The sound of the bagpipes from the Scottish Highlanders pass by and Ian knows he has to get to the street and join the celebration. The fire in his belly flares up at the sound of the pipes. He looks over at his friend who has also lost a leg from a battle long forgotten. He had been as despondent as Ian at the prospect of returning home. What could a farmer do with one leg, he often joked, as he tried to hide his despair.

"Hey Jack, can you hear that, lad? The war is over! We actually beat those bastards." Ian calls over to his friend. "I think we should join the celebrations. It is our victory, too!"

Jack looks at his friend and smiles. He is fond of Ian who helped him through the rough days and nights after the realization of his future without a leg impacted his fogged brain. For a long time, he longed to be with his friends in shallow graves alongside the trenches. Their pain and suffering were over but so was their vibrant life. The chaplain had spent long hours at his bedside instilling the miracle of life in this dark time the war had created. Finally, Jack accepted that one good leg was as good as two and started fighting for his life. After all, half of the hospital's patients had lost legs or arms.

"Did you suddenly grow wings, Ian? Do you have a plan to get down there with the crowd?" asked Jack.

"I will think of something. All we need are wheels and a batman. Those pipes have stirred my blood; I only wish I had my kilt," replied Ian. The need to be on the street was consuming him. As he looked around the hospital room, he spots me returning with a patient. Finally, he catches my attention and waves me over.

I approach the bed with a big smile on my face. The war is over and I can go home at last. I will be with my family again.

"What's up, Ian? Can you hear the celebrations down on the streets? Oh, it is a good day to be alive. General Haig is preparing a parade and inspection of the troops this afternoon." I can hardly wait to be free of my duties and join the crowds.

"Well, laddie, we are stuck here, are we not? Do you want some adventure? My friend and I want to see the action. Laddie," Ian hopes to convince me of his plan, "all we need is a way to break outta here!"

I have seen the antics these two have cooked up before so I smile and ask what they have in mind. I find it hard to refuse this rugged Highlander from Cape Breton.

"Well, t'is the pipes that stirred me up! I want to see 'em ag'in before I go home. Here's the plan, laddie. You get Jack and mysel' some wheels and get us to the street," replies Ian with a big grin. I let him think he has taken me in like the other schemes he planned.

"You know it is cold out there, Sergeant, been snowing a bit. Might be a problem finding something for you. But give me some time," and I wink and roll my eyes, "sounds like a good time. It is a celebration, after all!" I reply and disappear down the long line of hospital beds.

An hour passes and the street sounds continue to echo through the hospital windows. The patients that could walk are lined up at the windows watching the sights below. Ian has almost given up on his escape partner and turns to Jack. "Looks like the laddie aborted the mission, old chap. I was all stirred up to see the kilts and pipes ag'in." At that moment, he spots me and an orderly, each pushing a laundry cart, enter the room. "Ah, maybe we will get outta here yet."

It was a struggle but we finally get the soldiers into the laundry carts and make our way to the outside exit. As we enter the street, the noise is deafening. Ian looks around at the thousands of Londoners swarming around him. A wool blanket covers him to offset the chill of the November air. It was all the hospital could offer for clothing. All uniforms are burned because of the filth and lice from the battlefield. Sitting on a pillow placed on the bottom of the laundry cart, Ian looks out at the jubilant scene. Two young nurses come along carrying bottles of champagne and grab my arm.

"Quick, come with us," they shout.

I am dumbstruck. Could these pretty young women mean me? "Where are you going?" I ask curiously.

One of the ladies pulls harder on my arm. "The King is riding down the Esplanade to meet the troops. It is just two streets over. Bring your patients. Lydia, help the other chap."

Ian reaches up and takes the bottle of champagne. "This will warm me up," he says and winks at me. Eventually we push through the overexcited crowd until we find ourselves looking out at the street.

"Make way for a hero!" cries the girl called Lydia who is half drunk. A burly man stands in her way but she shoves past him and helps push the laundry cart in front. The occupants are jolted and tossed about in the rough ride but they are too excited to care. Many bystanders stare at us in amazement.

I am breathless as this is more than I had bargained for. I had not expected so many Londoners to be on the street. Bells are ringing in all the church steeples. As far as the eye can see, jubilant faces are pressed close to each other waiting to cheer the King. Thousands of flags wave vigorously as the crowd waits impatiently. *What a sight to write home to father,* I think as I pass up on an offered bottle of champagne which is being freely distributed throughout the crowd. I wonder where my older brothers are celebrating the end of the war. They are certainly missing a great party in London.

The Scottish pipe band comes into view playing a lively tune and behind them comes the reserve troops from Bramshott Training Camp. They look like new recruits dressed in their new uniforms but most are seasoned troops recently recovered from injuries and waiting to return to France. For them, this is a proud moment as they had fought hard and never doubted a victory. I scan the troops to get a glimpse of my brother Lenley who had come over a year before but is still at Bramshott with the 5th Canadian Division. Many of the conscripted recruits never saw the action in France; the call for their advancement never came before the war ended. When I last spoke with my brother, Lenley, I was amazed at how bitter he was for being overlooked. He will be marching today with the 5th Canadian Division but I cannot pick him out of the sea of khaki.

As if on cue, from the other end of the street, King George V and General Haig emerge on horseback. They ride toward the marching troops led by its commanding officer, Colonel Hughes. They will pass close by us and Ian McPearson wiggles and squirms trying to get higher in the laundry cart. "Laddie," he calls to me, "help me up so I can meet the King proper and not sitting down in a nightshirt." Several men standing close by size up the situation and without any prompting, grab the wounded soldier under the arms and lift him clear of the laundry cart.

When the King drew abreast of our little group, his attention is taken by the legless soldier yelling. "For King and Country! Long live the King!" Ian manages a sloppy salute as both arms are held by the men holding him in the air. King George V stops his horse and speaks to the General's adjutant who promptly dismounts and comes over to us. 'What is your name, soldier? His Majesty wishes to visit you later in the hospital." I am happy to pass on the information he needs and we watch the King proceed down the Esplanade on his fine horse. The black stallion is prancing as the noise of the crowd has excited him but the King sits him well. The cheers from the crowd are deafening for their appreciation of his fine display of horsemanship.

We are a weary group that finally makes our way back to the hospital hours later. Both patients are in a happy state; champagne and excitement has erased their pain and self-pity. Waiting for them is the medical officer who pretends to be angry about their escape but he had engineered the plan when I revealed the wishes of the two patients. "This is the best medicine for these soldiers," he told me. Surprised to learn of the King's planned visit later that evening, he immediately orders the staff to have all patients clean and comfortable.

The celebrations will go on for a week with dances and parades but I hope these two patients will be content to listen from the comfort of their beds. I wonder if they know they will soon be on hospital ships sailing home to Canada to face an uncertain future.

I am anxious to be relieved of my duties so I can join the celebrations in the street. Seeing the chaplain waiting for me when I return is a surprise. I was sure his duties in the hospital chapel today would take longer.

"Private Lantz, let's go to the Officer's Mess for dinner," he calls out after getting my attention. Everyone is excited about the news of the war ending and wants to talk to me. I break away with a promise to come back later and share my excitement.

"Sir, I was hoping to get the rest of the day off," I say as I approach the chaplain. "It is a jolly good time on the streets, you know."

"Yes, I know. Today is for celebrating but first I want you to have dinner with me," says Canon O'Brien as he leads the way to the Officer's Mess. While I am a bit disappointed that my plans are delayed, I cheerfully relate the King's response to seeing the wounded soldiers.

While we are eating a delicious meal, I keep wondering why the chaplain is so quiet. This is not his usual manner and I hope he doesn't ask me to delay my celebrating. I promised that pretty nurse I would meet her later.

"Gordon, I will speak to you like a father," the chaplain says finally, his face is very grave. "The news I must tell you is very important and I cannot let you go out with knowing."

I am just finishing my dessert and I look questionably at Canon O'Brien. A shiver runs up my spine. The two of us have been through a lot of exciting and scary adventures on the frontlines but he has never spoken to me like this before.

"Am I being sent home, sir? 'Cause the war ended?" I ask. It is my hope to go home.

"No, it will take several months to demobilize all the troops. That is a big job. I just received word that your brother Orrin was killed in action several days ago. There is no easy way to tell you. My information was that he died a hero and was decorated with the Military Cross for his bravery. I am so sorry, Gordon." The Canon's voice breaks as I look at him in shock. I cannot believe I heard the chaplain right. Orrin could not be dead and so close to the end of the war. I knew my brother was in the thick of the fighting but he had lots of men with him that would keep him protected.

"The Highlanders would not let him get killed, sir. They love my brother. Are you sure of this news, sir?" I ask. This is the first thought that comes to me in my confusion.

"Gordon, it grieves me to tell you this. My understanding was that a bridgehead was blown up and your brother's company was too close. They were taking the bridgehead, you see. He left half his men behind when he stormed the Germans' stronghold." As the chaplain explains to me what happened, my head starts to whirl. *It can't be true,* I keep thinking. The Canon continues, "The Highlanders brought his body back to headquarters, son, they could not leave him in the field. They did love your brother and were proud to serve under him." His words cut me like a knife and my face crumbles as the tears start rolling down my cheeks. I am shaken to the core. *Not Orrin. Not my kind loving brother.* I get a sharp pain in my chest and double over the dining table knocking dishes on the floor. Several officers glance my way and seeing the chaplain with me, offer an understanding smile.

"Where is he? Did they bring him to London?" Stupid with grief, I ask the chaplain this senseless question. As the pain subsides I rise to go to my quarters, but the chaplain puts a fatherly arm around my waist to support me. I did not realize how weakened I had become.

"I will help you, Gordon. But you know that fallen heroes are buried in the fields where they fall. We buried many while we were on the frontlines," he says gently. I try to act like a soldier but the news has broken me and I sob loudly as I leave the Officers' Mess. His gentle voice continues as we make our way to the barracks, "It does not matter where one's body lies, Gordon, the soul goes to heaven to be with God. I know this is hard news especially on Victory Day but you see God has a plan for us all. We may not understand this but I like to think that when God calls a young soul to heaven, he has a special plan for him. I prayed all afternoon for your brother's soul when I heard the news. You must have faith, son."

We reach my quarters, and I gratefully drop face down on the bed sobbing my heart out. I didn't hear the chaplain leave but some hours later, I stir from my dazed state and find the room dark and I am alone. The realization that Orrin will not return home with the rest of us brings on a fresh outburst of crying. *Why him? He was the best of us, so strong and kind.* Then I think of my father who had hoped that Orrin would follow his footsteps and become a minister. *Does he know yet?* I wonder. *This will devastate him! This bloody war!* It is quiet here in the barracks. I am far enough away from the street not to hear the celebrations that will continue all night. *I am probably the only soldier not celebrating tonight but I will honor my brother. I will write a letter to father and express my sorrow. That is what Orrin would want me to do.* I collect my thoughts and sit at the desk. It will be the hardest letter I have written in my young life. *How can I tell my father that his shining star has fallen? How cruel this world is.* I sit at the desk a long time before I finally make enough sense to compose a letter. After several attempts, I finally pour out my heart to my father.

My thoughts drift to when I left for the war in 1914, my father put on a brave front to wave to us as we were leaving on the train. But it is Orrin's parting remarks that surface in my memory. "Father, we will return; have no worry! God is with us." I now realize that we were so filled with dreams of glory that the reality of this war never dawned on us. What did we know of guns and human slaughter? I have been to the battlefields and seen its horrors. Suddenly I feel like an old man and I start to shake. The shock is wearing off leaving an enduring mark on my grieving heart.

****

FOOTSTEPS OF SERGEANT HAROLD LANTZ:

I am working at the mill when Hazel arrives breathless from her exertions. Her long brown hair is blown in tangles as she runs toward me.

"Harry, come quick. Father needs you. Hurry!" she yells.

I drop the log I have been wrestling with and race after her flying skirts. My mind is filled with questions but I am running so fast, I can't speak. We reach the kitchen door and as I open it, I can hear a commotion inside. In our haste, we both try to get through the door at the same time. I step back and let Hazel enter the kitchen with me close on her heels. I don't see our father, but James and Beecher are there. Beecher is wailing and hugging his dog tightly. I assume they have just come home from school. I turn to Hazel in confusion.

"What is the matter? Where is father, Hazel?" I ask her. My first thought is that he was injured by the new horse he had just bought. He had left for town at noon leaving me to work in the mill alone. By now, her sobs are hysterical and she is frantically waving at the letters on the table. I walk over to the table warily. A new fear is gripping me. Obviously father had picked up our mail on his return but only one letter has been opened. I look around the room but there is no sign of our father.

"Read it, Harry! Please tell me it is not true!" A fresh outburst of tears from Hazel sets off the boys' wails again.

As soon as I notice the War Office stamp on the bottom, I sink into a chair. My heart is beating so fast I have trouble breathing. *Oh God, which one?* My mind flits in all directions. *The Angel of Death* sits on our kitchen table and I am afraid to read which brother it has taken. My shaky hand finally picks up the telegram and I read the contents.

"The War Office regrets to inform you that your son, Lieutenant Orrin Lincoln Lantz, has been killed in action on November 6th, 1918. He died a hero and has been decorated with the prestigious Military Cross. We extend

our sincere sympathies to you and your family, Reverend Lantz. Sincerely, the War Office Administrator."

I lose all sense of place and time until the grandfather clock in the hallway chimes four times. I glance around the table where my younger siblings have gathered. They are in various stages of shock but Hazel is taking it the hardest. I go to her and wrap my arms around her trembling body. "I can't fix this, Hazel. Orrin lived in danger every time he went on the battlefield. But I never thought this would happen. He was such a good soldier!" The shock is starting to settle in and I can feel my resolve weakening. "Where's father?" I ask. Meanwhile Beecher is looking through the letters and pipes up.

"Look, here's a letter from Everett! Maybe it is a mistake and he knows the truth!" He pushes the letter into my hands. It is addressed to our father and, of course, I cannot open it without his approval. Just then the study door opens and our father enters the kitchen. His grief is evident and I shudder to see him aged to an old man. I rush over to give him my arm for support. After he is seated in his chair, he asks for a cup of tea. This request pulls Hazel together and she takes the kettle off the hot stove to pour water into the teapot. It is the end of November and our kitchen stove is our only source of heat. I really appreciate the comfort of its heat as a chill has settled over me. As we all sit at the table waiting for our father to say something, I push away the disturbing thoughts flooding my brain.

"Please pass me the letters, Harry," he finally requests. All eyes are on his trembling hands as he opens the letter from Everett. His voice is quivering too much to read it and he passes it to me. "Read it out loud, Harry. I think Everett will tell us what really happened."

I look at Everett's familiar handwriting and a surge of strength comes over me. I had hoped this day would never come but with six brothers in the war, I always knew one of us would make the supreme sacrifice. I never thought it would be Orrin and I start to read the letter out loud to my shocked family.

"Mons, Belgium

Dear Father:

    I have terrible news to tell you and I wish I was there with you now. Instead I sit on my bunk still on the battlefield. You probably received word from the War Office advising you of our dear Orrin's unfortunate death. I will tell you all I know as it will help you deal with your loss, I hope. I went to Mons on the night of November 11ᵗʰ to find my brother as I knew he was fighting in that area. My Regiment was camped further away. There was a great celebration going on. I found several of his comrades who were celebrating and they directed me to his commanding officer. I am sad to say but his commanding officer was drunk, as were most of the soldiers that night. Four years of fighting had come to an end so I guess they were justified. He, in turn, directed me to the General who, thank heavens, was sober and in his office. I must tell you, father, that our General Currie is an honorable man and God-fearing. He was very kind in telling me the news of Orrin's final battle. Orrin's company was in an assault to take a bridgehead which the enemy exploded and it killed everyone in Orrin's company. They got too close. The Germans often sacrifice their own lives to hold a position as we are the enemy to them. It seems that Orrin lived for a while as the men that were not in the assault carried him back to headquarters hoping he would survive. The General arranged for me to visit his gravesite this morning as I leave tomorrow for the Allied march to Germany. Part of their surrender was agreeing to an Occupation of British and Canadian troops for six months to make sure they do not try to re-muster their army. Orrin is buried in a peaceful field with poppies growing wild everywhere. It is on the outskirts of a large town in France he had helped liberate just five days before he was killed. This will become a permanent cemetery for Canadian soldiers, I am told. Beside him lie his comrades that died in the same battle. I can only say that he was much loved by his fellow soldiers and well respected by his commanding officers. Everyone speaks highly of him as a man and a soldier. I can leave this despicable battlefield knowing that my brother is resting peacefully after helping to end this godless war. I hope this will give you some comfort, father, as I know your grief will be great.

I will write you when I reach Germany for it will be a long march through Belgium. Our General Currie will lead the Canadian troops but of course, my regiment will be marching with the British. It is not my wish to go as I find no glory in babysitting the defeated enemy but orders are orders. I should be home next summer, God willing.

Please give my love to my siblings that are with you and I offer you a son's love in your time of great sorrow.

Affectionately, Everett"

It is very quiet as the news settles on us. I glance at Beecher who stares back with eyes as large as saucers. He finally hears a war story which is beyond understanding by his young years. I assume his imagination will go overboard with it and there will be tales at school tomorrow. Our father clears his throat. After instructing Hazel to prepare supper for the boys, he gently asks her to bring sandwiches and a pot of tea to his study. I glance at my sister who is pale and visibly shaken. I feel sorry for her but as my father gets up from his chair, I rush to his side. He asks me to follow him into his study. Fear grips my heart but I obey. This news has shaken me; memories of the war are flooding my brain. I realize now that I have been lulled into a false sense of peace since returning home.

Somehow the familiar smells of the leather chairs and books soothe my father and as he sits in his well-worn chair, a huge sigh escapes him. He looks at me carefully as if wondering about my health before he speaks.

"Harry, will you tell me what it was like over there? It was wrong of me to forbid you to speak of the war when you came home last year. I know it grieves you to relive your experiences but it will help me deal with Orrin's death. I beg you to tell me about him over there. I am dismayed that God would take him when he was destined to wear His raiment. I thought that my son had God's blessing. Could he have fallen out of Our Lord's favor?"

I can tell my father is trying hard to understand why Orrin died and not how he died. I gather myself for this ordeal. Speaking of the war no longer bothers me since I meet with other wounded soldiers who have returned and we discuss it freely. But trying to justify Orrin's death is beyond my skills and I am at a loss as what to say to my grieving father. We talk long into the night and when I finally seek the comfort of my bed, I am emotionally exhausted. Reliving the hell of the Great War did not bring me any peace of mind but it seemed to help my father understand how brave and loyal his devoted son was. I left him in the study long after midnight, eating his sandwich and drinking cold tea. But his grief had subsided and he had found some comfort in my words. He is convinced that while Orrin's body may lie in a grave in France, his soul has joined our mother's in the family grave on the hill behind his beloved white clapboard church.

****

I watch my father stand in the pulpit of his beloved church. It is a cold day in late November and he gazes lovingly at his faithful congregation. Only a few young men have returned from the war so the congregation is made up of older men, and women and children. But they are his dear friends and neighbors and they faithfully fill the hardwood seats every Sunday regardless of the weather. He knows their fears and their hardships as he visits them regularly during good times as well as bad times. As I look around, I am not surprised to see the adoration in their eyes for my father. Today is a memorial service for Orrin and I am worried about my father's fragile state.

"My dear friends," the Reverend's voice is subdued, "The *'Angel of Death'* has visited our small community many times in the past four years. We have lost beloved sons and brothers. We have all been touched by the horrific details of this war and we thank our Good Lord that it has finally ended. This week, I received word from the War Office that my beloved son, Orrin, was tragically killed in a battle a few days before November 11th. But my household was not the only one receiving bad news. The Henshaw family also received word that their son, Milledge,

191

died in battle as well on that fateful morning. This family has lost four of their five sons serving King and country. Their faith has been sorely tested but they are here today with their spiritual family praising God for delivering us from the evil of the Germans. This is a scene that is repeated in many churches across Canada. We must thank our good Lord for the safe return of our sons and brothers and for the souls of our departed loved ones. This war has tested our faith and I am pleased to say that our community has stood fast to our beliefs. We know that God's Love has been with us throughout all our anguish and despair. It is the foundation that has stood the test of time eternal. Let us pray and thank Him, our Savior, Jesus Christ, for our salvation."

My father looks lovingly at us seated in the front pews. Even Beecher is on his best behavior as he sits between me and his sister. I worry how pale and withdrawn Hazel has become since the news arrived.

Reverend Lantz continues his sermon. "I wish to close today with a poem that a young soldier wrote before he died from his wounds. My son, Harry, was working in the Dressing Station that day and tended to his mortal wounds. He gave Harry a poem which he had written only hours before he died as a thank you for his kind care. I think it is fitting to dedicate this short poem to all our brothers and sons whose bodies are buried on foreign soil but whose spirits are free to return to us.

"Farewell"
"No splendid rite is here — yet lay me low, ye
comrades of my youth I fought beside,
Close where the winds do sigh and wild poppies grow,
And where a sweet brook doth babble by my side,
Tis simple splendor, yet lay me tenderly to rest
where the guns no longer crow."

****

Calgary, Alberta
November, 1919

Dear Hazel:

I received your kind letter yesterday. Thank you for your concern. It has been a year since the war ended and for some Canadians, it has already been forgotten. I wish I could be so lucky. I was glad to hear that Gordon has been studying for the ministry. Father must be so pleased to have, at last, one son follow in his footsteps. I often wonder if Orrin would have returned to his studies had he not been killed. After neutralizing so many Germans, I find it hard to believe that he would have been able to take up ministry but we will never know, will we? I know Father thinks that Orrin's spirit lies in the small cemetery beside Mother but my dreams find him lost on the vacant battlefield. He is always searching for someone, reaching out a bloody hand and beseeching 'come with me'. I try to comfort him but it is not me he is seeking. I think he is a lost soul. My dreams have abated somewhat; my dear friend Elizabeth has been so kind. So Everett went back to the United States to live. Father must have been upset with that news. I suppose our younger brothers are old enough to help with the millwork now.

I am sorry to hear that money is a big issue. Perhaps working outside the home will improve for you. Hazel, you must start thinking about yourself. You have served Father well but you need to make a life for yourself as well. Have any other young men returned yet? They should all be demobilized by now, I would think. Try going to a dance or two.

I have news to share. I met one of my buddies from the Corps, John Teuridel, and we have taken an apartment together. It is small and a bit shabby but the War taught us to ignore luxury. I still sleep on the floor. I prefer that to a bed. There is only room for one army cot in our small space of a bedroom and I gave that to John. I know this sounds harsh but I am quite comfortable. We both work in a hospital as orderlies so our financial situation is fair. There are a lot of wounded soldiers convalescing at the hospital. They have been badly wounded and will take a long time to heal.

You ask me when will I come back home? I cannot say when that time will come. I am grateful that I am still wanted despite my failings. I do appreciate your caring and I am healing slowly. Someday I will get on the train going to Nova Scotia but I am uncertain how long that time will be.

Now I must close. Send my regards to Florence. She sent me a nice letter several weeks ago. I do not have much news to write even though she seems anxious to hear from me. I will pen a letter to her in a few weeks. Please take care of yourself and give my best wishes to everyone.

Your loving brother, Harry

P.S. I am glad you liked the book on English cathedrals. I only hope that you will see them someday. They are my fondest memory of the war.

THE END

Epilogue

On the eve of November 11, 1918, the Canadian Corps encountered heavy resistance on the outskirts of Mons; the German Army had dug in refusing to retreat further. By daybreak, the Allies had secured Mons. The Germans retreated outside the town and they camped there waiting for the Armistice deadline. The Battle of Mons has been debated by many historians. However the war diaries of the soldiers that were there and the communal cemetery in Mons which contains 57 Canadian graves speak of the sacrifices made on the last day of the Great War. The British fired the first shots in Mons, Belgium in 1914 which started the Great War. The last shots were fired by the Canadian Corps in Mons, Belgium to end the Great War in 1918.

General Sir Arthur Currie was harshly criticized for engaging the enemy so near to the deadline for the cease of the fighting. All commanding officers, both German and Allied Forces, had received written dispatches that a treaty had been signed and would be effective at the 11th hour, November 11, 1918. Not a single shot was fired after the deadline. General Sir Arthur Currie was credited as one of the greatest commanding officers in the Canadian Corps and had been knighted by King George V on the battlefield. He returned to Canada in late August 1919 after the completion of Canada's part in the Occupation of Germany. He was one of the last Canadian soldiers to return home. He arrived in Halifax, Nova Scotia without any official reception and walked to the train station alone to continue his journey home in Ontario. Few people paid attention to one of the finest and most competent of all Allied commanders in the whole war. He had taken command of the Canadian Corps in 1917 after the Battle of Somme. His brilliant strategies and daring plans shaped the Canadian Corps into a recognized fighting force earning its' nickname, *Shock Troops,* by the British generals. Sir Arthur Currie died in 1933 at 58 years of age. He was given a state funeral by the Government of Canada in recognition of his military achievements.

General Hon. Sir Samuel Hughes, Canada's Minister of Militia and Defense in 1914 organized the largest contingent of Canadian soldiers and equipment in two months that sailed to England in the largest Armada ever to cross the Atlantic Ocean. He fell out of favor with the Government of Canada before the end of the war. He died in 1921 without any recognition for his military achievements by the Canadian government.

The last Canadian hero to fall in battle was Private George Price of Falmouth, Nova Scotia. A Canadian monument stands in the city of Mons where he fell at 10:58AM on November 11, 1918, two minutes before the guns of war were silenced. His company had strayed too close to the main German Army on the east boundary of Mons. Private Price was crossing the street to join the rest of the men hunkered down in a ditch when a German sniper considered him a threat.

The Nova Scotia Highlanders were fierce fighters and feared by the Germans who dubbed them *The Ladies from Hell*. After their first battle which literally wiped out most of the regiment with the use of gas by the Germans, they were not allowed to wear kilts in battle nor have the pipers pipe them over the top. The British and Canadian generals decided it was better if the Germans could not distinguish where the Highlanders were in the trenches. But their war cries could not be silenced and many Germans, hearing their ancient war cry, ran from the battle in fear of them.

The Newfoundland Regiment which fought with the British also suffered high casualties; they proved to be courageous and hard fighters. King George V recognized their valiant contribution to the war by declaring them The Royal Newfoundland Regiment, a very rare honor but well deserved. The famous battle at Beaumont-Hamel in 1916 in High Wood killed eighty percent of the regiment. A replica of The "Danger Tree" that stood in No-Man's Land, where so many brave Newfoundland soldiers fell, stands today in their memory. It was their first engagement with the enemy and lasted only thirty minutes.

The Princess Patricia Regiment, Canada's finest and elite regiment of seasoned soldiers, fought beside the British during the war. Their courage and determination on the battlefield was tested many times as the regiment's losses were extensive. They rebuilt their regiment several times over the four years of fighting and never once left their position on the battlefield in defeat.

It became fashionable for the wealthy ladies in England to open unused wings of their fabulous mansions to wounded soldiers as convalescent hospitals. It was their way to aid the war effort. Lord and Lady Astor had a hospital built on their expansive estate in Taplow for wounded Canadian soldiers with the help of Canada's Governor General, the Duke of Connaught. The Duchess of Connaught's Red Cross Canadian Hospital was considered one of the best and many Canadian soldiers recovered from their physical and mental wounds in a totally holistic peaceful setting. Lady Astor only employed Canadian nurses. After the war, Lady Nancy Astor was elected for a seat in parliament, becoming the first female to sit in the House of Commons. She held that seat representing Portsmouth, where the first Canadian recruits arrived in 1914 and where Lord Astor had a summer home, from 1919 to 1945.

The Canadian Medical Services employed five hospital ships to evacuate sick and wounded soldiers from England home to Canada. These five ships made a total of 42 trans-Atlantic trips and transported 28,238 patients.

Of the seventy-five hospital ships and ambulance transports that supported the British and Canadians in transporting sick and wounded soldiers from France to England, seventeen were destroyed by German submarines or German mines even though they were clearly marked as hospital ships and carried no guns.

The No. 1 Canadian Base Hospital in Boulogne, France where thousands of wounded Canadian soldiers were treated throughout the War was bombed by the Germans in a two hour air-raid in May 1918. The nurses' wing was demolished. Sixty-five patients and staff were killed. Matron Elizabeth Pierce survived and returned to Canada after the war.

Lieutenant Orrin Lantz was awarded France's highest medal for valor, Croix de Guerre, (only 412 Canadians received one) by the French President for his part in the Battle of Passchendaele on October 28,

1918 just days before he was killed in action on November 6, 1918. He was also awarded the Military Cross for his gallant and distinguished service on the battlefield. Only 3,727 of these medals were awarded to Canadian soldiers throughout the four year war. Lieutenant Lantz is buried in the Valenciennes (St. Roch) Communal cemetery on the north-east side of the city where many Canadian soldiers are laid to rest. He was 25 years old.

Sergeant Harold Lantz, who returned home from the war *shell-shocked*, could find no peace. After the war ended, he left for Alberta where some of his comrades were and worked there for several years. When he finally returned home to Centrelea, Nova Scotia, he married Florence Hicks who had faithfully written him letters while he was in France and Alberta. They had two daughters and he spent the remainder of his life in his home community where he died at 79 years of age. He often served as Deacon in the Baptist Church his father loved so much.

Sapper Gordon Lantz returned home after the war ended and resumed his studies. An ordained Baptist minister, he took a parish in New Brunswick, married and had a family. On a visit to his father in Centrelea, Nova Scotia in 1932, he was killed in a car accident. He was 35 years old. His father George William Lantz, age 79, was in the car accident with him, and died the next day. They were on their way to visit Hazel, the only daughter and sister.

The older brothers, Havelock, Everett and Lenley Lantz, who were conscripted in 1917, moved to British Columbia after the war where they worked, married and had families.

The younger brothers, Hubert (Jim) Alexander and George Warren (Beecher) Lantz, both enlisted and fought in the Second World War. They both returned home after the war.

The brothers' sister, Hazel, married in her late 20's and moved away from the family. Although she started her own family, she always stayed close to her brothers.

Every battalion had its own chaplain or padre. These brave servants of God could be found everywhere on the front lines; dressing stations, hospitals, in the trenches, burial sites – no soldier died without spiritual comfort where possible. They were all volunteers; some received serious wounds or were killed in carrying out their ministerial duties.

The total Canadian fatal battle casualties during the war were 56,638, 13.5 percent of the 418,052 sent overseas. A total of 611,711 Canadian men and women enlisted during WW1. Approximately, 10,000 Canadian soldiers were treated and discharged for *shell-shock*. WW1 veterans found it difficult to speak of their traumatic war experiences.

The Spanish Flu broke out during the last year of the war and ended in 1919. It afflicted both Allied and German soldiers and killed more people, approximately twenty million worldwide, than WW1. When it first surfaced in the trenches in 1918, the British and American commanders thought it was German biological warfare or their use of mustard gas but the German troops were as sick as the Allied troops with many too sick to fight. With the end of the war and the wounded soldiers returning to Canada in 1919, the virus was carried with them bringing death to many Canadian families waiting for their loved ones to return from the war.

****

Afterword

While going through a box of old books in a century home that my mother had bought in the late 1990's, I found a small, insignificant red pocket diary written by a soldier in WW1. This diary had survived ninety years but I could tell it had been lovingly kept. My father was a veteran of this war so it immediately caught my attention and sparked the birth of *My Brothers' Footsteps*. The last entry in the diary was April 25, 1915 and I assumed the soldier had perished in one of the most historical battles in the Great War. Because he was an orderly in a Field Dressing Station which were often bombed, I decided to trace his footsteps. Thus began a remarkable journey and I discovered after reading many books on WW1 and locating his daughter that he did survive the war and that he was one of six brothers that had answered the call for King and country.

Writing this novel has been enlightening. Through research on the Great War, I learned the significance of being Canadian. Bringing to life the story of the six brothers was a unique experience for me. As their story progressed, individual characters surfaced and the story unfolded on its own terms. Literally speaking, the story wrote itself and I was carried along on its journey. I chose to use the real characters and true events but I fictionalized the conversations and interactions in a first person narrative. Researching their individual regiments allowed me to place them in specific historic battles. Their experiences in the war showcased their pain and courage, revealed their rage and frustration, and tested their faith in battles and death. Thousands of Canadian families watched their sons and daughters leave home to an unknown world but their loyalty and patriotism overcame their fear. Despite the loss of thousands of young Canadians that some historians claim a whole generation was slaughtered, the birth of a nation emerged from their blood spilled on foreign soil.

Canada will never forget the Great War and what it stood for. A single flower has become the symbol of the sacrifices made by our young men and women - the wild poppy and its blood red color. When I visited Austria several years ago, I was so thrilled to see the wild poppies growing everywhere. They grew along the highways, in the fields, in the corn patches. They were as common as our daisy in Canada. It transported me back one hundred years to the fields of wild poppies growing on the battlefields that were trampled by combat boots and squashed by bodies of patriotic men as they fell in battle. Today where these mighty battles were fought, the poppies still grow, proud and beautiful, to give us hope and to remember those who fought and died for freedom. *My Brothers' Footsteps* is written with great respect for those young men and women who a hundred years ago fought for freedom and sacrificed their lives so future generations of Canadians could live free of oppression. The characters are portrayed as themselves so that their names and their courage will not be forgotten.

To Honor A Fallen Hero

LIEUTENANT ORRIN LINCOLN
LANTZ, M.C., CROIX DE GUERRE
1892-1918

Enlisted with 85th Battalion on December 28, 1915. Promoted to Sergeant June 26, 1917; promoted to Lieutenant on June 28, 1918. Killed in action November 6, 1918 during the last battle fought by the 85th Battalion in the war.

One Hundred Years
By Gloria Marshall

One hundred years have passed
Since the battle cry of the 85th Battalion
Rang across this foreign land.
Brave and courageous,
These young men answered the call of their nation.
The guns are silenced now
And the fields are empty.
Once bloodied, they are green and fertile, and the wild poppies grow.
Our fallen heroes lie in shallow graves
And tombstones, stark and white, stand
Row after row across this scarred land.

One hundred years have passed
But every night at eight o'clock, without fail,
Their ghosts muster at Menin Gate
To the trumpet sounds of the Last Post
Where grateful citizens gather to wail.
If you visit these shallow graves
And are touched by a ghostly hand
Of a brave lad who died for his patriotic duty
Fear not, he is missing his homeland.

Glossary

Across the big pond: beyond the Atlantic Ocean, usually refers to England

Angel of Death: telegram from War Office advising son or daughter killed in action

Belgian rattlesnake: Lewis machine gun

Black Hand Gang: soldiers' slang for raiding party on a difficult mission

Blighty: England

Blighty One: wounded severely, sent to hospital in England and usually sent home from war

Box Barrage: Artillery bombardment upon small area

Brass Hats: high ranking officers

Bull Ring: Training ground behind the lines where recruits could be prepared for service at the front

Bully Beef: canned corned beef that was the principal protein ration

Chin-strapped: tired, exhausted

Dinko: mad, insane

Fritz: slang term for German soldier

Gearsman: tank crew member responsible for managing the gears

Gone West: term used by soldiers when a comrade dies in battle

Gunfire: strong tea laced with rum

Grubber: spade or entrenching tool

Hun: slang term for German soldier

Kamerad: friend (German)

Ladies from Hell: Germans called the Cape Breton Highlanders who they hated and feared

Land Creeper: tanks

Mills bomb: British #5 grenade

On the mat: called before the commanding officer

Pipped: struck by bullet

Pond Farm Particular: chest infections from weather and poor sleeping quarters at Training Camp on Salisbury Plains

Shell shock: psychological disorder caused by prolonged exposure to combat

Rest Camp: graves of fallen heroes

Taube: German airplane

Ticket: official discharge from army for medical reasons

Trench Foot: fungal infection of the foot which could become gangrenous, caused by standing in wet and cold trenches

Yellow Cross: German gas

Willie: tanks

Bibliography

Burton, Pierre, "Vimy – 1917"
  Penquin Books New York NY 1987

Canada in WW1: "85th Nova Scotia Highlanders-Passchendaele November 1917"
  Internet Research

Cook, Tim, "Shock Troops Canadians Fighting the Great War 1916-1918"
  Penquin Books Canada 2008

Cramb, J. A. MA, "Germany and England"
  John Murray London, UK 1914

Douglas, Tom, "Valour at Vimy Ridge Canadian Heroes of World War 1"
  James Lorimer & Company Ltd. Toronto, Ontario 1941

"First World War.com/diaries/1918/1917/1916"

Fussell, Paul, "The Great War and Modern Memory"
  Sterling Publishing New York NY 2009

Gilbert, Martin, "The First Great War A Complete History"
  Henry Holt and Company, New York, NY 1994

Gwyn, Sandra, "Tapestry of War-A private View of Canadians in the Great War"
  Harper Collins Publishers Toronto Ontario 1992

Herwig, Holger H., "The First World War Germany and Austria -Hungary"
  St. Martin's Press Inc. New York NY 1997

Hunt, Captain M.S., "Nova Scotia's Part in the Great War"
Nova Scotia Veteran Publishing Company Limited 1920

Lantz, Sergeant Harold, "War Diary 1914-1915"... "letter home in 1915"
Unpublished

Lantz, Lieutenant Orrin, "letter home in 1918"
Unpublished

"London Times"
Newspaper 1914

MacDonald, Lyn, "1915-The Death of Innocence"
Headline Book Publishing London UK 1994

Major, Kevin, "No Man's Land"
Doubleday Canada Limited Toronto Ontario 1996

Marteinson, Joe, "We Stand on Guard-An Illustrated History of the Canadian Army"
Ovale Publications Montreal, Quebec 1991

Morton, Desmond and J. L. Granatstein, "Marching to Armageddon-Canadians and the Great War 1914-1919"
Lester & Orpen Dennys Limited Toronto, Canada 1989

Reid, Gordon, "Poor Bloody Murder-Personal Memoirs of the First World War"
MO Oakville Ontario 1980

Scott, Canon, "The Great War As I Saw It"
Clarke & Stuart Co. Ltd. Vancouver, B. C. 1934

www.Canadian Great War Project: "The 1st Contingent-CEF Life on Salisbury Plain"..."Obituary of General Sir Arthur Currie December 01, 1933"... Nursing sister Elizabeth Pierce"

www.cbc.ca/history: The Conscription Crisis 1917... Under Suspicion-Imprisonment of Immigrant Canadians

www.dailymail.co.uk.news/: Shell Shock: From Panic Attacks to Mental Paralysis

www.canadahistory project.ca/: Vimy Ridge 1917

www.greatwar.co.uk/battles: Battles of Western front 1914-19

www.greatwar.co.uk/timeline/ww1-events-1914

www.wikipedia.org./: The Halifax Explosion December 6, 1917... List of Canadian Battles during the First World War... Second Battle of Passchendaele... Aldershot Garrison, England... Margaret, Maid of Norway... Westminister Abby, England... London Coliseum...Taplow Village, England...Clividen... Lady Nancy Astor, Vicountess Aster... Intercolonial Railway... Canadian Corps-WW1... Chemical weapons in World War 1...Raid on Scarborough, Hartlepool and Whitby 16 December 1914... Ross Rifle... Hon. Sir Samuel Hughes... List of Infantry weapons of World War 1... Hever Castle, England...Private George Lawrence Price... Battle of the Canal du Nord-1917... Battle of Hill 70-1917... General Douglas Haig... Union Jack Club... Beaumont-Hamel Newfoundland Memorial

About the Author

GLORIA MARSHALL, published poet and artist,
born in a small lumbering community
of New Ross, Nova Scotia.

A soldier's war diary that survived a
hundred years prompted her to give it a voice.
The words recorded by this soldier were
similar to the stories told to her as a child by
her father, a veteran of WW1 and WW11.

This is Gloria's first novel and she has written it with a
passion that only a first novel can produce. From
the war diaries and their letters home, she followed
these brothers' footsteps. The amazing journey is a
compelling and heart wrenching story which she eloquently portrays.

Gloria resides in Halifax, Nova Scotia. Retired from a 25 year career in
Office Administration, she enjoys family time with her grandchildren.
Her two passions are writing and painting.